Buzz Malone had been struck by lightning once when he was fifteen years old.

The doctors had said it was a miracle he'd lived.

Buzz wondered what the odds were of a man surviving such an ordeal twice in his lifetime, because he felt as if he'd just been struck again.

He's your son.

Kelly's words rang in his ears like a thunderclap. Shocking. Dangerous. Damning. He wanted to deny them, give voice to the outrage inside him. Instead he stared at the woman he'd spent three years loving more than life itself and the last few trying desperately to get out of his system.

Slowly he turned to face her. "You kept my *son* from me."

"I never meant to hurt you."

Buzz didn't have time to acknowledge the fury burgeoning inside him. Right now, there was a young life at stake. A life he had every intention of saving. His son's life.

Dear Reader,

Things are cooling down outside—at least here in the Northeast—but inside this month's six Silhouette Intimate Moments titles the heat is still on high. After too long an absence, bestselling author Dallas Schulze is back to complete her beloved miniseries A FAMILY CIRCLE with *Lovers and Other Strangers*. Shannon Deveraux has come home to Serenity and lost her heart to travelin' man Reece Morgan.

Our ROMANCING THE CROWN continuity is almost over, so join award winner Ingrid Weaver in *Under the King's Command*. I think you'll find Navy SEAL hero Sam Coburn irresistible. Ever-exciting Lindsay McKenna concludes her cross-line miniseries, MORGAN'S MERCENARIES: ULTIMATE RESCUE, with *Protecting His Own*. You'll be breathless from the first page to the last. Linda Castillo's *A Cry in the Night* features another of her "High Country Heroes," while relative newcomer Catherine Mann presents the second of her WINGMEN WARRIORS, in *Taking Cover*. Finally, welcome historical author Debra Lee Brown to the line with *On Thin Ice*, a romantic adventure set against an Alaskan background.

Enjoy them all, and come back again next month, when the roller-coaster ride of love and excitement continues right here in Silhouette Intimate Moments, home of the best romance reading around.

Yours,

Leslie J. Wainger
Executive Senior Editor

Please address questions and book requests to:
Silhouette Reader Service
U.S.: 3010 Walden Ave., P.O. Box 1325, Buffalo, NY 14269
Canadian: P.O. Box 609, Fort Erie, Ont. L2A 5X3

A Cry in the Night
LINDA CASTILLO

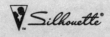

INTIMATE MOMENTS™

Published by Silhouette Books

America's Publisher of Contemporary Romance

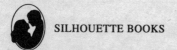 **SILHOUETTE BOOKS**

ISBN 0-373-27256-1

A CRY IN THE NIGHT

This edition published by arrangement with Harlequin Books S.A.

® and TM are trademarks of Harlequin Books S.A., used under license.
Trademarks indicated with ® are registered in the United States Patent
and Trademark Office, the Canadian Trade Marks Office and in other
countries.

Visit Silhouette at www.eHarlequin.com

Printed in U.S.A.

Books by Linda Castillo

Silhouette Intimate Moments

Remember the Night #1008
Cops and...Lovers? #1085
*_A Hero To Hold_ #1102
*_Just a Little Bit Dangerous_ #1145
*_A Cry in the Night_ #1186

*High Country Heroes

LINDA CASTILLO

grew up in a small farming community in western Ohio. She knew from a very early age that she wanted to be a writer—and penned her first novel at the age of thirteen during one of those long Ohio winters. Her dream of becoming a published author came true the day Silhouette called and wanted to buy one of her books!

Romance is at the heart of all her stories. She loves the idea of two fallible people falling in love amid danger and against their better judgment—or so they think. She enjoys watching them struggle through their problems, realize their weaknesses and strengths along the way and, ultimately, fall head over heels in love.

She is the winner of numerous writing awards, including the prestigious Maggie Award for Excellence. In 1999, she was a triple Romance Writers of America Golden Heart finalist and took first place in the romantic suspense division. In 2001, she was an RWA RITA® Award finalist with her first Silhouette release, *Remember the Night*.

Linda spins her tales of love and intrigue from her home in Dallas, Texas, where she lives with her husband and three lovable dogs. Check out her Web site at www.lindacastillo.com. Or you can contact her at P.O. Box 670501, Dallas, Texas 75367-0501.

Chapter 1

Kelly Malone knew better than to panic. Even as she felt its razor claws dig into her, she fought its powerful grasp. Panic made smart people do stupid things. Stupid things that ultimately led to mistakes. She couldn't afford to make a mistake. Not when her child's life was on the line.

Gripping the steering wheel with white-knuckled hands, she stared through the windshield into the black abyss ahead and pressed the accelerator to the floor.

She'd grown up less than twenty miles from the eastern edge of this beautiful, unforgiving land. White River National Forest had been her home for thirty-one years. Her father had been a smoke jumper; her mother a park ranger. Kelly knew the area like the back of her hand, respected its capricious nature. She knew and loved the people who lived here. Over the years she'd known of a dozen lost children. She'd even helped look for a few of them herself. She knew most of those children were found safe and sound.

None of them had ever been *her* child.

The thought sent a spike of fear straight through her heart to coil in her gut like a reptile whipping its spindly tail. "He's going to be all right," she whispered fiercely. "He's going to be okay."

Kelly knew the value of remaining calm and rational— even if the situation had already spiraled out of control. But the side of her that was a mother first scoffed at the idea.

Her child was missing.

It was her fault.

And there was only one man in the world she trusted to find him and bring him back. A man she'd once loved with all her heart. A man she'd hurt terribly. A man whose life she was about to change forever.

A fresh wave of terror slashed her, choking her, bleeding the last vestiges of calm from her veins. Adrenaline sparked like fire and zipped along her nerve endings like a lit fuse. Hysteria beckoned, but she knew once she entered that shadowy place, she'd never climb out.

The headlights sliced through the blackest night she'd ever seen, but Kelly didn't slow down. Driven by the primal instinct to protect what was precious, she drove like a madwoman through the inky darkness, her single-minded determination slapping down any notion of her own safety. Though the night was mild—even in July, temperatures in the Colorado Rockies could vary wildly—she felt cold, chilled from the inside out, as if her blood had been replaced with ice.

She would never forgive herself if something terrible happened to her little boy.

The wind tore at her car, shoving it from side to side like a child's toy, but she didn't slow down. Her tires protested with a squeal as she skidded around a dangerous curve she knew better than to take at such a high rate of speed. To the west, lightning split the sky, shattering it like crystal, illuminating bony trees and rocks the size of dinosaurs.

Kelly withheld a sob at the thought of her child huddled and alone on a night like this. Eddie had never been afraid of the dark, but thunder had always scared him. It tore her up inside knowing he was out there, alone and frightened and cold. The thought reached into her, a fist breaking through her ribs, gripping her heart and squeezing it so brutally she couldn't breathe.

She nearly missed the narrow lane cut into the forest. Her foot punched down hard on the brake. The car fish-tailed, but she cut the steering wheel hard to the right and forced it back under control. Gravel spewed high in the air as she pointed the vehicle toward the cabin and gunned the engine.

She wasn't even sure if this was the right place. It had been almost five years since she'd been here. She'd heard from the friend of a friend that he'd taken the old cabin and fixed it up. Five years ago, it had been uninhabitable.

The porch light loomed into view like a buoy in a raging sea. The place looked different, but she recognized the old SUV. A sound of relief escaped her, a strange and animal-like sound in the silence of her car. She brought the vehicle to a sliding stop a few yards from the front porch and jammed it into Park. Flinging open the door, she hit the ground running.

Above her the sky exploded, lightning spreading like white capillaries. She smelled rain, but the sky wasn't re-linquishing the water the forest had been crying out for since spring. The wind kicked dust into her eyes as she ran toward the cabin.

Please, God, let him be home.

The frantic thought pounded her brain. She crossed the porch in two strides, then slapped her palms hard against the wooden door. Once. Twice. "Buzz! Help me! Buzz, please!" She barely recognized her own voice.

A light flicked on at the rear of the cabin. Kelly waited eternal seconds, her heart hammering against her ribs so hard she thought it would explode.

An instant later the door swung open.

She saw slate-gray eyes, a wide chest covered with a sprinkling of dark hair and faded jeans that hugged lean hips and muscular thighs. Even lost and drowning in terror, she felt the impact of him, like a punch between the eyes that dazed the unwary.

Kelly wasn't unwary when it came to Buzz Malone.

She pushed by him. Her entire body vibrated as she walked into the foyer. She felt wild and out of control standing there inside his tidy cabin. She could only wonder how she must look to this man who never lost control.

Taking a calming breath, she spun to face him, sought his gaze. Six feet two inches of male pride and ego and one of the most complex—and difficult—personalities she'd ever encountered stared back at her. His gray eyes held a hint of ice, but his expression was etched with equal parts surprise and concern and that iron restraint that had cost them both so much when they were married.

"I'm in trouble. I...I need your help." The words tumbled from her brokenly, breathlessly. "Please, you've got to help me."

Brows drawn together as if he'd just been posed an impossible question, Buzz Malone stepped closer, but he didn't touch her. "You're bleeding. Are you hurt?"

She'd forgotten about the cut on her temple and shook her head. "I'm fine. There's a...lost child. Eddie. W-we were at the campground for my family reunion. We were hiking and I fell...."

"Calm down, Kelly. Just tell me what happened." With the impersonal touch of the cop he'd once been, Buzz took her arm and guided her over to the kitchen table. "Who's Eddie?"

Kelly melted into a chair. Because her hands were shaking uncontrollably, she put them flat on the table in front of her. "Eddie...." She closed her eyes, uttered a silent, heartfelt prayer. "He's my son. He's lost in the woods. The park rangers are looking. They notified a Search and Rescue outfit out of Boulder, but four hours have passed and they haven't found him. I want you there. I know if anyone can find him, you can."

If he hadn't known she had a son, he gave her no indication. "Where is he lost?"

"The eastern trail. When I slipped, I hit my head and must have passed out. I don't know how long I was out, but when I woke up, he was...gone. I called out to him, covered the area on foot, but...." The horror of that moment rushed over her, shaking her so hard she saw stars. "He's such a brave little guy, he probably went for help."

"How long were you out?"

"I don't know. Maybe ten minutes."

"Did you look for him right then and there? He couldn't have gotten far in ten minutes."

"I searched the entire area, calling his name. I called the ranger station immediately from my cell phone. I stayed near the spot where I fell and looked for about an hour. When the park ranger arrived, I went back to the campground and told my sister and her husband's family. They started looking, too. I went to the ranger station, and they called in Boulder One Search and Rescue."

"Boulder One is good."

"Not as good as you."

Buzz sighed, understanding. "They're a relatively new outfit. They don't have night vision equipment."

"You do."

"How old is he?"

Kelly closed her eyes tightly, then met his gaze. "He's four years old."

It was the first time she'd ever seen Buzz pale. Not Buzz Malone, the cool-eyed ex-cop who'd seen it all and never showed emotion. This time, however, he paled all the way down to his chiseled mouth. He recoiled, his gaze sharpening on hers. In the depths of his eyes she saw the questions, the hot spark of suspicion, dawning realization.

Kelly wished she hadn't had to witness it.

Buzz wasn't an emotional man. That had always driven her crazy back when they were married. The man had distant down to an art form. Cold was his middle name. If Kelly hadn't known him so well, she wouldn't have noticed the clenching of those granite jaws. The flash of shock in his steely eyes. But because she knew him, because she'd once loved him, she saw all those things, and the sense of dread that dropped over her was nearly enough to send her to her knees.

"What the holy hell are you telling me?" he snapped.

Kelly's pulse pounded like a freight train. The roar of blood through her veins mingled with the rumble of thunder outside until she couldn't hear. It was a struggle to hold his gaze, but she managed, if only by a thread. "He's your son, Buzz."

Buzz Malone stared hard at her. "I don't have a son."

Kelly stared back at him, a hundred words tumbling through her mind, a thousand emotions ripping through her heart. *I'm sorry. I wanted to tell you. I reached for the phone a hundred times. You never wanted either of us.*

None of the words were adequate. It was too late. The damage was done, but she knew the hurt wasn't over.

"I'm sorry," she whispered.

Incredulity filled his gaze followed by a flash of pain so clear it hurt her just to look at him.

But Kelly didn't have time to lament; Buzz Malone

didn't have time to hurt. Not tonight. All that mattered now was getting her son back. They would deal with the fallout after he was found.

It didn't matter that her ex-husband would never forgive her. That both their lives would be irrevocably changed. That the truth would tear their lives apart one more time. She'd decided in that first hour as she'd searched frantically for her little boy that she was willing to risk everything to find him. That included her own peace of mind and a future she'd been working toward since the breakup.

Vaguely, she heard Buzz curse. The roar in her ears turned into a loud hum. The lights dimmed. Her overloaded brain was simply going to short out. Her heart couldn't possibly keep up this insane rhythm. She'd never fainted before, but she feared that in a second she was going to collapse in a broken heap and sink to the floor at his feet.

But she didn't. Instead, she squared her shoulders, met that hard gaze with one of her own and said, "Eddie is your son. I'm sorry you had to find out like this. But I need you to help me find him. Right now."

Buzz Malone had been struck by lightning once when he was fifteen years old. One minute he'd been standing on a rock ledge looking out over Pike National Forest during a summer storm. The next he'd been lying on the ground disoriented and confused, with second-degree burns on his arms and feet.

The doctors had said it was a miracle he'd lived.

Buzz wondered what the odds were of a man surviving such an ordeal twice in his lifetime, because he felt as if he'd just been struck again.

Her words rang in his ears like a thunderclap. Shocking. Dangerous. Damning. He wanted to deny them, give voice to the outrage boiling inside him. But for the first time ever, the power of speech failed him. He stared at the woman he'd spent three years loving more than life itself, the last few years trying desperately to get out of his system and the world rocked violently beneath his feet.

"What the *hell* are you talking about?" He asked the question, but Buzz had already done the math. If the child was four years old, there was no doubt of his parentage. Kelly might not have been able to live with Buzz, but she'd always been fiercely loyal. There hadn't been anyone else. Not for Kelly. Certainly not for Buzz.

She looked down at her hands twisting in her lap, and bit her lower lip, the way she always did when she was upset or in trouble. Buzz figured the conversation they were having qualified for both of those things—and then some.

"I'm sorry I didn't tell you. I just...at the time, I couldn't," she said.

"Tell me *what?*" He knew damn good and well what she was about to say. But his brain refused to believe it. His mouth refused to say the words aloud. He didn't want to hear it, but he knew more than anyone just how futile wishes could be.

How in the name of God could she have done such a thing?

"I wanted to tell you a thousand times," she began. "But I didn't think you'd want to know."

Slowly, he turned to face her. "You kept my *son* from me."

"I never meant to hurt you."

"*Hurt* isn't the right word."

"Oh, I forgot," she choked. "Buzz Malone doesn't hurt like the rest of us mortals—"

"You stole four years of my son's life from me. I'm too angry with you to hurt."

"You made it clear, Buzz. You never wanted children. You didn't want me."

Uttering a nasty curse, he turned away from her and

stared blindly into the kitchen, his heart ricocheting like a bullet in his chest.

"Don't you dare turn away from me," she said. "Not now."

Clenching his jaws against the shock rocking his brain, he turned back to her. "You had no right to lie to me."

"I didn't lie."

"Don't play semantics. You lied by omission."

"You made your choice when we were married. I simply made it easy for you to walk away."

"You're the one who did the walking." But he was guilty, too, because he had merely stood there and watched and didn't do a damn thing to stop her.

Tears shimmered in her eyes when she looked up at him. "I can't talk about this right now. I can't, Buzz. Please. I'm begging you. Just…for God's sake, help me find him."

The need to know everything—every detail about his son—was an ache in his chest, but he knew she was right. The backcountry at night was no place for a young boy.

"Okay," he heard himself say. "Jesus. Okay. I'll find him. Let me make some calls. Give me a minute to get dressed." A moment to pull himself together.

Buzz knew her revelation was going to change his life, and he knew that ultimately it would hurt him in ways he could only imagine. In ways he'd never, ever wanted.

He felt the shakes descending. Tremors that started in his hands, then spread to his arms, his legs. Simultaneously, he felt the emotions snarling in his gut like a big cat rudely wakened from a deep sleep. Shock. Disbelief. A keen sense of betrayal that cut as jaggedly as any fang. The slow burn of fury spread through him like a flash and for a moment, he grappled for control.

Buzz didn't have time to feel betrayed. He didn't have time to acknowledge the fury burgeoning inside him. He didn't have time to feel anything at all. A hundred questions jammed into his brain, but he shoved them back. He would dig the answers out of Kelly later. Right now, there was a young life at stake. A life he had every intention of saving.

"I want to see him," he said.

She blinked at him. "What?"

"A picture." She looked on the verge of shock, but he refused to feel compassion. He refused to feel anything at the moment or risk the emotions threatening to overwhelm him. "Do you have a picture?"

Bending her head, she opened her purse and rummaged frantically inside. An instant later, she produced a three-by-five-inch color photo. "This was taken a couple of months ago."

Buzz stared at the photo, aware of the low roar of blood coursing through his veins, the hot zing of anger fusing with a throng of pain. He saw a little boy with freckles and dark-brown hair and an impish smile that was crooked and ended with a dimple in his left cheek. He saw innocence and tried not to think of all the terrible things that could happen to a child. In the mountains alone at night or in a world that could be merciless to the innocent.

Moved more than he wanted to be, a hell of a lot more than was wise, he looked away from the photo, then turned away from her so she couldn't see the emotions he knew were plainly visible on his face. "I'll want answers later," he said. "You owe me an explanation."

"I know I do. Just…after we find him."

Without looking at her, he snatched up the phone. His fingers trembled as he punched in the numbers to Rocky Mountain Search and Rescue Headquarters.

Senior medic John Maitland picked up on the first ring.

Buzz identified himself, his voice sounding strangely calm. He could hear raucous laughter in the background. The blare of rock and roll. The familiarity of those things gave him a badly needed sense of control, and he held on to it with all his might. "This is a call out. Code Red. I want everyone in house geared up and standing by. I'm on my way. ETA ten minutes."

"I'll put out the call to the team." John hesitated, as if sensing something wasn't quite right. "What's going on?"

"A lost boy up at White River. Four years old. I'm going to swing by on my way to the East Ranger Station."

"White River? I heard the call on the radio. Isn't that out of our jurisdiction? Boulder One SAR took it—"

"I don't give a damn about jurisdiction," Buzz snapped. "We're on it. Just do it."

Silence hissed for half a beat. "Yes sir."

"I want the chopper standing by. A winch team. I want weather reports. Night-vision equipment. Get someone over to the ranger station with a terrain map. I want Jake Madigan and a dozen volunteers on horseback ready for a grid search. I don't give a damn how many favors you've got to call in. Just get me some men. You got that?"

"Loud and clear."

Buzz slammed down the phone, turned to face Kelly. She stared back, her face ashen. He saw the imprint of her teeth on her lower lip. For the first time he noticed the bruise forming beneath the cut on her temple. The blood had clotted, but the wound still needed to be cleaned and dressed. "You ought to get yourself checked out at the hospital. You could be concussed."

"No."

"I can drive you over to Lake County—"

"I'm not going to the hospital. I can't leave knowing Eddie is out there all by himself. He's probably scared and hungry and cold…oh, *God!*"

He stared at her, seeing clearly the terror in her eyes, the torture in her heart. He felt his own version of panic punch him in the chest hard enough to take his breath. "It's only been four hours. We'll find him. He's going to be all right."

He didn't know that for sure, but he wasn't going to let his
mind go in that direction. He picked up the phone. "I'll
call Chaffee County Sheriff's Department and have them
bring in dogs. You got something with his scent?"

She jerked her head. "The socks he wore yesterday are
at the campground."

"That'll work." Buzz made the call to Chaffee County,
then dialed the Ranger Station at White River where a
search was already under way and told them he would be
there within the half hour.

"He's only a little boy, Buzz. He's sweet and smart
and...." Rising abruptly, she turned away, put her face in
her hands. "I can't stand not knowing where he is. I've got
to find him. I've got to go—"

"I need you to calm down and keep your head, Kel."

"I'm trying. Dammit. I'm just...scared."

"I know."

She looked at him with ravaged eyes. "I'm sorry you
had to find out like this, Buzz, but I didn't know where
else to go." She put a trembling hand over her mouth. "I
know we have a lot to work out. But right now I just want
him back."

Buzz barely heard the words over the pounding of his
heart. He tried to comprehend everything he'd been told,
but the meaning was too huge to absorb, too devastating.

After he finished the call, Buzz looked down at his hand
clenching the phone, saw that it was shaking violently. He
stared at his ex-wife. She'd always been a strong woman.
She knew her mind and never failed to speak it. That was
one of the things he'd always loved about her. Tonight,
however, she looked as if that spirit had been crushed. Her
coffee-brown eyes were wild with terror and ravaged by
guilt. If she shook any more violently he figured he was
going to have to pick her up off the floor. Because he didn't
want to have to do that, he rose and walked over to her,

set his arms on her shoulders. "Sit down before you fall down. I'm going to get dressed. Pack some gear."

"I don't want to sit down. I can't stay. I'm going back to the ranger station—"

"I'm going with you, damn it, and you're going to wait for me." He guided her toward the chair. "Sit down."

"Don't you have to go to headquarters to put your team out?"

"They're standing by. You and I will make a stop at RMSAR on the way to the ranger station." Noticing that her teeth were chattering, he scowled. He could feel tremors coming through her shoulders and into his hands. "Sit and pull yourself together. I'll be ready to go in five minutes."

She stared at him as if she was so at odds with the concept of sitting at a time like this that the sheer thought of it rendered her unable to do so.

"We'll find him," he promised, pushing her down into the chair.

Her shoulders felt frail beneath his hands. But Buzz knew she was anything but frail. She might weigh a hundred and ten pounds fully clothed and soaking wet, but her personality packed the punch of a linebacker. He'd been knocked senseless a time or two by that personality and had quickly learned size didn't always matter.

"He hasn't had dinner," she said hoarsely.

"He got any supplies?"

"Snacks. Raisins and a peanut butter sandwich in his backpack. A few cookies. A little box of juice."

"What else?" Plucking a flannel shirt off the back of a chair, Buzz jerked it on then stepped into his hiking boots.

"A flashlight. Bunky Bear, a little stuffed bear."

"That's good. Jacket?"

"Yeah, but it's not waterproof."

"It's not going to rain. Another dry front."

She jumped with a clap of thunder. "He's afraid of storms."

Buzz tried to think like the cop he'd once been, like the Search and Rescue professional that he was, but there were too many emotions banging around inside him to manage it. He definitely wasn't thinking objectively. He couldn't get a handle on this, could barely form a coherent thought, let alone come up with a plan.

Grabbing his jacket off the arm of the sofa, Buzz turned to get his bag of gear—and nearly ran into Kelly. He hadn't seen her rise, and the sudden contact stunned him, sent another shock through his system. For an instant she was so close he could smell her. A combination of citrus and the out-of-doors and the mysterious scent of woman. The familiarity of it struck him like a blow. He knew better than to let her affect him. Not at a time like this when she was frightened, when his own world had just been turned upside down, and an innocent young life hung in the balance. But when he took a deep breath, her essence enveloped his brain and brought back memories he had absolutely no desire to think of now.

Steeling himself against the power of those memories, he turned away abruptly and headed for the door. His head was spinning. Not only because of the shock of learning he had a son or that his young son was in danger. But because even after almost five years of being away from his ex-wife, she still wielded the power to make him shake inside and outside and every place in between.

Chapter 2

The drive to Rocky Mountain Search and Rescue Headquarters was a tense, silent affair, and Buzz felt every second that ticked by like a death knell. He'd been in some tight spots back when he was a cop. He'd come to within an inch of losing his life five years ago when a sixteen-year-old with a Saturday-night special had come out of nowhere and put a bullet in his spine. But even during that horrible instant when he'd known he was seriously—perhaps even fatally—hurt, Buzz hadn't been as scared as he was tonight.

The repercussions of Kelly's news rocked him to his foundation. And even though Buzz had never wanted children, he knew he would do everything in his power to protect what was his and bring that little boy home.

Back when they were married, Kelly had wanted children. Boys or girls, it never mattered to her. Buzz had seen too much of the dark side of the world to want to bring an innocent child into it. His own childhood had been a nightmare of neglect and subtle psychological abuses. Buzz had survived, but he'd known at a very young age he would never have children. Four years as a detective in the Child Abuse Division of the Denver PD had solidified that decision. He'd made his position clear to Kelly in the three years they'd been married. It had always been a point of contention between them. Kelly would never agree, but Buzz believed his not wanting children was one of the main reasons their marriage had failed.

Lord have mercy, he hadn't expected this to happen.

Rocky Mountain Search and Rescue Headquarters was lit up like a football stadium when Buzz turned into the driveway. Not bothering to park away from the building in his usual spot, he drove the SUV through the grass and brought it to a sliding stop ten feet from the front entrance. Kelly had her door open before the vehicle had even come to a complete stop.

He knew she was going through hell right now. As angry as he was with her, he would never wish that kind of pain on anyone. He'd never even met his son, yet the instant he'd known, Buzz had felt the connection. A link that was instinctive and primal and ran deep to a place inside him he'd never ventured to explore.

He reached the door first, shoved it open with both hands. The door swung wide with a bang. Aaron "Dispatch" Henderson sat at the communication station, manning the VHF radio. Buzz made eye contact with him, saw wariness enter the younger man's gaze. Neither of them spoke as Buzz stalked past. He could only imagine how he must look. Back when he'd been a cop, his fellow officers had jokingly called him "scary" when he was angry or intent on a case. Tonight, Buzz bet he looked downright terrifying.

He walked briskly down the hall, his boots thudding solidly against the wood planks. He heard Kelly moving behind him, but he didn't slow down. The light was on in the galley, and he knew that was where his men had congregated to wait. Working his coat off as he walked, he tossed it at the coat rack, heard it fall to the floor. He didn't stop to pick it up.

He entered the galley and halted. Four sets of narrowed eyes swept from Buzz to the woman behind him and back to Buzz. He saw the questions in their expressions, but he had no intention of answering any of them. Not tonight. Not until they'd found his son.

Medic John Maitland stood at the front of the room, dressed in his bright orange flight suit. Next to him, Tony "Flyboy" Colorosa, also geared in his flight suit, was pinning a topographical map of White River National Forest on an easel. Jake Madigan and junior medic Pete Scully hovered over the map, but their heads were turned and they were looking at Buzz as if he'd just beamed down from another planet.

Vaguely, Buzz was aware that he was breathing heavily. That his shirt clung damply to his back. He wondered if he was the only one who could hear the jackhammer rhythm of his heart.

"Winch team and night vision are RTG," John said, using the shorthand term for "ready to go."

"Chopper is standing by," Tony added.

Realizing he had yet to explain the situation, Buzz gave himself a quick mental shake and started toward the front of the room. "Take your seats," he snapped.

The four men shuffled into their seats.

For the first time since he'd begun his career with RMSAR four years earlier, Buzz felt as if he wasn't in control of the situation. He fought for objectivity, to attain the clarity of mind that had made him such a good cop, such a good team leader—but he knew it was a useless endeavor. When he raised his finger to the map, his hand shook.

"We've got a lost boy. Four years old." He indicated the general location on the map. "White River National Forest. East slope." Pulling in a deep breath, he looked at Kelly. "They'll need a description. You're familiar with the area. I'd like you to point out the exact location. Give us the circumstances."

Buzz watched her approach, aware of the dull thud of his heartbeat. In the harsh light of the galley, she looked pale and badly shaken. The cut on her temple stood out in stark contrast to her ashen complexion. The bruise forming beneath was going to be brilliant once it bloomed. She'd shed her coat in the foyer, and for the first time he realized just how bad the fall she'd taken must have been. Her jeans were dirty at the left hip and torn at the knee. The flannel shirt she wore had come untucked at one side and hung ungracefully to mid thigh.

He might be angry with her for lying to him about their son all these years, but he damn well was going to make sure she got checked out by a doctor before this was through. Damn hard-headed woman.

"This is Kelly Malone," he said.

Absolute silence filled the room. The four men watched her carefully and with great interest as she took her place at the front of the room and let out a shaky breath. Her brown eyes scanned the male faces watching her.

"Eddie is four years old," she began. "Dark hair, brown, cut short. Gray eyes. He's wearing a white Denver Broncos sweatshirt and a pair of blue jeans. White sneakers. He had a green jacket tied around his waist, but he might be wearing it now. His backpack is blue." Setting her purse on the table, she pulled out her wallet and dug the photo from it with trembling fingers. "I've only got one picture. It's a couple of months old, but it's a good one." She looked longingly at the photo, then closed her eyes briefly. Without looking at it again, she handed it to John Maitland.

"Where did you last see him?" Jake Madigan asked.

Taking Kelly's arm, Buzz eased her toward the map. "Did you say the eastern edge of the park?" he asked her.

She nodded, then turned to study the map.

Buzz could feel her shaking, knew she was holding onto her composure by only a thread. A very thin thread that wouldn't hold much longer. He didn't want to be there when it snapped, but knew he'd rather it be him than someone else.

He was aware of the men watching her, could practically feel the curiosity bubbling in the room. He knew they were wondering if their surly team leader had an ex-wife and a child he'd never told anyone about. Holy hell, this was a mess.

Forcing his mind back to the matter at hand, he gently squeezed her arm to let her know she was doing all right. That they were going to get through this. That they were going to get their son back.

Kelly gave him a grateful look, but her hand shook violently when she raised it to point out the hiking trail where she'd fallen. "Right here."

"That's the eastern edge of the hiking trails," said John Maitland. "Terrain gets rough to the north."

She nodded. "We were on the southernmost trail. About two miles from the campground."

"How long has he been gone?"

"Almost four and a half hours." Her voice cracked with the last word.

Knowing she couldn't take much more before she broke, Buzz moved her gently aside and stepped forward. "Flyboy, what's the weather situation?"

"There's a front to the northwest. Weather Service is

expecting sustained winds of fifty knots. It's going to get rough when that sucker blows through.''

''What's the flying time frame?''

''I'd say we have a couple of hours of fly time before I have to recall to base.''

Buzz's curse was interrupted by Jake Madigan's. Buzz looked over at the tall man wearing the battered Stetson. ''That's not the only problem,'' the cowboy said.

The hairs on Buzz's nape stood up. Next to him, Kelly jerked her head toward Jake. Buzz shot the other man a questioning look.

Jake sighed, glanced from Kelly to Jake.

Buzz understood what the other man was trying to say an instant too late. Kelly darted around the table and walked over to Jake. Chin jutting, she raised her hand and pointed a finger in the general direction of his face. ''Don't you dare keep information from me just because you think I can't handle it. I need to know what's going on.''

Grimacing, Jake removed his Stetson, then looked helplessly at Buzz. ''Well, ma'am…uh, with all due respect—''

''What problem?'' she pressed.

Realizing abruptly what Jake was about to say, Buzz stepped forward and put his hands on Kelly's shoulders. ''We're professionals, Kel. Let us take care of this. We'll find him.''

''No.'' She whirled on Buzz. ''Don't try to keep me out of this. I'm not going to sit this out.'' She turned back to Jake, who looked as if he'd just backed into a cactus. ''Damn it, tell me what the hell is going on.''

Jake sighed, shot Buzz a questioning look.

Knowing his ex-wife wasn't going to back down, Buzz gave him a minute nod.

''The ranger station up on Ruby Lake reported a fire a few hours ago,'' Jake began. ''There was a lightning strike. With the drought and high winds, the fire is gaining momentum. It's still small at this point, but it's burning uncontrolled and heading this way.''

Kelly put her hand to her mouth to stop the sob that bubbled out, but she didn't succeed. Her free hand went to her stomach, as if she'd been gut-punched. ''Oh, God. Oh, no.''

Buzz pressed his fingers into her shoulders. ''Kelly, the fire is small. Chances are the firefighters will be able to contain it. Let us take care of this. These men are the best. They've got to go to work. Right now. I'll have Dispatch take you to the hospital to get that bump checked—''

''I'm not leaving Eddie.'' Shaking off his grasp, she turned to face him, a waif ready to take on an army. ''Don't ask me to stay out of this. I know the area. I know the trails. I've got to be out there, looking for him.''

''You were knocked unconscious, damn it. You're not going to do anyone any good when the adrenaline wears off and you find yourself flat on your back with a concussion.''

''The only thing that's wrong with me is that I've lost my son.''

''You're scared spitless and bleeding and running on nerves and your own hard head—''

''Don't you dare try to shut me out of this. I'm not going to sit it out.''

''You're out of control.''

She advanced on him, shaking so violently she didn't trust her legs. ''You're damn right I am! I thought you might feel the same way, but obviously, your heart is still as cold as it ever was!''

She hadn't meant to go there. Hadn't meant to say those words or make this any more personal than it already was. Her control broke with an almost audible *snap!* The tears came in a rush. A useless, humiliating show of emotion that wasn't going to accomplish anything except give her a wham-banger of a headache and prove to the men in this room she wasn't going to be much help. She struggled valiantly to staunch the sobs that wrenched from deep in her chest, but they were powerful and shook her from head to toe.

Realizing the room had gone utterly silent, Kelly sucked in a breath and stopped herself cold. Buzz stared at her as if she'd just announced that she was an alien and would be moving back to her own planet in another galaxy at the end of the week. Tony Colorosa and Pete Scully had found something fascinating in the wood planks of the floor. John Maitland stared at the map. Jake scratched at a non-existent stain on the felt of his hat, his brows knitting as if in intense concentration.

Knowing her credibility was on the line, she let out the breath she'd been holding and addressed the men. "Eddie also has a flashlight with him. Since it's dark, he may have it on. It's plastic and not very bright, but the batteries were new, so it should be working."

Buzz cleared his throat. "If that's all…."

She jerked her head. "Please, find him. I want him back."

He addressed his team. "Let's get this show on the road, gentlemen." He looked at his pilot. "Do your best for me, will you, Flyboy?"

"Piece of cake." Some of the cockiness went out of Tony's expression when he glanced at Kelly. "We'll find him, Ms. Malone."

Because she couldn't speak, she nodded her thanks and within seconds, the men had grabbed their canvas equipment bags and rushed out the rear entrance, leaving an uncomfortable silence in their wake.

Without speaking to her, Buzz left the room and picked his coat off the floor in the hall. Kelly followed. "I'm sorry I broke down like that," she said.

"You're entitled."

"I know this is hard for you, too."

He turned to her, striking her with a gaze as sharp and cold as an alpine winter. "Whatever you do, don't apologize."

"Buzz…."

"I still plan to rake you over the coals."

"Well, I certainly don't want to miss out on *that*."

Buzz shot her a thin smile. "That's one of the things I've missed about you, Kel."

"What's that?"

"Your smart mouth."

"Not something to base a relationship on, I guess."

"I guess not." Grimacing, he started toward the door. "Let's get out to the site."

"I hope it doesn't rain, Bunky Bear." Eddie Malone shone the flashlight on the stuffed animal's face, wishing the little bear could say something back. "Mommy always told me thunder was just this big guy up in the sky throwing thunderbolts, but I didn't really believe it. I didn't tell her 'cause I didn't want to hurt her feelings, but I thought that was a really dumb story."

Bunky Bear stared back at him with his one good eye and a little smile on his mouth that always made Eddie laugh. But Eddie wasn't laughing tonight. He was scared. More scared than he'd ever been in his whole life.

It had all started when he'd dropped Bunky Bear down that big hill. He'd tried not to cry, but he'd wanted his bear back. Mommy had climbed down after Bunky, but the branch she was holding onto had snapped and she rolled and rolled all the way down the hill. It had scared Eddie even more when he called out to her and she didn't answer. When he'd climbed down after her, she was asleep. He tried to wake her, but she wouldn't wake up. He knew he shouldn't cry, but it scared him so much he just couldn't help it. He'd sat down beside her and cried for a long time.

Then he saw the cut on her head and thought he should go for help. Isn't that what Captain Kudo on "Kudos and Kids" would do? Knowing it was the only way to save his mom, Eddie had grabbed Bunky Bear, stuffed him in his backpack and started back toward the campground where Aunt Kim would know what to do. He'd thought for sure he was going the right way. But it seemed like he walked forever and never got back to the campground. Then the wind had started blowing, and it started getting dark.

Snuggled up against Bunky Bear, Eddie shivered and huddled deeper into his jacket. "Don't worry, Bunky Bear," he said. "Mommy's okay. She's a good hiker and knows everything there is to know about camping and stuff."

The rumble of thunder in the distance made his teeth chatter. He looked up, saw the sky flicker. Around him, the treetops swayed and whispered. He wished it wasn't so dark. He hadn't been quite so scared when the sun was shining.

He wished Mommy would hurry up and find him so they could go home.

Buzz didn't bother with the speed limit on the way to White River Campground, and the trip took less than half an hour. Using his cell phone en route, he checked in with the ranger station where the base camp for the search had been set up, as well as the Lake County Sheriff's Department to see how the search was progressing. Neither agency reported any sign of Eddie. Another call to his contact at the Chaffee County Sheriff's Department told him a team of scent-trained bloodhounds would be brought in at first light. Buzz hoped to God they found him by morning.

If they didn't, he hated to wait that long to bring in the dogs, but he knew how difficult nighttime searches were.

Next to him, Kelly stared into the darkness beyond the window as silent and still as a mannequin. The tension coming off her was palpable. Buzz felt his own tension like a knot being drawn ever tighter in his chest. But as angry as he was with her, another side of him felt a pang of compassion every time he looked at her and saw the profound sadness in her eyes. He wasn't going to let her down.

A hundred questions rang in his head. Even though Buzz knew now wasn't the time to raise them, there was a small part of him that wanted to know everything about his son. He wanted to know how tall he was. What he liked to eat. His favorite stories and movies and toys. If he took after his mother—or, God forbid, him. Another side of him—the side that was an ex-detective and had worked some of the worst child abuse cases in the city—cringed at the thought of bringing something so precious as a child into a world that was many times less than kind to the innocent.

Feeling the urgency press into him with an almost physical force, all too aware of the minutes ticking by and the fire raging just a few miles to the north, Buzz looked at his watch, felt another snap of tension go through his system. Eleven o'clock. Eddie had been missing for five hours now. As an ex-cop, and now a Search and Rescue professional, he knew all too well how much could happen in five hours.

Where are you, son?

Surprise rippled through him that he was now thinking of this child as his son. He wondered how smart that was when he didn't have any idea how he was going to handle being a father—if he would even get the chance, if he wanted it at all.

The campground was humming with activity when Buzz drove into the parking lot. Park rangers and volunteers and sheriff's deputies hustled about, talking into their radios and looking harried. Buzz parked the truck next to a Lake County sheriff's van and shut down the engine. Next to him, Kelly reached for the door handle.

"We're going to hit the trail, so make it brief," he said.

Nodding once, she slipped out the door. Buzz gathered his gear and got out of the truck. He was in the process of slipping his pack over his shoulders when a tall man dressed in khakis and a button-down shirt rushed toward Kelly with a determined stride. Buzz couldn't see much of him in the dim light cast from the single sodium vapor lamp overhead—just enough to recognize the glint of male interest in his eyes.

"Any word?" Kelly asked the man.

"Nothing yet." He opened his arms to her. "I'm sorry."

She went into his arms without hesitation.

Standing next to the truck, Buzz watched the exchange, trying in vain to ignore the hot snap of jealousy.

"I came straight over from the office," the man said to her. "Your sister called and talked to my assistant. I wish you'd called me."

"There was nothing you could do."

"I could have been here for you."

"God, Taylor, I'm so worried. It's been over five hours."

"I'm sure they'll find him." The man eyed Buzz over Kelly's shoulder, taking his measure much the same way a contender did in the minutes before a boxing match.

Buzz stared back with his best bad-cop glare, wondering if it would be considered politically incorrect of him to wipe that superior expression off the other man's face with his fist. Buzz wasn't a fan of politically correct.

Never taking his eyes from Buzz's, the man lowered his hand to the small of Kelly's back in a silent message that wasn't lost on Buzz.

She's mine.

"You holding up okay?" the man asked her.

"I'm all right," she said. "I just need to find him."

"You're cut—"

"It's nothing."

Buzz refused to identify the brutal twist of emotion in his gut. He was *not* a jealous man. Never had been. Hell, he wasn't even possessive. Not that he had a right to be in the first place. He and Kelly were through. She was free to see whomever she chose. Just because Buzz had never quite reconciled himself to the fact that their divorce meant things were over between them for good didn't mean he was going to let the possibility that she was having a relationship with this bespectacled corporate jerk cloud his judgment.

Easing back from the man, Kelly turned to Buzz. "Taylor, this is Buzz Malone."

The other man stuck out his hand. "Taylor Quelhorst. Glad to meet you."

Buzz hesitated an instant before accepting the handshake. If the other man knew Buzz was the father of the child in question, he gave no indication.

"You're a retired policeman." Taylor squeezed Buzz's hand.

Buzz squeezed back. "Ex-detective."

"Buzz and I are going to hike the trail where Eddie was lost," Kelly said.

Taylor released Buzz's hand abruptly and gave her a sharp look. "I was planning to take you back to the motel where I'm staying."

"No. All my things are here. You go. I'm going to join the search."

"Well, then, I'll go with you."

"You don't have any gear," Buzz cut in, then motioned toward Taylor's Italian loafers. "You'd just slow us down."

The other man's annoyed gaze swept from Kelly to Buzz, and then back to Kelly. "Do you want me to go—?"

"No, I want you to go back to the motel," she said firmly. "Make sure the rangers and sheriff's department have the number there, so they know how to reach you."

"They do."

"All right." Pulling away from him, she sighed. "You've got my cell number. Please, call me the instant you hear anything." Her eyes intensified. "Anything."

"You got it." Leaning forward, he kissed her gently on the cheek.

Unwilling to witness any more of the exchange, Buzz turned away and started toward a couple of sheriff's deputies holding a thermos of what he hoped was coffee. He might be divorced from Kelly, he might even be fine with it, but he sure as hell didn't like seeing another man put his hands on her.

A moment later, Kelly drew up beside him. "All right. I'm ready. Let's go."

All too aware that he was annoyed as hell and his heart rate was up to a dangerous level, Buzz risked a look at her, but he didn't slow down. "You finished with Mr. Corporate America?"

"His name is Taylor Quelhorst, and he's my boss."

"Seems friendly."

"We're friends. He cares for Eddie."

"I'll bet."

Buzz stopped walking on reaching the two deputies. Setting his pack on the ground, he offered his hand. "I'm Buzz Malone with RMSAR."

A young, muscle-bound deputy grinned and shook his hand enthusiastically. "You guys found that lost Boy Scout last summer. Good going. We're glad to have you here."

"This is the lost boy's mother, Kelly. What's the stat?"

After introductions were made, one of the deputies

poured coffee from a thermos and handed a cup to Kelly, another one to Buzz. The other young man updated Buzz and Kelly on the search. "No sign of the subject yet. Someone reported tracks up on Cougar Ridge, but they didn't pan out. We've had so many volunteers, the area is pretty trampled. Most of the volunteers have gone home for the night, but they'll be back first light. What are you folks going to do?"

"We're going to hike up to the site where the child was initially lost."

Grimacing, the deputy glanced down at Kelly. "You sure you want to do that in the dark? You can't see much. You'll have a better chance of spotting him tomorrow if you're fresh."

Buzz knew the deputy was experienced enough to know that many times the parents of lost children exhausted themselves early and then weren't much good to anyone— including the child—thereafter. What he didn't know was that Buzz intended to make sure Kelly got some rest tonight whether they were on the trail or not.

"I've got a halogen spotlight and a whistle." Buzz finished his coffee and passed the empty cup back to the deputy.

"That'll help." The deputy collected Kelly's cup as well. "You got a radio with you?" he asked Buzz.

"VHS. What frequency are you guys using?"

"Emergency channel 16. All agencies involved."

"Got it."

"You folks be careful."

Hefting his pack, Buzz slipped it over his shoulders and started toward the darkened trail. Kelly had to trot to keep up with his long stride.

"I don't have a pack," she said.

"I've got everything we need in mine."

"I didn't know you had a whistle," she said. "That's a good idea. I wish I'd thought of it."

"I do this for a living now, remember?"

She didn't answer, but Buzz knew what she was thinking. The way he made his living had been another point of contention between them—they'd had a lot of those when they'd been married. Early in their relationship, the love between them had been so strong it didn't matter that he was a cop and spent his days wrestling with armed criminals who wouldn't think twice about capping a cop. But the dangers of his job had taken a heavy toll on their marriage.

After the shooting, Kelly had made it clear she could no longer take the pressures of being a cop's wife. With a bullet lodged mere millimeters from his spinal cord, Buzz hadn't been able to go back to active duty. The department had offered him a desk job, but the position held little appeal. Kelly had wanted him to take the corporate security job that had been offered to him by an established firm out of Denver. But the thought of sitting behind a desk all day, devising ways to keep employees from stealing pencils was about as exciting as his own funeral. When the team-leader position with Rocky Mountain Search and Rescue had become available, Buzz had jumped at the opportunity. That had been the proverbial straw that broke the camel's back.

Buzz had never fully understood why she hadn't been able to accept his need to be on the front line. He suspected her father had a lot to do with it. Buzz had never met Jack McKee, but the man was a legend. He'd been a smoke jumper back in the early 1980s. A breed of man who lived for the rush and the heady taste of danger that came with putting his life on the line. They'd called him Jumpin' Jack Flash back then. He'd been the best of the best. Courageous. Daring. Kelly would have been about fifteen when he'd died. Buzz didn't know the details, but he'd heard that

McKee's chopper went down on the front line of a forest fire. Her brother had been on board too. Both men had perished.

Knowing what he did about her father and brother, Buzz figured Kelly deserved a man who didn't like gambling with fate. The worry and sleepless nights had torn her apart during their marriage. When she'd asked for a divorce, he hadn't contested it. He'd let her go, first, because he couldn't stand to hurt her, second, simply because she'd wanted to go. She wanted him to change, but Buzz hadn't been able to stop being who he was no matter how much he loved her.

He'd moved on with his life, but there had been no other women. No woman would ever come close to touching him the way Kelly had. Buzz knew no other woman ever would.

Even frightened and disheveled with a cut on her temple and pain in her heart, Kelly was still the most beautiful woman he'd ever known. That was a hell of a thing for him to be noticing at a time like this.

No, it wasn't a comforting thought at all to realize that the divorce hadn't diminished his attraction to her. They might be compatible when it came to the bedroom, but all compatibility ended there. Sex was the only facet of their marriage that they'd agreed upon unequivocally. It hadn't been enough.

With a long night stretching out ahead of them, Buzz figured he would be wise to keep that in mind.

Chapter 3

"This way."

The sound of Kelly's voice jerked him from his reverie. Buzz's flashlight illuminated a fork in the trail. Kelly motioned left. "How far are we from where you fell?" he asked.

"Maybe another quarter mile or so."

"This was a long hike for a young kid."

"He's a bundle of energy, Buzz. I know him. I know his physical capabilities, and I know what he likes. He's always been fascinated by the outdoors. Trails. Camping. Animal tracks. Even flowers. We were having so much fun, I just didn't realize how...." Her voice trailed off.

Buzz practically felt the rise of guilt. "I didn't mean to imply that this is your fault, Kel."

"I know. I just...if I'd just used my head, none of this would have happened."

"You know what they say about hindsight being twenty-twenty."

She shot him a grateful look. "Yeah."

They walked in silence for a while, the only sound coming from their feet on the trail and heavy breathing. "Do you know the tread pattern on his sneakers?" Buzz asked.

"The deputy said the tracks had been—"

"You never know when you might get lucky."

She didn't hesitate. "Small circles with an arrow pointing toward the toe."

"That ought to be easy enough to spot."

"I didn't see any when I looked, but I was pretty frantic. I could have missed something."

Buzz tried to approach this mission with the same emotionless determination with which he approached other missions, but the cool objectivity he'd always been able to achieve eluded him. He couldn't stop thinking that it was *his* son out there this time. A little boy who was too young to keep himself safe. A child who still carried his stuffed animal with him.

"This is the place."

Buzz halted. Kelly stood a couple of feet away, her breath puffing out in a thin white cloud. The night had grown cool. A preschooler with nothing but a light jacket to keep him warm would be cold.

Dropping his pack to the ground, Buzz dug the whistle out of his jeans pocket and blew into it twice in quick succession.

"Eddie!" Kelly turned in a circle, looking out into the surrounding darkness. "Honey, it's Mommy!"

Putting the whistle back in his pocket, Buzz put his finger to his lips. "Quiet, Kel. The whistle carries farther than a voice. Let's just listen a moment, and see if we get a response."

She nodded, then stood motionless and stared into the surrounding darkness. For a full two minutes, Buzz listened to the chirping of crickets, the call of an occasional night bird, the crack of a twig beneath the weight of a fat raccoon, the rustle of an owl's wings as it swooped down to pluck an unsuspecting mouse from the grass.

"Exactly where did you fall?" Buzz asked.

"To your left. Eddie dropped Bunky Bear down the ravine. He's had that bear since he was born, and he was upset."

"Don't tell me you went after it."

"The bear fell only a few feet down."

Shining the light down the incline, Buzz frowned. It was steep and rugged, but not vertical. "You should have known better than to try something like that without a partner."

"I thought I could get to it, then get right back up. But I grabbed a branch. The branch broke...." She shrugged. "Well, there's that hindsight thing again."

Buzz knew all too well about hindsight.

"I'm going to go down there and have a look around," he said.

"Buzz, what did you just tell *me?*"

"I've got an adult partner. You."

"I'm not EMT certified."

He shot her a small smile. "I'm not a rookie."

"No, you're just foolhardy."

"Same goes, evidently."

She frowned at him. "I guess I had that coming."

"You did." He handed her the spotlight. "Keep the light out of my eyes and on the ground below me so I can see, okay?"

Nodding once, she accepted the spotlight. "Be careful."

The light flickered over her delicate features like firelight. Her gaze met his, and Buzz felt his heart give a weird little lurch.

Kelly wished he wouldn't look at her like that. Like the world was at his beck and call, and she was right at the center of that world. She was no longer the idealistic young woman who'd fallen crazy in love with him a lifetime ago. She wasn't the same woman he'd married. Wasn't even the same woman he'd divorced. The world had taught her a few things since then. Lessons Kelly wouldn't ever forget. Lessons that had made her too smart to make the same mistakes all over again.

But looking into his eyes, she *believed* everything was going to work out. The fierce determination that was so much a part of him, the force of his personality, his inability to take no for an answer. All of those things made her believe they were going to find Eddie unharmed. That was why she was here, she realized. If anyone could find her son, it was Buzz. So she'd come, even though she'd known both of them would pay a price.

Kelly had never been able to pretend when it came to Buzz. The mere power of his gaze wrenched the truth from her no matter how painful, no matter how deeply she tried to lock it away. She knew this was going to change their lives irrevocably. And as much as she didn't want to admit it, she knew from experience that sometimes things didn't work out for the better.

Trying not to think of the darker possibilities, she watched him step into the rappel harness and loop the nylon rope through the carabiner, then anchor the end to a sturdy-looking pine. She knew better than to notice the way that harness accentuated his long, muscular thighs and lean hips. But she noticed anyway. And the sight of him, even after all these years, still made her mouth go dry.

"Kel, the spotlight."

She jumped at the sound of his voice, jerked the light to the steep incline just below him. "Be careful of the rocks," she said.

"I'm always careful." Never taking his eyes from hers, he stepped backward toward the ledge. Glancing quickly behind him, he stepped down and disappeared over the edge. She could hear the nylon rope humming through his gloves as he descended, his hiking boots thudding against the rocky face of the ravine. Holding the spotlight steady, she guided him over jagged granite, through juniper and the spindly roots of the occasional pine that clung to the side of the mountain, all the way to the ravine floor thirty feet down.

"I'm in!" came Buzz's shout a moment later.

The rope went slack and Kelly knew he'd disengaged the rappel harness. She squinted through the darkness. "Do you see anything?" she shouted.

She could hear him breaking through brush. Hope burgeoned until her chest was so tight she couldn't breathe. *Please, God, let my son be down there. Let him be all right.*

The need to hold Eddie tight and safe in her arms was an ache so deep she almost cried out with the pain of it. That need twisted inside her now, like a knife, cutting her at the very core of her being. She knew better than to get her hopes up, knew how acute disappointment could be, but her heart kicked hard at the thought of getting him back safe and sound.

"I need for you to put on the harness."

Kelly started so abruptly at the sound of Buzz's voice, she nearly dropped the spotlight. She'd been so embroiled in her thoughts, she hadn't seen him climb back up the ravine wall. One look at his face, and fear snarled like a rabid beast inside her. She tried to shove it down, refusing to give it free rein, but it was a cold, mean fear and clamped over her like a predator's jaws.

"What is it?" she blurted. "Is he down there? Is he—?"

"Easy, Kel." Buzz grimaced. "He's not there. But he was. I almost missed it, but there's a sneaker print."

"Are you sure? He was there? But how did he—" She

closed her eyes, a strangled sound escaping her. "How did he get down that ravine?"

"Looks like our little guy climbed down."

"But…it's so steep. How did he…." Because she didn't want to think of her son braving such a treacherous climb, she let the words trail.

"Maybe he climbed down to help you."

The thought of Eddie trekking down that dangerously steep ravine to help her ripped at her, tearing her from the inside out. She'd sworn she wasn't going to cry or succumb to hysterics, but the thought of her little boy risking his life to help her when she'd been hurt shattered the last of her control.

She put her hand over her mouth to smother a sob. "Oh, God, Buzz. He's so brave."

"Easy, Kel. Just take it easy for me, okay?"

"I want him back."

"I know, honey."

Kelly closed her eyes tightly against the tears, but they squeezed through her lashes and ran unchecked down her cheeks. The sob that tore from her throat didn't sound at all like her. Not like Kelly Malone who'd been standing on her own two feet since she was fifteen years old. Not the young girl who'd lost not only her father, but her brother and then spent the rest of her teenaged years taking care of the broken woman who had once been her mother.

But the pain was too great and refused to be bridled. Wrapping her arms around herself, Kelly doubled over, felt a sob wrench from her throat. "Where *is* he?" she cried.

"Shh. Kel, hey, settle down. I want you to take a deep breath for me, okay?"

She tried to suck in a breath, but all she managed was a keening sound that echoed off the trees like the cries of a dying animal.

"Kel…."

"I want my son."

"Come here."

She barely heard the whispered words over the tide of grief within her. But slowly they penetrated the fog of pain, the fear of the unknown, and registered in her brain. *Come here.* An offer of comfort when she desperately needed it. She knew what it was like to be wrapped within those strong arms. To have that gentle voice reassure her. For those hands to caress away her pain and fear. She knew better than to give in to that kind of temptation. But Kelly was tired of being strong. Tired of being alone. For a little while, she wanted to step into that strong embrace and just be held.

Buzz took the decision away from her. Without bothering to remove his rappelling harness, he reached for her. Strong hands closed around her arms and pulled her to him. Kelly started to protest, but he shushed her gently. She didn't remember falling against him. Or wrapping her arms around those rock-solid shoulders. She knew getting close like this was dangerous business, that she should pull away. But the next thing she knew he was holding her close, molding her body to his and she was helpless to resist. All the while the scent of his aftershave curled around her brain, reminding her of how right it had once felt to be wrapped within this man's embrace.

"I need him back, Buzz. It's killing me." She was sobbing now. Wrenching sobs that bubbled up from somewhere deep inside her where the pain was unbearable and her body and heart could no longer contain it.

"We'll get him back."

"He's everything to me."

"Shh. We'll find him." Gently, he stroked the back of her head. "Let it out, honey. Just cry it out. I've got you."

Kelly didn't want to cry. Not again. But the pain had been hammering at her for nearly six hours now. The element of the unknown beckoned her beleaguered mind to conjure unspeakable possibilities. She simply couldn't bear it if something terrible happened to her little boy.

"Promise me we're going to find him," she whispered. "Please, promise me."

"Kel—"

"Say it," she said fiercely. "I want to hear you say it."

"I promise. We'll find him. Just…be still a moment, okay?"

The rush of tears ended as quickly as it had descended. In its wake, Kelly felt calmer. Still afraid, but somehow stronger. Purged.

"Better?" Buzz asked.

She wasn't sure why the question embarrassed her, but it did. Kelly wasn't a helpless female, couldn't bear for this strong man to think of her that way. "I didn't mean for that to happen," she said. "I don't usually have emotional meltdowns."

"Considering the circumstances, I won't hold it against you."

Tilting her head back just enough to look at him, she smiled thinly. "I appreciate that."

"You've been holding it together remarkably well. You're doing just fine."

Only then did she realize his arms were still around her, and he was close enough for her to feel the warm brush of his breath against her cheek. Awareness zinged through her. She felt the hard planes of his body against hers, his warmth radiating into her, taking away the chill that had sunk all the way to her bones. He smelled of soap and man and the subtle scent of an aftershave that brought back a jumble of memories she was crazy to think of now.

Realizing she'd nearly trespassed into territory best left alone, she eased away from him. "Where did you see the sneaker print?" she asked.

"At the base of the ravine."

"Where do you think he went?"

Buzz studied her intently in the ribbon of light cast by his flashlight. "I don't think he climbed back up that wall."

The words registered slowly. Kelly's pulse spiked, and she took another step back. "Do you think the volunteers that came through earlier missed him?"

"Maybe. Boulder SAR is a relatively new outfit. A lot of the guys are rookies. Lots of energy and training, but they lack experience."

A starburst of hope exploded in her heart. "They didn't look in that ravine, did they?"

"Maybe not."

"I need to go down there."

"All I've got with me is a light tactical harness. It's pretty basic; nothing fancy. Think you can rappel down?"

It didn't matter if she remembered how to rappel or not. Come hell or high water she was going down there. She just wouldn't tell him she hadn't touched a rappelling harness since they'd scaled Deep River Gorge together over six years ago. She knew him too well to tell the truth. "Of course I can."

"The harness is minimal. Lightweight. Think you can handle it?"

She nodded, already reaching for the harness and stepping into it. "No problem."

Reaching around her, he looped the rope through the caribiner and doubled it back over the pine tree. "I'll spot you from up here. Keep the light on you."

"Okay."

"When you reach the ravine floor, unharness yourself and I'll pull it up and meet you down there."

Impatient now, Kelly walked over to the edge of the ravine and looked over her shoulder at the darkness below.

"You sure you're okay with this?" Buzz asked. "If you're not, we can rig something and go down together."

"I'll be fine."

"Just keep a grip on that rope." He plucked off his leather gloves and handed them to her. "Use these."

Kelly put the gloves on, gripped the rope the way he'd taught her all those years ago, then turned to face him. "I'm ready."

"Trust your equipment, Kel. Feel your way down with your feet. Trust the rope."

"Okay, okay," she said impatiently. "Let's go."

But for all her bravado and the heady rush of newfound hope, her legs were shaking. When she'd fallen earlier in the day, the fall had seemed endless. Her body remembered every rock and every broken root that had punched her on the way down. Knowing she was about to descend the very same ravine with nothing more than a nylon rope and the vague memory of a previous rappelling experience to back her was unnerving. But the fear of falling was nothing compared to the fear of never seeing her son again. She had to do this.

Wrapping the rope once around her leather-clad knuckles, she backed to the ledge, then stepped down into the ravine. Instantly she realized the darkness was going to make her descent infinitely more difficult. But knowing she didn't have a choice, she slid her feet inches at a time. First her right foot, then her left. Branches poked at her back and legs as she broke through the brush. Adrenaline spiked through her when her hiking boots slipped on the slick granite. She dangled for an instant before swinging her legs forward then pushing off against the rock face.

By the time she reached the ravine floor, every muscle in her body quivered with exertion.

"You okay?" Buzz shouted down to her.

"Fine." Stepping out of the harness, she slipped off the

gloves and tied them to the harness. "Go ahead and pull the harness back up."

An instant later, the harness bumped back up the rock face.

Slipping the flashlight from her fanny pack, Kelly flicked it on and shone it down on the ground. Her heart turned over when she saw the barely discernable sneaker print in the dust. Small circles with an arrow pointing toward the toe. Buzz had been right. Eddie had been here. Guilt nipped at her that she'd missed it earlier. If she'd seen it and searched the ravine, she might have been holding him safe in her arms right now.

Needing to be close to him, Kelly dropped to her knees and pressed her fingers into the dust. "Oh, sweetheart. Mommy's coming for you." Bowing her head, she whispered a prayer for the good Lord to keep her son safe until she reached him.

She was still kneeling when Buzz slid the last few feet down the ravine wall. "Kel?"

The first tinges of exhaustion pressed into her as she got to her feet. Kelly looked up at him, surprised to see the raw concern in his expression.

"You okay?"

She nodded. "I'm fine. I just need to find him."

Tugging the radio from his belt, Buzz jerked out the antenna, adjusted the squelch and barked into it, "This is Tango Two Niner, RMSAR Homer One, do you read? Clear."

"Hey, Tango, this is Dispatch. Any luck?"

"I've got tracks, and I'm wondering if Eagle is out and about. Clear."

"National Weather Service issued a wind advisory. Eagle went back to her nest. Sighting negative. What's your twenty?"

"I'm three miles from remote camping. East ridge of White Water."

"It's oh one hundred, Buzz. Dogs will be there at oh six. Please advise."

Kelly listened to the exchange. She'd always known that Buzz was the kind of man who would be good at what he did, no matter what it was. He was competitive and driven and a perfectionist to the extreme. But somehow, the breadth and width of what he did—and how good he was at it—hadn't fully penetrated until now. At that moment, she knew she'd done the right thing by going to him. He was the best of the best. He loved what he did, he chose his team wisely, and she knew if it was the last thing he did, he would find her son.

"Advise Lake and Chaffee counties of our twenty. Let them know we found tracks. We're going to camp for the night. Over and out." Buzz switched off the radio and shoved it back into his belt.

Kelly just stood there a moment before realizing she was staring at him and that he was staring back. "I'm not camping," she said.

"You're dead on your feet," he returned evenly.

It was true, but that didn't mean she was going to admit it. It sure as hell didn't mean she was going to sleep while her son wandered around lost. But Buzz was the kind of man who took care of things. The kind of man who liked to be in charge, liked to be in control. If he knew she was exhausted, he would make sure she got rest—even if that meant calling the search to a halt until morning. Kelly didn't intend to let that happen. "I'm not tired," she said.

"It's 1:00 a.m."

"I want to keep looking."

"We need to find a place to camp for the night. Get a couple of hours of sleep—"

"Dammit, Buzz, I'm not going to stop! We just found

his tracks, for Pete's sake. If we keep going we could find him before morning."

"If we don't find him by morning, you'll be about as much use to me as a broken rope."

Kelly heard the logic in his words. She wasn't a fool. She knew she had to pace herself. But the part of her that was a mother first couldn't bear the thought of stopping to sleep when her little boy was huddled somewhere all alone, cold and hungry and afraid.

Shaking with the need to find him, she walked over to Buzz and met his gaze with an equally powerful one of her own. "Give me one more hour. Please. If we don't find him, we'll make camp and get some rest."

Buzz sighed, his jaw flexing. "I'm going to hold you to it."

"One hour. That's all I'm asking."

He looked past her, toward the small footprints in the dusty earth. "Is that where you came to after the fall?"

She nodded. "He must have come down the ravine to see if I was okay."

He shone the spotlight over the area. "Let's see if we can pick up a trail."

Re-energized now that they had found a tangible clue, Kelly nodded and slipped her flashlight back into her fanny pack to conserve the batteries. She'd only gone a few steps when Buzz's voice stopped her.

"He went this way."

Kelly watched his spotlight play over tall grass and sparse trees where the terrain sloped gently. She could see how a young child would think the slope led down the mountain. But the fact of the matter was that the downward incline had taken him in the wrong direction, away from the campground to a higher elevation and some of the most rugged high country in the state.

"You can barely see it, but there's a path in the grass." Buzz shone the spotlight over the meadow.

Kelly squinted, trying not to think of how scared he must have been. "He thought the downward slope would take him back to the campground," she said.

"Smart little kid."

He takes after his father. The words almost slipped out, but Kelly stopped herself just in time. Now wasn't the time to tell Buzz how many times Eddie had reminded her of him. She couldn't talk to this man at all about the child she had chosen to keep a secret. The child he'd never wanted. She had a pretty good idea how Buzz felt about that—angry and betrayed and justifiably so.

When they were married, Buzz had made it clear he didn't want children. She understood why. Though he'd never revealed the details, she knew about his own childhood. About the abuse he'd suffered at the hands of his father. She also knew about the four years of hell he'd gone through when he'd worked the Child Abuse Division of the Denver PD. He never talked about it, but she knew what those years had done to him. She had been there when he'd wakened in the dead of night, his hands shaking, his body slicked with sweat. In the end, Buzz had made his choice. He'd chosen the job over her, over family, and stuck like glue to his resolve never to bring a child into the world. Kelly hadn't been able to live with that, and their marriage had slowly fallen apart.

She wondered how he would react when she told him she would be moving to Lake Tahoe next month. She wondered if he'd thought about whether or not he wanted to know his son. She wondered if he would travel to California to see him or settle for a two-week visit during summer vacation. She wondered if he would relinquish a relationship with his son for his own selfish peace of mind.

Without speaking, they started into the meadow, Buzz's

spotlight playing over the grass, sparse juniper and the ever-present rock from which the mountains had garnered their name. Lightning flickered on the horizon to the north-west. Kelly tried not to think of Eddie out there all by himself and facing the threat of a thunderstorm.

"Why didn't you tell me about him?" Buzz asked after a moment.

Kelly thought she had been prepared for the question. Since Eddie's birth, she'd rehearsed her answer a thousand times. But all those carefully constructed responses withered on her tongue when she looked into Buzz's eyes. Back at the cabin, she'd seen the emotions behind those eyes. Now those emotions were gone, replaced by ice, perhaps even a thin layer of contempt. But he was so hard to read, had always been hard to read, she couldn't be sure. And whatever defenses she'd built around herself in the last hours nearly crumpled beneath the power of his gaze.

"You never wanted children," she managed to say.

"You did."

"What's that supposed to mean?"

"I guess that could be translated as I'm wondering if you got pregnant on purpose. Maybe you figured you needed a baby, but you didn't need me."

"You know I wouldn't do that."

"That's exactly what you did."

Her temper jumped, like a big, wild cat hit with a jolt of electricity. Stopping abruptly, she turned to him. "Don't you dare lay all the blame at my feet. In case it's slipped your narrow mind, it takes two people to make a baby!"

"You were always…. I thought you were on the pill."

"I went off the pill the day the divorce was finalized. You came to me twice after that. Twice! Both times we…. That last time…." She let the endings of both sentences hang, not wanting to think of the wrenching sadness and blinding, desperate passion they'd shared that final night.

Buzz had made love to her with a desperation so powerful it scared her. It was the last time they'd been together, the last time she'd been with anyone, and she'd always known in her heart that was the night Eddie had been conceived.

Buzz switched off the spotlight. Kelly wondered if it was to conserve the battery—or to keep her from seeing his expression.

"You kept him from me, Kel," he said. "I didn't think you were capable of something like that."

"Because you didn't want him. Because you didn't want me."

"Did you come to this conclusion before or after you decided to walk?"

"You're the one who made the decision," she said breathlessly. "You made your choice. I merely followed through."

"I had a job to do, and I did it the best way I knew how."

Kelly struggled to pull oxygen into her lungs. Her heart bucked and stomped in her chest. She hated fighting like this. Hated opening up those painful old wounds. It had been bad enough when they were married. But with her son lost and the fear pounding like a drum inside her this was infinitely worse.

"It's not that simple," she said after a moment. "There was nothing simple about our marriage."

"Marriage is cut and dried. Either you stay and try to work things out. Or you walk away and don't look back. We both know which choice you made."

Her temper rose like hot mercury. Memories rained down on her, pieces of her life that had gone up in smoke, fluttering down like smoldering ash, burning her. "I walked out because I know what men like you do to the people who love them."

"Now I guess we're getting to the heart of the matter, aren't we?"

"You put me through three years of hell, Buzz."

"Oh, for chrissake!"

"I saw you the night they brought you in on that stretcher. You had a bullet in your back. You were bleeding internally. You couldn't even breathe on your own, for God's sake! You nearly died that night. The doctors didn't know if you'd ever walk again."

"I was a cop, Kel. Cops get hurt sometimes. It goes with the territory. I couldn't stop doing my job just because you didn't like it."

She didn't tell him those were the same words her father had used to placate her mother. The same words her brother had used the last time she'd seen him alive. They'd scoffed at her worry. She couldn't tell him that she would rather lose him on her terms than on the more vicious terms set forth by fate. "You had a choice."

"I made the only choice I could," he snapped.

"Yes, you did. And that was when I knew it wasn't going to work."

"That's when you realized you didn't have the guts to stick by me."

"Don't lecture me about guts!" The anger came with such force that her voice shook with it. "You turned down that corporate security position for the job with Rocky Mountain Search and Rescue. This could have turned out differently."

"Don't blame what happened between us on fate, Kel. Maybe it wouldn't have worked out no matter what I did for a living."

She stared at him, speechless, not sure how to disagree without opening doors she knew were better left closed and locked.

"You made a conscious decision and stuck by it," he said.

"I stuck by it because I don't want my son to have his heart ripped out by a man who doesn't have the good sense to know when to retire. A man who would eventually draw the short straw. And I know Eddie will never have to see his father die before he's old enough to understand how exactly final death is."

"I guess you think it's better that he doesn't have a father at all?"

She thought back to when she'd lost her own father and brother. She'd only been a teenager, but she'd never forgotten the agony of that day or the dark months that had followed. Her mother had never been the same, and had quietly faded away until she was nothing more than a shell of the vibrant woman she'd once been. While her sister, Kim, had gone away to college, Kelly had cared for their mother, and she'd sworn she would never let her own children suffer the same fate.

"Yes," she said quietly. "I do."

Buzz remained silent, but his eyes never left hers.

Shaken by the exchange, by the truths on both sides and the echoes of pain clanging through her heart, Kelly tugged the flashlight out of her fanny pack and moved ahead of him, shining it over the tall grass. "I'm not going to discuss this with you now."

Not waiting for a reply, she found the subtle trail in the grass and followed it. A moment later, she heard Buzz behind her. She knew eventually they would have to talk about how they were going to handle this. About whether Buzz wanted to be part of his son's life. About whether Kelly could accept Eddie bonding with a man who spent his days jumping out of helicopters and rappelling down sheer cliffs and putting his life on the line day in and day out. Just as her father and brother had all those years ago.

Kelly knew that before this was all said and done she would have to decide if she could live with the very real possibility that she might one day have to watch her son have his heart ripped out by a man who thought he was immortal.

Chapter 4

Buzz was too angry to talk, so he lagged behind a few feet. He'd promised to give her an hour before stopping for the night, but an hour came and went and he didn't mention it. He knew she was exhausted and running on little more than nerves and that steel determination he saw in her eyes every time he looked at her. But the truth of the matter was he didn't want to have to sit down and look into her eyes and see all that pain or, God forbid, talk about how they were going to handle their having a son.

He knew that's what would happen if they made camp. He simply wasn't up to talking. He was too angry. Too off-kilter. Too damn…everything to do anything but make the situation infinitely worse. He figured they may as well keep walking until they were both too tired to talk.

The three-quarter moon was sinking low in the west when he finally spoke. "Kel, let's pack it in for the night."

He'd expected her to argue, felt a sharp retort sizzle on the tip of his tongue in preparation. But surprising him, she stopped and just stood there, staring into the darkness as if listening for a cry in the night that never came.

Her face glowed pale in the dim moonlight, her eyes dark and troubled. When he stepped closer, he saw the exhaustion and defeat and the tired remnants of fear in her eyes and a pang of compassion gripped him despite his efforts to remain distant.

"We'll sleep for a few hours and start again first light," he said.

"It's so cold," she said tonelessly. "I wish it wasn't so damn cold."

For a moment, Buzz thought she was referring to herself, then realized her own physical comforts were the last thing on her mind. She was worried about Eddie. The night was uncomfortably cold, but it wasn't harsh enough to cause hypothermia to a child with a jacket. As long as he wasn't wet.

Because Buzz didn't know what else to do to comfort her, he dropped his pack and stooped to dig out one of two compact thermal sleeping bags he'd packed. Rising, he handed one to her. "Unzip this and put it around your shoulders."

She obeyed without objection. Then, huddled within the blanket, she just stood there, staring into the darkness, listening, waiting.

Buzz had been through some intense moments with Kelly. But in all the years he'd known her, he'd never seen her like this. Bleak and filled with despair and utter hopelessness.

At a loss as to what to do next, he looked around and spotted a semi-protected area where they would be out of the wind. Picking up his backpack, he walked over to it and began unpacking. He removed the stove first and lit the wick. The flame cast yellow light on the surrounding trees and nearby outcropping of rock. A few feet away,

Kelly sank down on a fallen log and put her face in her hands. She didn't make a sound, but Buzz saw her shoulders shaking, and he knew she was crying. Jesus, he hated seeing that. He'd seen plenty of women cry over the years. He'd long since grown used to female tears. But to see this strong, stubborn woman reduced to tears tore at him like a sharp-fanged little animal.

"We've got to believe he's going to be all right, Kel. Don't let your mind get away from you," he said after a moment.

When she raised her head and looked at him, tears shimmered like wet diamonds on her cheeks. "I ache inside. I've never hurt like this before. If something happens to him, I'll never—"

"Don't go there, damn it," he interjected harshly. "Don't say it. Don't even think it."

"I'm sorry I'm such a basket case."

"Don't apologize. This isn't easy. For either of us."

Rather than upset her, his harsh tone seemed to bolster her control. Rising, she approached him and knelt in front of the stove to warm her hands. "Is there anything I can do to help?"

Buzz passed her his backpack. "I brought some protein bars. Get out a couple, so we can eat. Put down the tarp." He could have very well done those things himself, but he knew Kelly well enough to know that she functioned better if she was busy, no matter how minute the chore.

While she did that, Buzz pulled the first-aid kit from his pack and set it atop a relatively flat rock. "Come here," he said.

"That's not—"

"I'm the EMT," he said. "Let me worry about the first aid, all right?"

She handed him one of the protein bars. "I'm too tired to argue with you."

"Well, that's a first."

"Don't get used to it."

A reluctant smile tugged at the corner of his mouth. "Keep that blanket around your shoulders and sit down."

Relief slipped through him when she sat down without an argument. Buzz removed an antiseptic cleansing pad, some antibiotic cream and a large square bandage. "Any headache or blurred vision?" he asked.

"No."

"Nausea?"

She shook her head.

He cut her a hard look. "The truth, Kelly."

She sighed. "A little bit of a headache, but it's only because I've been crying."

He wasn't sure why it was so hard to look at her. Wasn't sure if it was her beauty or the grief he saw in the depths of her gaze. But as he knelt in front of her to get a look at the cut on her temple, he found himself barely able to meet her eyes.

"I'm going to check your pupils." Without giving her time to respond he put his hand gently against her crown, then flashed the light first in her left eye, then in her right. "As far as I can tell, you don't appear to have a concussion."

"I could have told you that."

"Well, after we find Eddie tomorrow, I'm going to personally haul you into Lake County Hospital and make sure you get a CT run."

Her gaze met his, the play of emotions in her eyes touching him despite his staunch resistance. "Thank you for saying that. I mean, about finding him."

Realizing it was probably best not to talk to her when he was this close, Buzz disinfected his hands then applied a thin layer of antibiotic cream to the cut. He tried not to notice the sweet scent of her hair that rose up with her body heat into the cold night. He damn well ignored the fact that his heart rate was up, and that it didn't have anything to do with high altitude or physical exertion—or even a lost little boy.

He unwrapped the bandage and pressed it to the cut, sealing the adhesive as he did so. Throughout the process, Kelly didn't so much as flinch, just watched him with sad, devastated eyes.

When he finished, Buzz rose quickly, paced over to the stove and adjusted a flame that didn't need adjusting. He wasn't sure exactly what was going on in his head, but he didn't like it. He wanted to believe it was the shock of learning he had a son that had him twisted up inside. But Buzz was honest enough with himself to realize that keeping close quarters with his very attractive ex-wife was making an already complex situation infinitely worse.

"Kel, why don't you lie down on the tarp and try to get some sleep?" he said.

When she didn't answer, Buzz walked over to her, and put his hand on her shoulder. "Kel?"

"I'm not going to be able to sleep," she said.

"You've got to try."

After a long moment, she raised her gaze to his. "I'm too scared to sleep," she whispered. "How can I sleep knowing Eddie is out there in the wilderness all alone?"

"You can do it because you know you're going to need your strength and a cool head to get through this. You can do it because you raised a smart kid. And because you know I'm damn good at what I do."

A wan smile touched her mouth.

"I'm not going to let either of you down." Slipping his hand under her arm, he helped her rise. Kelly didn't fight him. Gently, he guided her to the tarp, then slipped her sleeping bag off her shoulders and spread it on the tarp.

"If you can't sleep, just lie down and rest. It'll be light in a few hours."

He wasn't sure if her legs buckled or if she went down on her own power, but he was surprised nonetheless when she acquiesced. Once she was inside the sleeping bag, Buzz pulled the edge more squarely over her and walked over to the stove and doused the flame. At his own sleeping bag, he lay down.

Around him, the night sang a peaceful symphony. The familiarity of it should have calmed him, but it didn't. Buzz was as revved up as a jet engine, his mind replaying everything that had been said and done in the last hours.

Across from him, Kelly lay silent and still. The moon cast pale moonlight over her silhouette. Even in the dim light he could make out the curve of her hip, the dark shadow of her hair. The wind shifted, stirring the leaves of the tree above them, and he thought he could smell the sweet scent of citrus and woman that he remembered so well. The familiarity of it took him back to the last time they'd been together. The little house where they'd lived as husband and wife.

That last night, they hadn't even made it to the bedroom, shedding clothes and inhibitions and resolve.... They'd ended up in the hall, disheveled and crazed with lust. She was the only woman who could do that to him. The only woman who could make him lose control as if he were some kind of randy teenager dealing with his first case of hormones. They'd ended up making love on the stairs, in the landing, on the desk just inside the study....

Buzz's body stirred, a deep, purring heat that disturbed him deeply. Shifting restlessly beneath the blanket, he turned onto his side away from her and closed his eyes. He knew better than to think of her in sexual terms. The woman had stolen four precious years of his child's life

from him. Buzz didn't want to forgive her. He didn't want
to care for her. He sure as hell didn't want to want her.

But he did want her. His body ached for her. A familiar
ache that had haunted him for all these years. Buzz figured
he could live with it because there was no way he could
overlook what she'd done, no way he would ever let himself get tangled up with a woman he couldn't forgive.

Buzz woke to a scream. Scrambling out of his sleeping
bag, he jumped to his feet, blinked the sleep from his eyes.
He looked down, saw that Kelly had left her sleeping bag.

Where the hell was she?

Dawn brushed pink and gold on the rocky peak above
where they'd camped. A yellow finch chirped angrily from
the branch of a lodgepole pine. The breeze rustled the tall,
dry grass from the meadow.

Had he dreamed the scream?

"Buzz!"

The terror in her voice sent him into a dead run. He burst
through the brush, around an outcropping of rock and into
a stand of aspen and pine. A hundred scenarios rushed
through his brain. Panic nibbled at his spine, but he shoved
it back. Buzz Malone was a professional. He didn't panic.
Wouldn't panic because he knew a little boy's life could
very well depend on his keeping a cool head.

"Kelly, where are you?" he shouted.

"Over here! Please, Buzz! *Hurry!*"

His sock-encased feet pounded over the dry earth. He
broke through thick underbrush, the branches scratching
him like sharp tentacles. An instant later, the forest opened
to a clearing. The sound of rushing water met him. He
stopped. Held his breath. Listened.

"Buzz! Over here!"

Twenty yards away, he saw a flash of blue near the water. Kelly. He dashed toward her, keenly aware of his heart

hammering against his ribs. Fear gripped him like a vice as he stumbled over river rock and into the icy water.

"What happened?" he shouted.

The water level was low. Kelly stood next to the muddy bank, her arms wrapped around herself, looking down at the ground.

Buzz reached her a moment later. Her eyes met his. The ravaged expression in her face devastated him. He saw pain and terror and the dark fringes of panic in the brown depths of her eyes. All the caution he'd been feeling the night before left him abruptly. He went to her, put his hand on her shoulder, heard himself say her name.

Her hand trembled when she pointed at the muddy bank.

Buzz looked down at the perfect imprint of a cougar's paw.

Kelly looked wildly around, felt her control leave her like a physical departure. She stared down at the print, horror zinging through her like a gunshot, her heart pounding pure terror.

"Eddie!" she cried. *"Eddie!"* Panic resonated in her voice when she screamed his name. She tried to squash it down, get a grip on it, put it in a compartment for later, but it reared up inside her like a maddened beast, took her in its jaws and shook her violently.

"Eddie! Sweetheart, where are you?"

She turned in a circle, looking frantically for something, anything, any sign of her son. Trees and brush and rock blended into a single, dark threat as her gaze skimmed the surrounding woods. The shadows within mocked her, refusing to give up their secrets. Every sound taunted her, a child calling out.

On the other side of the stream, she spotted a disturbance in the sparse yellow grass. Her heart stopped for a beat, then banged hard against her ribs. The next thing she knew she was running, through shallow water that ran swift and cold around her ankles. She scrambled over rocks, slipping on moss and tripping over loose stones the size of basketballs. Vaguely, she was aware of Buzz calling her name, but she didn't slow down, and she didn't stop.

Wet sand sucked at her hiking boots when she reached the bank, but Kelly was in good physical condition and muscled her way up it. Calling out to her son, she paused, breathing hard, shaking uncontrollably, her every sense honed on her surroundings. She wasn't sure what caused her to look down, but when she did everything inside her froze into a solid mass of ice. A perfect imprint of Eddie's sneaker was set into the dry earth. Right next to it, several drops of bright red blood glistened dark and wet.

Kelly stopped breathing. Her blood stalled. The sound of the birds and swiftly moving water faded to a dull roar. Around her, the trees and underbrush and jutting rocks blurred into a kaleidoscope of black and gray. Terror like she'd never felt in her life enveloped her, a dark smothering hand that shut down her senses one by one. She felt it cover her, pressing down, constricting her heart and lungs and squeezing until she couldn't breathe.

"Eddie!" Feeling wild inside, she looked around, felt the steely grip of helplessness clench her. A few feet away, another drop of blood glistened darkly. Farther in, another footprint beckoned her to follow.

She broke into a run, then into an all-out sprint. Branches clawed at her face and clothes as she tore down the trail. Sounds choked from her throat, but she didn't care. Her mind whirled with the possibility that she would find her little boy safe and alive and crying for her. Tears blurred her vision as she darted between two boulders and entered a copse of lodgepole pine. Hope and desperation churned and exploded inside her until she convinced herself she would reach her child any second, that she was so close she could smell his little-boy scent, hear his voice crying out to her.

"Kelly!"

She'd nearly forgotten about Buzz. For the first time she heard him behind her, breaking through the brush. She could hear the heavy pound of his footfalls against the earth, his labored breaths, the occasional curse....

An instant later, a heavy hand clamped over her shoulder. On instinct, she spun around, tried to jerk away. "Oh, God, Buzz! There was blood! On the bank! Oh, God!"

Buzz maintained a firm grip on her shoulders. "Take it easy, Kel."

"I've got to find him. Let go of me!" She tried to twist away from him. "He needs me!"

"Calm down, damn it. Pull yourself together!"

She stared at him, aware that she'd lost control, that she didn't have a clue why she was running or where she was going. "He's crying for me," she said.

"Kelly...."

"Let go of me. I need to find him. Don't try to stop me."

"Easy. Just...Jesus, Kel, take it easy."

"Let go of me!"

"I want you to calm down. Take a deep breath for—"

"I've got to find him," she cried. "He's nearby. I can feel it."

"Kelly! Damn it."

Somewhere in the back of her mind she knew she'd lost it. That she'd slipped down that slippery slope into hysteria and was tumbling headlong into a place she didn't want to go. She knew it was going to cost her credibility. The logical side of her brain knew it was foolish to fight him; she knew Buzz was only trying to help. Intellectually, she knew all of those things. But terror and panic and a mother's desperation overwhelmed logic. Something inside her brain shorted out and all she felt was the primal need to find what was precious.

"Let go of me!" She lashed out with her fists, but Buzz was ready and deflected the blows. "Please, he needs me."

"Stop it." He shook her hard enough to make her head snap back.

Angry now, she put her weight into it and shoved him. She might as well have been shoving at a mountain because he didn't budge.

"Kel, pull yourself together."

She stepped back, trying to dislodge his hands, but the heel of her boot caught on a fallen log behind her. She stumbled. Her arms shot forward as she fell back, her hand snagging the sleeve of Buzz's jacket.

"What the—" His sock caught on the same log, and they went down in a tangle of arms and legs.

Kelly landed on her back atop a cushion of pine needles and prickly tufts of buffalo grass. Muttering a curse, Buzz came down on top of her, breaking his fall with his arms on either side of her. An instant later, she was staring into gray eyes set into the hardened planes of a face that was at once troubled and concerned. In the back of her mind, she was aware of heavy breathing. She could feel a heart raging, but he was so close she couldn't tell if it was his or hers. Her legs were drawn up slightly and her knees were apart. Somehow, Buzz had managed to land between her legs.

Something in the way he looked at her snapped her back. She blinked, shook herself. A breath shuddered out of her. Slowly, she became aware of him pressed intimately against her. His solid weight was strong and reassuring and achingly familiar. The panic that had exploded out of control a moment earlier faltered, then retreated, a formidable army temporarily defeated.

In its place, a new awareness zinged like a hot bullet.

She told herself it wasn't possible to feel anything but fear and desperation and pain when her son was missing and in danger. She tried desperately to deny the slow spiral of warmth that crept past the ice that gripped her. Finding Eddie was the only thing that mattered. But the familiar press of Buzz's body against hers banished the last vestiges of panic, reminded her that while she might be afraid, she was still alive. She was still human, still a woman—and she hadn't been held for a very long time.

The power of the moment stunned her. His closeness, the warmth of his body, the scent that was uniquely his made her realize that she was still vulnerable to him. And that no matter how badly she'd wanted to believe it, she hadn't gotten this man out of her system in the time they'd been apart.

Chapter 5

"Are you all right?" Buzz finally asked.

The words came to her as if through a fog and from a great distance. Blowing the hair from her eyes, she risked making eye contact. His face might have been expressionless to a person who didn't know him. But Kelly knew him. Had memorized every hard angle and plane, and she didn't miss the flash of heat in his eyes. She wanted to believe it was anger, but she knew it wasn't, knew it was much more dangerous and infinitely more complex. And she knew there was no way in hell she could let this go on.

"I'm okay," she said in a voice that sounded amazingly normal. "Let me up."

His grip on her wrists relaxed. "You're not going to go off on me again, are you?"

"I didn't go off on you," she snapped.

Pulling away slightly, Buzz scowled at her.

She looked away, shamed that she'd lost control. She

could only imagine what he thought of her, this man who lived for the high that came with emergency situations. A man who looked down on people who were too weak to handle it. She wondered if that's what he thought of her now. That she was weak, that she couldn't handle it.

"I'm sorry I lost it," she said after a moment. "I don't normally do that."

"It's okay. This has been…stressful to say the least."

She remembered the blood and shuddered. "I was okay. I mean, I'd walked over to the stream to splash some water on my face. I was feeling all right. I was ready to go. Then I saw those cougar tracks." She closed her eyes for a moment, fighting to control an imagination that would drive her insane with worry if she let it. "There's blood, Buzz. For a moment, I thought…I thought…"

"Don't go there, Kel. He's all right," he said fiercely.

"How do you explain—"

"The blood could be from any number of things. The cougar could have nabbed a squirrel, for God's sake."

She prayed that was the case.

"We're going to find him," Buzz said. "And he's going to be fine when we do. You've got to believe that."

A dozen emotions rushed through her brain when she looked into his eyes and saw that he wasn't saying empty words on her behalf. Buzz didn't make nice; he didn't pretend for the sake of others. He believed what he was telling her, and he meant it. The realization took her panic down a notch. "Thank you for saying that," she said.

"Kel, you've got to trust me." Buzz stared at her for an interminable moment. "I've got to be able to count on you, too."

Kelly stared back, desperately trying not to acknowledge how much being close to him like this had bolstered her. His hips were nestled snugly between her legs. She could feel the hard ridge of him against her most intimate part.

It shamed her that she would notice such a thing at a time like this. What kind of mother did that make her? She tried to convince herself she needed the physical contact on an emotional level. But she knew that wasn't quite true.

Sex had been the one aspect of their marriage that had never failed them. Even when things were bad, sex had always been…breathtaking. It had healed a lot of wounds between them. She supposed that's why it had taken her so long to realize mind-blowing sex couldn't fix a broken marriage. She wasn't quite sure whether Buzz had ever realized the same thing.

He'd come to her several times after the divorce was final, and he'd made no bones about what he wanted. There were no pretenses for Buzz Malone. Even knowing they could never live together as husband and wife, Kelly hadn't been strong enough to turn him away.

She'd gone off the pill in a last-ditch effort to convince herself that she would never be with him again. That it was over between them not only physically, but emotionally as well. Kelly knew her going off the pill had been more of a symbolic gesture than anything else. A surefire way to sever that last, lingering tie. But the break hadn't been clean. When Buzz had shown up at her door at two o'clock in the morning with desperation in his eyes and taken her into his arms, Kelly went willingly. She'd vowed to turn him away, convinced herself she didn't need him anymore. But when he'd kissed her, her resolve had crumpled.

They'd ended up in bed and for a few short hours, they'd forgotten about the rest of the world. In the morning, Buzz was always gone. Kelly had hated herself afterward. For being weak. For being vulnerable. For always feeling too much. But in the few short hours when he'd held her in his arms, she'd almost believed they were going to make it. Almost.

She flinched when he raised his hand and pulled a twig from her hair. They spoke simultaneously.

"Sorry I fell on you," he said.

"Sorry I tripped you."

She forced a short laugh, but it didn't break the high-wire tension that had fallen between them. This wasn't a good time for her to be taking a trip down memory lane.

With the effortless grace of a man in top physical condition, Buzz got quickly to his feet, then offered his hand. "Let's get back to camp and pack up."

Kelly accepted his hand and let him pull her to her feet. For the first time she realized her boots were soaking wet. Her feet were cold. Mud clung to her backside, and she had leaves in her hair. "I must look like a crazy person," she said with a laugh.

"You look like a worried mother," he said. "Stop being so hard on yourself, okay?"

She glanced at her watch, amazed to see that it was only a few minutes past 6:00 a.m. It seemed as if Eddie had been missing forever.

"We'll pack up, and cross back over the creek and take that path you found," Buzz said. "He can't be too far away."

A fresh burst of hope leapt through her. "Okay," she said and they started toward the camp.

Buzz had always prided himself on having a level head. He was a cautious man, not prone to idiotic behavior or lapses in judgment. He was the kind of man who relied on logic to guide him through a world that was as complex as he was basic. The kind of man whose emotions never entered the picture when it came to making important decisions. He could count the number of mistakes he'd made in his lifetime on one hand. It didn't elude him that most of those mistakes had to do with Kelly.

That his hormones would betray him was the ultimate irony. Sex was the one aspect of his relationship with her that he'd never been able to control. An area where all the good sense and logic he prided himself on possessing didn't mean squat because once he touched her he didn't give a damn about any of those things.

He'd come within an inch of kissing her a moment ago. Worse, he didn't think he would have wanted to stop with just a kiss. He never wanted to stop with just a kiss when it came to Kelly.

He could still feel the heavy pool of blood in his groin. Still feel the softness of her body beneath his. The sweet brush of her breath against his cheek. She'd been terrified and panic-stricken, and the need to calm her was like a living thing inside him. It hurt to see her that way. It hurt even more not being able to do anything about it.

That he was out here in the middle of nowhere looking for his own son gave the situation a cruel twist. How could he be thinking of Kelly in sexual terms given what she'd stolen from him? How could he still want her when she'd made her feelings perfectly clear five years ago? Was he that big a fool?

Buzz still couldn't quite grasp the fact that he now had a son. An innocent little boy with eyes so like his own he couldn't bear to look at the photograph. Damn it, he'd never wanted children. The truth of that made him feel like a son of a bitch. But he knew how cruel life could be to an unwanted child.

Russell Malone hadn't wanted children either, and Buzz had spent his childhood paying for his parents' mistake. His mother had died during childbirth, and Buzz's father, overcome with grief and bitterness, had blamed the child he'd never wanted. For sixteen years, young Buzz had paid in every way an abused child could pay. He'd learned when to hide by the time he was six. Learned to duck punches before his tenth birthday. He learned to take those punches by the time his teen years rolled around.

He still couldn't bring himself to think of those days. Couldn't think of Russell Malone without getting a knot of hate in his gut.

Yes, Buzz knew first-hand the terrors this world could offer an innocent child. Four years with the Child Abuse Division of the Denver PD had solidified his resolve never to have children. He'd seen things during those years he could barely acknowledge even now. Things that shocked him and shamed him. Things that had given him nightmares for months afterward. He thought of all those things now— the nightmares innocent children faced every single day of their lives—and wondered how a woman he'd once loved could do something so deceitful.

Cursing under his breath, Buzz packed the lantern into its case and shoved it into his backpack. He could hear Kelly behind him, packing her things, but he didn't look at her. There were too many emotions boiling inside him, and Buzz needed to keep those emotions bottled. He didn't want them to come out because they were dark and volatile and wouldn't do either of them any good. Kelly was already on edge. All she needed was a spark and she'd go off like a bomb.

"I'm ready."

He turned to her and frowned. She looked better than she had a right to. Her color had returned. She'd pulled her brown hair into a ponytail. Dirt marred the knees of her jeans, but she'd tucked in her shirt and brushed off the leaves. No, she shouldn't have looked so damn good. But she did, and the fact that he noticed ticked him off more than anything she could have said.

Without speaking, he pulled the radio from its case and summoned Rocky Mountain Search and Rescue Headquarters. "Homer One this is Tango Two Niner. Can you give me a stat on our lost boy?"

"Dispatch here, Buzz. We just heard from White River. No sign of the subject. Grid search in progress just north and east of you. Clear."

"Where's Eagle?" he asked, referring to the Bell 412 chopper.

"Eagle left at first light. Flyboy did a sweep of the area, but the Forest Service needed a swoop and scoop just north of you. It's an emergency situation up there. A dozen homes burned this morning. Sixteen people had to be evaced."

Buzz hadn't wanted Kelly to hear that. They didn't need yet another emergency piled on top of the one they were already dealing with. Without looking at her, he turned and walked a few paces away from her. "How bad is the fire?"

"It's small right now. Only a couple thousand acres have burned. But it's not controlled and another front is coming through this afternoon. Winds are going to be bad, Buzz. Fifty, sixty knots. Going to send the fire south fast. Things might get a little crazy."

Buzz knew all too well what those kinds of winds would do to a fire in drought conditions. Even a light breeze could turn a relatively controlled fire into an out-of-control inferno if things were dry enough. He and Kelly and Eddie were directly south of the area Dispatch was referring to. For the first time, true fear gnawed at his stomach like a starving rodent. "Front going to be dry?"

"That's affirm according to Weather Service."

"Damn." Buzz scrubbed a hand over the stubble of his beard. "Kel and I are on the east side of the campground. We found tracks last night, then again this morning. Let the base camp know, all right? I think we're close, but we could use some volunteers up here."

Dispatch hesitated. "Boulder One is working the fire."

Buzz closed his eyes, caught himself, hoped Kelly didn't see the reaction. "We lost all of our help?"

"That's affirm."

"How many people we got looking for the boy?"

"Jake Madigan is out with a few people on horseback just to the west of you. Dog team from Chaffee County is en route. John Maitland and Scully are in the ATV to the south."

"Roger that, Dispatch. Clear." Cursing, Buzz shoved the radio into its case and latched it to his belt. When he ran out of things to do, he turned to Kelly.

She was standing a few feet away, staring at him as if he'd just hung up with the executioner. Her eyes were large and dark and knowing in the pale oval of her face.

"Where's the chopper?" she asked evenly.

"There's a fire to the north. Forest Service asked Flyboy to evac some families."

"They're not going to help us?"

"The fire takes precedence, Kel."

"How bad is the fire?"

He considered her for a moment, weighing his options, wondering how much he could tell her without setting her off.

"Don't you dare hold out on me," she snapped.

"I'll level with you if you can keep a handle on it."

"I can handle it. Just...." Her voice broke. "Damn it, Buzz. I deserve to know what we're up against."

"The fire's to the north of us and burning out of control. There's a front coming. Winds are expected to kick up to about fifty knots."

"Rain?"

Buzz shook his head. "It's a dry front."

"It's coming this way, isn't it? South. Of course it is."

He nodded, hefted his backpack and slipped his arms through the straps. "Let's go."

"How long do we have?" she asked.

"Kel, you know how unpredictable fires are."

Her hands shook when she reached for her fanny pack and clipped it to her belt. "All right," she said. "Let's go find Eddie."

To someone who didn't know her, she might have looked like she was about to set off on a Saturday-morning hike. But Buzz knew her all too well, knew her intimately, remembered every detail about her because he still dreamed about her.

He saw clearly the pain and fear in her eyes. The tension in her shoulders when she moved. The unsteady hands. All of that punctuated by the determined set of her mouth. It was hard for him to watch her hurt, even harder not to do anything about it. Every cell in his body screamed for him to go to her, to hold her for a moment and tell her everything was going to be all right.

But he held his ground. He knew if he gave in to the need to touch her, to make everything all right—even if it wasn't—he might open a door he'd worked very hard to close. A door he would be a fool to open now, no matter what lay on the other side of the threshold.

Chapter 6

By noon, the winds had shifted out of the north, and Buzz could smell smoke. A call to Rocky Mountain Search and Rescue Headquarters told him the southernmost line of the fire was now only six or seven miles to the north of where they stood. Throughout the afternoon hours, the sky had darkened, casting eerie gray light over the forest. Ash fluttered down from the slate sky like dirty snow, a constant reminder of the danger bearing down on them.

"This is the third time we've been through this area."

Stopping next to the small creek that ran along the trail, Buzz looked over at Kelly and felt that all-too-familiar punch-in-the-gut sensation that got him every time he looked at her. Considering they'd been walking for six hours without food or rest—and with no sign of Eddie—she was holding up amazingly well.

They'd run into another search party near Panther Creek a couple of hours earlier and chatted for a few minutes. Nobody had said what they were all thinking, but Buzz saw it in the other men's eyes: The little boy should have turned up by now.

"Fourth time," he corrected and tugged the collapsible water container from his backpack. He drank deeply, then handed it to Kelly.

She took the bottle, but she didn't drink. "I don't understand how his tracks could just disappear."

"Neither of us are trackers, Kel. We missed something. That's all. We'll make another sweep. He'll turn up."

He saw a fresh wave of worry leak into her features. He was beginning to see the trend. She was fine as long as they were moving. Once they stopped, her mind began to torture her with terrible possibilities.

"Drink," he said firmly. "I don't want you getting dehydrated.

Sighing, she raised the container to her lips. Buzz watched her drink, the slender column of her throat moving rhythmically as she swallowed. At some point, she'd removed her flannel shirt and tied it around her waist. The T-shirt she wore was dirty in places and torn at the shoulder, but neither of those things detracted from the slender form beneath. He remembered every curve and secret place with painful clarity. And the way she looked at him when she was aroused, the heat of her flesh beneath his hands....

From where he stood a few feet away, he could see the outline of her bra and the faint points of her nipples through the thin material. She'd never been into fancy lingerie when they'd been married, but he swore he saw the delineation of lace. The image gave him pause, made him wonder if she bought that fancy underwear for someone to see. The thought stuck in his craw like a piece of glass. In the back of his mind, he wondered if she was seeing that jerk back at the campground, if it was serious. He wondered if she realized the man he'd met back at camp was interested in being more than merely her friend.

Buzz knew it was stupid, but the thought of her with someone else ticked him off. Damn near made him queasy. But he could tell by the way Taylor Quelhorst had looked at her that he was definitely interested. Any man in his right mind would want her.

His gaze traveled the length of her as she drank. She was thinner than he remembered, with a little bit more muscle definition in her arms. He wondered if she still liked to run. When they'd been married, she used to get up early and run every morning. Then she'd come home, and if he was still in bed she'd join him and they'd make wild, passionate love. They'd shower together and make love again beneath the spray....

Realizing he was just standing there, staring at her—and that she'd noticed—he eased the backpack off his shoulders and let it fall to the ground.

"What are you doing?" she asked.

He frowned at her, then lowered himself onto a comfortable-looking slab of granite and worked the stiffness out of his ankles. "I'm going to sit down and eat one of these protein bars. I suggest you do the same."

"We can't stop now," she said. "Damn it, Buzz, it's getting late. We can circle around again. Use the whistle—"

"We're going to stop and rest for a few minutes."

"I want to keep going."

He would have snapped at her if she didn't look so damn good standing there, killing him with those eyes and all those curves he was a fool to be noticing now. "If you've got half a brain you'll sit down and rest while you can, Kel. We've got a long night ahead of us."

She stood her ground. "I'm not tired."

Ignoring her, Buzz rummaged through his backpack, found two protein bars and tossed one to her. She caught the bar, then stalked over to a flat-topped rock a few feet

away where she ripped off the wrapper. She ate without
pleasure, all the while her eyes scanned the surrounding
woods.

Buzz had to admire her; she'd done well considering the
circumstances. He knew what parents were like when children turned up missing. Most were more of a hindrance
than a help when it came to the search. He should have
known Kelly would be different. She might be missing her
son and scared spitless, but she'd taken control of the situation as best she could. Kelly had never been one to sit
on the sidelines. When she didn't like something, she
changed it. Or tried to, anyway. Buzz supposed her take-
no-prisoners attitude was one of the factors that had led up
to their divorce. She hadn't been able to change him.

Not that Buzz was the most flexible man in the world.
He wasn't.

He thought about Eddie and wondered how in God's
name he was supposed to be a father. He didn't know the
first thing about fatherhood. It wasn't like he'd ever had a
role model. Russell Malone had done most of his talking
with his fists. What the hell kind of father would Buzz
make? How did a man go from childless divorcé to having
a young son with a sexy-as-sin mother he'd never managed
to get out of his system?

They ate in silence for a few minutes, the only sound
coming from the strong north wind hissing through the
pines above.

"Tell me about Eddie," Buzz said after a moment.

Kelly looked over at him as if the question had startled
her. "What do you want to know?"

"Well, what's he like?"

She smiled, but it was fringed with a deep sadness. Buzz
had forgotten how pretty she was when she smiled. She
hadn't exactly had a lot to smile about in the last hours.

But even sad and tired and unhappy as she was, he could still feel the power of her smile tugging at him.

"He's sweet and smart and incredibly intuitive for such a little guy." Her smile deepened. "He likes Matchbox cars and Labrador retrievers, and he wants to be a race-car driver when he grows up. He likes Little League. Shortstop. He hates carrots. Loves rocky road ice cream." Tears shimmered in her eyes when she looked over at Buzz. "He's got freckles on his nose. A mole just behind his ear. A wart on his left thumb. I cut his hair a couple of weeks ago and his bangs are crooked." A breath shuddered out of her. "He's a world-class snuggler. He likes to get in bed with me on Saturday morning and turn on the television. We snuggle and eat Cap'n Crunch and watch cartoons with Brandy, our dog."

Buzz didn't want to bear witness to the hurt he saw in her eyes when she talked about her little boy. *Their* little boy. Aware that his heart was beating too fast, he looked down at his boots, hoping she didn't break down and cry. He wasn't sure how he'd handle it if she did.

"You got any more pictures? I mean, with you?" he asked.

Wiping the tears from her cheeks with her sleeve, she reached into her hip pocket and pulled out a small folding wallet. "I took these last year when we got our Labrador pup."

Buzz reached for the photos. Something shifted hard in his chest when he looked down into the laughing eyes of the little boy. "He looks like you."

"He looks like you, too. The eyes, mostly." Rising, Kelly knelt beside Buzz and pointed to a photo of Eddie in the pool with a gangly black dog. "He's a good swimmer. Strong. And he loves Brandy."

"Dogs are good for kids."

"He reminds me of you."

Buzz wanted to look at her, but he didn't dare. Not when she was so close he could see the shimmer of her hair in the dim sunlight.

He cleared his throat. "Must be that race-car driver thing."

"No. His mannerisms. The way he thinks. He already wants to conquer the world."

Buzz forced a laugh, but it was an odd, humorless sound. "Sounds like he takes after you."

"I don't want to conquer the world."

"You just want to control it."

She laughed. "Maybe that's why we couldn't make things work."

"Or maybe we both just have really hard heads."

"That, too."

He looked at her, realized they'd broached a subject he had no desire to discuss. Quickly, he moved to change topics. "Who's Taylor Quelhorst?"

"I work for him. I met him last year when I was doing cross-country ski tours in Breckenridge."

"What are you doing now?"

"I'm an assistant manager at the Snow Moose Lodge."

"Nice place." Buzz whistled. "So you work together?"

"Not really. Taylor owns the lodge."

Taylor, Buzz thought. Not Mr. Quelhorst, not Taylor Quelhorst, but Taylor. It was none of his damn business, but he wanted badly to tell her just how he felt about her being on a first-name basis with a man who looked at her the way Quelhorst did. But he knew it would only cause an argument. After all, Buzz didn't have a claim on her one way or another. Damn it, he didn't *want* that kind of relationship with her. They'd tried once and it hadn't worked. He was crazy to be feeling like a jealous teenager.

"Sounds like you've done well for yourself," he said after a too-long moment. "You still living at the house?"

The pretty little house just west of Denver they'd bought together as newlyweds seven years ago. The two-bedroom, one-bath matchbox with the tiny yard and leaky kitchen sink. The house where they'd made love in every room, including the living room closet.

"Actually, I put the house on the market last month," she said. "The commute…it was just too long."

Buzz wasn't sure why, but that hurt. "And you didn't see fit to discuss it with me?"

"It's my house. I didn't see any reason—"

"What about my son? Maybe you could have considered him."

She blinked at him. "Buzz, I didn't think you would mind. I mean, you made it clear you didn't want the house."

"Maybe I do mind. Maybe you don't know me as well as you think you do." Angry now, he turned away from her, willing his pulse to slow. He knew he was acting like an idiot, but he couldn't seem to get a handle on his temper. "Did you buy another house?" he asked. "An apartment? What?"

"I rented a condo in Breckenridge, but it's only temporary."

Buzz shot her a questioning look.

Kelly took a keep breath, like a woman on a high diving board about to plunge twenty feet into cold, deep water. "I'm relocating to Lake Tahoe."

"Lake Tahoe is in California," he said stupidly.

"We're moving." She looked down at the crumpled wrapper in her hand. "Next month."

For an instant, he wasn't sure he'd heard her correctly. But he saw the answer in her eyes, felt the truth like a dull knife plunged into his solar plexus. "I see," was all he could manage.

"Taylor just opened a small resort in Tahoe. Skiing in

the winter. Horseback-riding and hiking in the summer. The grand opening is next month. I'm going to be running the place for him. It's a good opportunity for me. I mean, it's not like I have ties in Denver holding me back.''

For a moment, Buzz couldn't say anything, didn't know what to say. All he knew was that yesterday he'd been told he had a son. Today, he was being told the son he'd never met was moving five hundred miles away. He wasn't exactly sure how he was going to handle being a father, but he suddenly knew enough to realize he didn't like the idea of a long-distance relationship with his boy.

''When were you planning on telling me?'' he asked.

She wrapped her arms around herself in a defensive posture. ''I don't think this is the time to discuss this.''

''Evidently, you didn't think any time was a good time to discuss this, did you?''

She stared at him, stricken. ''I can't talk about this right now.''

Buzz tried hard to get a handle on his temper. He knew she was right; now wasn't the time to open this particular can of worms. Things were tense enough with Eddie missing. But his temper boiled every time he thought of her leaving town with his son and not telling him.

''Maybe you were just going to leave and not tell me. You're good at that, aren't you, Kel?''

''That's not the way any of this happened.''

''Yeah?'' Furious, he rose and stalked over to her. ''I guess you didn't notice the way he looks at you.''

She gaped at him. ''The way *who* looks at me?''

''Quelhorn.''

''You mean *Quelhorst?*''

''Whatever.''

''Our relationship is strictly professional,'' she said.

''Strictly professional until he decides he wants more.''

''Buzz, where the hell is this coming from?'' She rose,

smaller, but every bit as furious. "Even if I was involved with him, I don't see what business it is of yours. We're divorced, remember?"

Buzz had sworn he wasn't going to let her do this to him. He wasn't going to let her tick him off. Swore he wasn't going to let her push his buttons. But if there was any one person in the world who could set him off, it was Kelly. Aware that his heart was pounding, that he was feeling cranky and mean and scared—and that his hands were clenched into fists at his sides, he spun on her. "It's my business because I'm Eddie's father," he growled.

"That's a role you never wanted."

"You took any choice I might have had away from me." Breathing hard, he paced away from her. The next thought that occurred to him turned him back around, had him stalking over to her. "What have you told Eddie about his father?"

She blinked at him again, as if the quick spin of topics was confusing her. "I haven't told him anything. He… hasn't asked."

"What are you going to say when he does, Kel? You know he will sooner or later."

"I haven't decided—"

"Haven't *decided?*"

"Buzz—"

"Maybe you're planning to tell him Quelhorn is his daddy. That his daddy is a goddamn pencil-necked—"

Chin jutting out angrily, she stalked closer until her face was less than a foot away from his. "What do you think I should tell him, Buzz? That his father is an adrenaline freak and spends his days trying to get himself killed?"

"That's crap and you know it."

"That you think you're some kind of superhero? Maybe I could tell him about the night you got shot. The night some kid put a bullet in your spine. Another millimeter or two and it would have severed the cord. Maybe I could tell him how you almost died that night.''

"I was a cop, Kel. It's part of the job. I accepted that.''

"I didn't.''

"Cops get hurt. You knew that going in.''

"That's not going to happen to my son.''

"He's my son, too.''

"In that case, maybe I'll tell him you turned down a decent corporate security job because you're addicted to adrenaline. All the people who love you can go straight to hell because you don't give a damn what they think or how much they suffer or who you leave behind if you get yourself killed. Maybe I'll tell him you chose Rocky Mountain Search and Rescue over our marriage because it chafes your ego to sit behind a desk.''

"I did not choose RMSAR over our marriage. You gave me an ultimatum.''

"And you made your choice.''

"I did what I had to do!'' he shouted. "What I do has nothing to do with ego. It has to do with who I am, and with the fact that you never got over losing your father and brother.''

She paled at the mention of her father. Buzz knew he'd hit a nerve. They'd never discussed the details of the chopper crash that had killed her father, Jack McKee, and her older brother Kyle. But Buzz had heard the rumors, heard the stories. He knew it must have been tough for her; she'd only been a kid. But he also knew he couldn't change who he was simply because she couldn't live with it.

"Don't bring my father or brother into this,'' she said in a quivering voice. "This is between you and me.''

"I think we both know your father and brother are at the heart of the matter,'' he said quietly.

"You're forty years old, Buzz. When are you going to

grow up? You can't spend the rest of your life jumping out of choppers and rappelling down cliffs!''

"You can't spend the rest of your life being afraid."

"I'm not the one who's afraid. You are."

Buzz couldn't remember the last time he was so angry he shook. But he was now. That it was Kelly who'd gotten him to this point irked him to no end. She'd always known which buttons to push and he could clearly see that the time away from him hadn't changed anything.

Grinding his teeth, he turned away from her, stalked over to his backpack and scooped it up. "We're burning daylight," he said.

"Fine." She hurled the water bottle at him.

Buzz caught it with one hand, tucked it into his backpack then slung the backpack over his shoulders. His heart was still pounding when he started down the trail.

"The sky looks funny, Bunky Bear."

Eddie Malone huddled against the rocks and hugged the stuffed animal, trying not to think about how scared he was. He'd drunk the last of his juice when he first woke up, and already he was thirsty. He'd eaten his peanut butter sandwich for breakfast, and now he only had one cracker left. He wanted to save it for later, but he was hungry, too.

What was he going to eat when he ran out of crackers?

The thought made him want to cry, but he didn't. He'd cried a lot already and all it did was make his cheeks burn. His eyes and throat were burning, too. He didn't think that was from crying, though, but because of the smoke. The air smelled like it did when he and Mommy had a fire in the fireplace.

Thinking of his mommy made him whimper. Oh, he wished he could find her. All he wanted to do was go home.

"Mommy!" he called out. "I'm scared! Where are you?"

He'd had a bloody nose earlier when he was crossing the creek. He hadn't even noticed until he looked down and saw blood on his shirt. Mommy always told him to pinch the end of his nose and tilt his head back, so he'd sat down with Bunky Bear and done just that until it stopped.

A screech drew his attention to the sky. Eddie looked up to see a big bird wheeling overhead. He wondered if it was an eagle. He'd never seen an eagle before.

Even though the sun was still out, the sky was darker than it had been the day before. Maybe there was a storm coming. He thought about thunder and almost started crying again. He didn't like storms, so he hugged Bunky Bear tighter and started to hum the song Mommy had taught him when they'd driven on that really far drive to the mountains where she was going to be working in a really cool place.

"One, two, three, look at me. I'm a happy cowboy. Four, five, six, ropey tricks, are easy for a cowboy...."

For the hundredth time, he wondered where his mommy was. He knew she was going to be worried. He hoped she wasn't mad. He couldn't help it if he was lost. He'd been trying so hard to find her. He wondered if she was still where he'd left her. He hoped she'd woken up and gone back to the ranger station.

Turning slightly, Eddie set Bunky Bear on the rock opposite him, so he could see him better. "Mommy knows all about the woods and camping," he said. "She's the smartest mommy in the whole world, Bunky Bear. Don't worry. She's not even going to be mad. She's out looking for us right now. Probably has a bunch of people helping her. Really smart people who wear hiking boots and cowboy hats and know all about the mountains and stuff."

The thought of his mommy made him smile. He looked up at the sky again, felt the first fringes of fear at the thought of the coming darkness. Or a storm.

Last night had been so scary. Even though he had a

jacket, he'd been cold. So cold he hadn't been able to sleep. And he'd heard all sorts of noises. Strange growling sounds. Rustlings in the bushes.

The thought of spending another night alone scared him so much Eddie began to cry. "Don't cry, Bunky Bear," he said, sniffing loudly. Reaching for the stuffed animal, he hugged it close and started to sing the song again.

Chapter 7

Kelly found the candy bar wrapper just before dusk. Lingering several feet behind her as they clamored over rocky terrain, Buzz saw her kneel.

"He was here!" she cried. "Buzz! Oh, my God! He was here!"

Holding the wrapper up as if she'd just found the world's largest diamond, she rushed toward Buzz, covering the rugged terrain at a dangerous speed. She was breathless, smiling, her face lit with new hope when she reached him. She waved the wrapper like a victory flag. "This was in his backpack. Buzz, he was here!"

Without waiting for him to reply, she spun and cupped her hands to her mouth. "Eddie! Honey, it's Mommy! Where are you, sweetheart!"

Grasping the whistle hanging from the chain at his neck, Buzz put it to his mouth and blew three times in quick succession. The ear-splitting sound echoed off the treetops and the rock face on the other side of the creek. A flock of birds flurried into the air a dozen yards away.

"If he's within earshot, he'll hear the whistle," he said.

As if holding her breath, Kelly turned in a circle, her eyes skimming the surrounding forest and rock. "He's got to be close," she said. "Even if he can't hear us, he's got to be close."

"Let me see the wrapper," Buzz said.

She passed it to him, but her attention was riveted to the surrounding vistas. Buzz studied the wrapper. Residual chocolate had melted on the inside. A few tiny ants had discovered it and scurried about the paper. Judging from the amount of chocolate consumed by the ants, he guessed it had been on the ground an hour, maybe two.

He blew the whistle again. Three long durations. Then they listened. He could practically feel the excitement coming off Kelly. While the wrapper was good news, he knew it wasn't a guarantee that they would find him any time soon.

Buzz was in the process of handing her the water when a voice came over his VHF radio. "This is Homer One. You there, Tango?"

Buzz slid the radio from his belt. "I'm here."

"Flyboy just called in with an update on the situation up north."

Instinctively knowing why the man on the other end hadn't used the word *fire,* Buzz turned away from Kelly and lowered his voice. "What've you got?"

"Twelve homes burned last night near Meredith. Two firefighters are missing. Flyboy's out looking, but it doesn't look good."

Buzz cursed. Damn, he hated it when the good guys lost one of their own. "I'm four miles south of there. We've got plenty of smoke."

"Fire's moving fast, Buzz. Front came through and everything went to hell."

"How many people we got left looking for the boy?"

"They've expanded the grid search. Jake Madigan is out with a few other volunteers. Maitland and Scully are still out in the ATV." The man on the other end paused. "They needed the chopper to find the two firefighters, so Flyboy is gone."

"Roger that."

"Any sign of the kid?"

"That's a negative."

"We're not going to quit, but in light of the conditions up there, you might consider sending the mother back. That fire's burning uncontrolled. Things could get squirrelly."

Buzz sighed. He knew Dispatch was right; he knew the time had come for him to send Kelly back. Just as he knew he was going to have a knock-down-drag-out fight on his hands. Holy hell. He couldn't think of a more impossible situation.

"Flyboy is going to do a fly by on his way to base when he fuels," Dispatch said. "He'll keep an eye out for the kid."

"Tell him I appreciate that."

"Will do. Good luck."

"Over and out." Buzz flipped off the radio and was in the process of sheathing it when Kelly came up beside him.

"What did they say about the fire?" she asked.

He looked at her, felt that familiar punch-in-the-gut sensation that always made him feel as if he'd just stepped out of the ring after being trounced by a sumo wrestler. He wished she'd stop looking at him like that. Like something good was about to happen when he was fresh out of good news.

Buzz had been around the block enough times to know good didn't always prevail. Even when it came to the innocent. Especially when it came to the children....

Shaking off the memories, he fought his way back to the present and relayed the new information to her.

She stared at him, her eyes wide and filled with denial and a measure of defiance. "Four miles is a long way."

Buzz didn't say anything.

"That just means we've got to hurry. We've got to find him quickly. Buzz, we're close. I—"

"Kel, that means the fire could come roaring through here in a matter of hours."

"What are you saying?"

"I'm telling you I want you to go back to the ranger station. It's not safe for you up here. If the wind shifts or the leading edge of the fire moves more quickly than expected, we could get into trouble."

She backed up a step, put her hand out as if to fend him off. "I'm not leaving my son up here."

"Kel, if you don't go back voluntarily, I'll be forced to take you back myself. That's time spent that I could have been looking for Eddie."

"I'm not leaving until I find him. I mean it, Buzz. Don't try to make me, because I'll fight you."

"I can't risk your getting hurt, Kel. We've already lost two firefighters. These guys are good at what they do, and the fire still got them. It's burning out of control and coming this way. I can't let you stay."

"I'm not leaving Eddie."

"I can work faster if I'm alone."

"I can keep up with any pace you set."

Buzz growled in frustration. "I understand why you don't want to leave, Kel. But come on. I'm a professional. Leave this to me. I'll find him."

She stared at him, stricken. "My God, how can you expect me to leave my child out here all alone?"

"He's my child, too, damn it! If something happens to both of us, who is he going to have?"

That stopped her. Buzz saw the battle raging inside her, the battle between a mother's instinct to save her child and the logic that dictated her own survival. When she turned to him and squared her shoulders, he knew instantly which had won. And he prayed it didn't end up costing both of them their lives.

"I'm not leaving. I'm sorry if that's not the answer you wanted to hear. But I can't leave him. I can't."

Buzz stared hard at her for a long time. His first instinct was to fight her on this, overpower her if he had to in order to keep her safe. But for the first time in a long time, he understood where she was coming from. He understood the need to protect what was precious.

Feeling a new urgency pressing down on him, he slung the backpack off his shoulders and pulled out the topographical map of the area, then glanced down at his watch. Seven o'clock.

"We have about two hours before dark," he said as he spread the map. He set his finger at the point where they stood. "We're here." He slid his finger a fraction of an inch. "This is where we found his tracks in the sand. And this is where you fell."

Kelly looked down at the map. When she set her hand at the point where they'd found the tracks, Buzz could see that her hands were shaking. She looked up at Buzz, her eyes large and frightened. "He's following the stream," she said.

"That's why we haven't been able to find him. He's been sticking to the rocks. That's why he hasn't left many tracks. He probably feels protected that way. There are lots of nooks and crannies he can fit into."

"How far are we from the stream?"

"Not far." Buzz pointed toward the cliffs to the north. "Just on the other side of that rock face. If he's near the water, he won't be able to hear us, either."

She cut him a questioning look.

"The water there runs swift. It's loud. If he's stopped

nearby, he won't be able to hear the whistle over the sound of the water."

"Let's go." She started to turn away, but Buzz grabbed her arm.

"From here on out, we move quickly," he said. "No more breaks. We drink while we walk. I'll refill at the creek. I've got some chlorine tabs, so we should be okay. We've got to push, Kel, and we've got to push hard. In another two hours it will be dark. Visibility may be nil by morning. Smoke will be a problem. If the fire comes this way...." Not wanting to finish the sentence, Buzz shrugged.

She was already nodding her head vigorously. "I can do it," she said. "I'm in good shape, Buzz."

Buzz knew exactly what kind of shape she was in—he'd seen the way she filled out those jeans and that T-shirt. Yeah, her shape was the one thing he didn't want to think about it. He also knew that even if she wasn't in top physical condition, she would look for her child until she dropped from exhaustion—and he wouldn't hear a sound from her until her body hit the ground.

"Let's go," he said and started down the trail.

"Eddie!"

Kelly shouted for her son until her voice was hoarse. Buzz used the whistle every five minutes or so. It seemed as if they'd been following the creek forever. Darkness had long since fallen, but neither of them acknowledged it. The wind whistled through the treetops, carrying with it the pungent tang of smoke. In the distance, she could hear the rush of white water over rocks. It had been their constant companion since they'd started following the stream. There hadn't seen a sign of Eddie since she'd found the candy wrapper, and she fought despair with every step she took.

Where on earth was he?

"Eddie!" she cried.

"Kel."

"Sweetheart, it's Mommy! I'm here! *Eddie!*"

She jolted when strong hands landed gently upon her shoulders. She'd been so focused on her surroundings, on looking for her son, she hadn't even realized it when Buzz walked up to her.

"It's almost 2:00 a.m.," Buzz said. "Let's stop for a couple of hours and get some sleep."

"I won't be able to sleep," she said automatically.

"Then we'll just sit for a while and rest."

When she only looked at him, he grimaced then raised his hand and tucked a strand of hair behind her ear. "Kel, you're exhausted."

"I'm okay. Damn it, I'm fine."

"You can barely stand upright."

"I appear to be doing just that."

"Just because you can walk doesn't mean you're worth a damn as far as seeing what you need to see."

"I can keep going."

"What about tomorrow, Kel? What about the next day?"

"I'll…we'll have him by then," she said, trying not to hear the desperation in her voice.

"You've got to rest or you're not going to be any help to anyone, including Eddie. I want you sharp, not zoned out because you refused to listen to common sense. Come on."

For the first time that day the heavy hand of despair pressed down on her. Up until now, hope and progress had fueled her. She hadn't even been tired. But suddenly the lead weight of fatigue dropped over her with such force that her arms and legs were too heavy to move. Her feet throbbed. Her back ached. Worst of all, she felt as if her heart were about to break.

Turning, she looked at Buzz, saw the same bone-deep

fatigue in his face, and she realized she didn't even have the energy to argue with him.

"This is all my fault," she whispered. "If I hadn't gone after Bunky Bear. If I hadn't fallen—"

He raised a finger, pressed it firmly against her mouth. "Don't let me hear you say that again."

"If I hadn't taken him on such a long hike—"

"Don't get into the what-ifs, Kel. It's a waste of energy, and counterproductive as hell. You're going to need all the energy you can muster in the coming hours."

She knew he was right. But she couldn't help but think that none of this would have happened if she hadn't gone down that ravine in the first place.

"He can't be far away," Buzz said.

"This is his second night." Pain knifed through her at the thought of her little boy enduring a second night of hunger and cold and fear. "He probably doesn't have any food left. He's probably out of water. He's going to be hungry and thirsty and cold. Oh, God, I can't stand thinking—"

"He's a strong little boy, Kel. Sure, it's hard, but he'll get through it. I've searched for children in these mountains before. They're amazingly strong and resilient and smart. Even the young ones. Let's just stay calm and keep our heads, okay?"

She nodded, knowing he was right, but still felt as if she was coming apart inside.

He looked around and pointed toward a relatively flat area protected from the wind by jutting rock. "Let's set up camp over there."

Kelly nodded, but she couldn't keep her eyes from skimming the surrounding trees and rocks. There were a thousand places where Eddie could have taken refuge. He could have fallen and be lying somewhere unconscious. He could have slipped off one of the boulders and into the rushing water. Or the cougar that had left the tracks could have…

The pain nearly doubled her over. She stopped walking, had to concentrate on catching her breath.

"Don't let your mind get the best of you, Kel."

Startled, she looked up at him. He'd always been adept at reading her. She wondered if he had any idea of the terrible thoughts streaking through her mind at this moment. That she was frustrated and terrified and so exhausted she wanted to sink down to the ground and cry.

She started to turn away, but he grasped her wrist and made her stay. "Most people think it's the physical strain that exhausts them during searches," he said. "But it's not. It's the emotional strain that puts people down. That renders them useless. Don't let that happen to you. I need you."

The words echoed between them for an interminable moment. Nothing else he could have said could have bolstered her more. She wondered if he really still knew her that well. Or if it was a psychology thing he'd learned in the course of his law-enforcement or search-and-rescue training. Whatever the case, it worked, and she would never forget that he'd done that for her.

For an instant, she just stood there, staring at him. Seeing the man she'd married a lifetime ago. A man she still thought about every day. A man she saw every time she looked at her little boy. A man she'd loved desperately once upon a time.

He stared back at her with those hard, emotionless eyes. Eyes that were as cold and hard as iron. Eyes that could cut with the ruthlessness of a blade. But they were the same eyes she'd seen soften to smoke. His features were in shadow, but she could still make out the narrow slash of his nose. The stern cut of a jaw that was a little too square and a lot too uncompromising. The mouth that rarely smiled. The same mouth that had kissed her countless times when they'd been married. A mouth that knew every inch of her body intimately.

He wasn't a handsome man, but the combination of features and the force of his personality attracted her as no other man ever had. As no other man ever would. She knew that in her heart. Knew she would never love another the way she'd loved Buzz Malone. It made her sad to think that that was behind her. That she would never experience again what she'd experienced with Buzz.

How could a man she'd loved so deeply so long ago still move her like this? A man who was all wrong for her? Who had turned her life upside down because he didn't have the good sense to keep himself safe? A courageous man who would risk his life for a stranger, but wasn't brave enough to bring children into their lives?

She didn't intend to touch him, but the pull was too strong, like a full moon tugging at a restless sea. He jolted when her knuckles grazed his cheek. His eyes sharpened to flint, but he didn't move away. He gazed steadily at her, unmoving, as if her touch was something to be endured and not enjoyed.

"Thank you for...this," she said quietly. "For being here."

His jaw flexed beneath her fingertips. "He's my son, too."

Aware that her heart was beating heavily in her chest, that she was standing less than a foot away from him with her hand on his cheek, she stepped back. She wasn't fast enough to prevent what she'd known would happen next.

Buzz reached for her. "Come here."

A current of tension went through her when his fingers closed around her biceps and he pulled her toward him. She knew better than to get any closer, but over twenty-four hours of psychological and physical stress had shredded her defenses. She stood before him, trembling, her own heartbeat drowning out the roar of the water fifteen yards away.

"Don't cry," he said softly.

She hadn't even realized she was. "I'm not."

One side of his mouth curved. "Must be allergies."

She choked out a sound, a laugh or a cry, she didn't know which, but it loosened something inside her. A shudder rippled through her when he brushed a tear from her cheek with his thumb.

"I'm just going to hold you for a moment, okay?" he said.

Unable to speak, blinking back tears, she nodded, wondering if he would ever know how desperately she'd needed to be held at that moment.

His arms enveloped her like a protective cocoon. Kelly knew they shouldn't be doing this. Buzz was as wrong for her as a man could be. She didn't want to open doors that were best left closed and bolted. She didn't want him to get the wrong idea. She didn't want him back in her life. She and Eddie were about to move to Lake Tahoe. There was no room in her life for a man who had put her through the wringer—and wouldn't hesitate to do it again if she let him.

But the solid warmth of his body against hers made her forget all the reasons she shouldn't need to be held. The scent of pine and the out-of-doors mingled with his own unique scent and drugged her like a powerful narcotic.

"Kelly...."

Pleasure quivered in her stomach when he whispered her name. Her arms went around his shoulders. She'd forgotten how muscular he was, how hard those muscles were. They felt like carved stone beneath her hands. He wasn't excessively muscled, but he'd always been a giant to her.

Turning her head, she pressed her face into the flannel

at his chest and closed her eyes. "I'm scared," she admitted.

"So am I."

"Tell me again we're going to find him."

He stroked the back of her head. "We're going to find him."

"Promise me."

"I promise."

In that instant, the wind whistling through the treetops and the rush of the water from the stream faded to background noise. Her senses honed in on the man who now held her in his arms. They were standing body to body. She could feel every angular plane of him against her, as hard and solid as the mountain upon which they stood. She could hear the steady thrum of his heart in her ear, as mighty as the rushing water just a few yards away. A heart that was beating too fast and keeping time with hers.

Kelly had forgotten how powerful those feelings could be. It had been five long years since she'd been held like this. Since she'd been held by Buzz Malone. He might be a hard man, but when he put his arms around her she always felt as if she were the only woman in the world. He made her feel safe and cherished and loved—even when deep down inside she knew she wasn't any of those things.

His arms tightened around her, and an alarm began to clang in the back of her mind. She knew she should pull away. She'd lived with this man and knew how quickly things could spiral out of control. But her emotions were in tatters, her self-control hanging by a ragged thread she could only pray didn't break. For the first time in a long time, she needed to be held. Right or wrong, she didn't heed the alarm, she didn't pull away, and she let herself be held.

Kelly knew fully that touching him like this—getting close to him—was like mixing gasoline and nitroglycerin.

Buzz had always liked living on the edge. He made his living tempting fate.

She should have known he would be the one to strike a match.

One instant, they were locked in a comforting embrace. The next his hands were on her face, cupping her, pulling her to him. Kelly saw the intent in his eyes. A voice of reason called out for her to stop what she knew would happen next. But before her brain could send the words to her lips, he lowered his mouth to hers.

The kiss spoke of desperation and fear and the profound connection between a man and a woman who share the bond of a child. His mouth moved over hers, a little too quickly, a little too hard. He'd never been a gentle lover and his intensity had invariably overwhelmed her when they'd been married. With Buzz, it was all or nothing in every facet of his life, and that included sex.

The realization should have been enough to jump-start her common sense and give her the will to push him away. But the feel of his firm mouth against hers sent her thoughts stumbling drunkenly through her brain.

He deepened the kiss without warning. His teeth clicked against hers. He invaded her with his tongue. She tasted male heat and urgency and a dozen other things she refused to recognize. She accepted him, welcomed him into her mouth. He skimmed his hands down her back to cup her backside. Growling low in his throat, he moved against her.

Pleasure shot sparks through her brain at the feel of his hard shaft against the cleft between her legs. Need jumped through her like a jolt of electricity from a hot wire. Her breasts grew heavy as arousal coursed like liquid fire through her veins. The power of it stunned her, made her incredulous, disturbed her.

Kelly had never considered herself a sexual person. She didn't need sex in her life, didn't need it to be happy or to feel whole. But she'd forgotten what it was like to be kissed like this. Buzz Malone kissed her as if his life depended on it, as if her life depended on it and the rest of the world was at stake.

He didn't give her the chance to think about it too long. His hands roamed restlessly over her back to her hips. Holding her in place he moved against her.

Pleasure shocked her brain. She felt the answering tug deep in her womb and her body went liquid. She knew she should stop this, knew it was insane to give in to the needs spiraling out of control inside her. The words formed in her brain. But his mouth and the feel of his body against hers was like a narcotic, slowing her thought process and extinguishing the last remnants of her control.

He didn't ask for permission before he slipped his hands beneath her T-shirt. A warning screamed in the back of her head an instant before his hands closed over her breasts. Her gasp of surprise came out as a sigh of pleasure. She'd always been sensitive there, and he'd always known exactly where and how to touch her. He was doing it now, she realized, skimming his thumbs over her aching nipples through the thin material of her bra until she was shaking violently.

She closed her eyes against the pleasure, felt a cry bubble up from inside her. Every nerve ending in her body sang when he slipped his hands beneath her bra. His palms were warm against her flesh. His fingertips were calloused and rough against her nipples. Her breasts swelled beneath his hands. She arched when he stroked. Groaning, he whispered something incoherent against her ear. Kelly felt herself go damp between her legs, felt her control falter and tumble and begin to spin....

The alarm in the back of her mind wailed for her to stop this before things went too far. There were a hundred reasons why she shouldn't do this. She might still have feelings for him, but Buzz Malone was not the right man for her. He was not the right man for her son. Those years of living with him—and having her heart ripped out every time he took his life into his own reckless hands had taught her a terrible lesson. A lesson she refused to forget, no matter how wonderfully he kissed.

Sanity intervened like a cruel slap. Kelly jolted, as if waking from a deep sleep. ''I can't,'' she said, pulling away from Buzz.

He let her go. She took two steps back, aware that her heart was racing, that they were both breathing as though they'd just run a marathon. She stared at him, appalled by what she'd let happen, and struggled to pull herself back together.

Oh, God, how could she do this when her little boy was out there lost and all alone?

Guilt crashed down on her with the force of an avalanche. As if reading her thoughts, Buzz started to reach for her. Kelly raised her hands as if to fend him off and took another step back. ''Don't,'' she said.

''I'm sorry,'' he offered.

''It was my fault, too.''

''I know what you're thinking, Kel,'' he said. ''Don't.''

If she hadn't been so scared and worried and guilt-stricken, she might have laughed.

''Don't feel guilty,'' he said. ''People react to stress in different ways. Some people need to be alone. Some people reach out.'' Shaking his head, he looked down at the short span of dry earth between them. ''Don't feel guilty for reaching out.''

''My son is missing,'' she said. ''And I'm…'' She couldn't finish the sentence. Damn it, she didn't want to say out loud what had just happened between them. ''What kind of mother does that make me?''

"That makes you human," he said fiercely. "You're a good mother."

"This can't happen again," she said. "For too many reasons to count."

He scrubbed a hand over his jaw. "Yeah," he said.

Tension built for perhaps a full minute. Slowly, their breathing returned to normal. Kelly found her eyes drawn to the trees and rocks surrounding them. She glanced at her watch, realized they'd only been stopped for ten minutes. A lot could happen in ten minutes.

"I'm going to build a fire," Buzz said.

The words jerked her from her reverie. "You can't build a fire. It's bone-dry, and there's a no-burn rule right now."

"If Eddie can't hear us calling for him over the sound of the water, maybe he'll see the fire. I can't use a flare, but I can damn well build a controlled fire."

The exhaustion she'd been feeling earlier returned. A hundred emotions squirmed uncomfortably in her chest. Hope. Fear. A mother's desperate love for a child that could be in imminent danger. Sharp-edged attraction to a man who'd proven to her a hundred times over that he was all wrong for her.

"Can I help?" she asked after a moment.

"Why don't you gather some kindling?" he said. "I'll gather some stones and larger wood. We'll make camp. We'll eat and rest for a couple of hours, then resume the search."

It went against her instincts to stop searching—even to eat—but she knew Buzz was right. As she set about hunting suitable kindling, she began to pray.

Buzz spent ten minutes building a fire. He considered putting up the one-man tent for Kelly—more because he wanted something to do than from necessity—but figured he ought to take his own advice and get some rest. Besides, they wouldn't be stopped long enough for her to get any use out of the tent, anyway.

Instead, he set up their sleeping bags on either side of the small fire, then busied himself with setting up and lighting the cooking stove. He'd thought keeping busy with the mundane business of setting up camp would keep his mind off the kiss—what it meant in terms of his having moved on with his life—but his efforts were futile.

Damn it, he wasn't some school kid dumbstruck with hormones. He was a forty-year-old man. Mature enough to know that messing around with his ex-wife was a very bad idea. She might appeal to him on a physical level, but Buzz knew that beneath that enticing exterior was a truckload of trouble he had absolutely no desire to deal with. She'd made it clear she wanted nothing to do with a man who made his living putting his life on the line. He was crazy to be lusting after her at a time like this. She'd neglected to tell him about his son, for God's sake. Robbed him of the opportunity to be a father to Eddie. How could he be attracted to a woman who'd betrayed him in such a terrible way?

Buzz's body wasn't as discriminating as his mind.

Five years was a long time for a man to be alone. He'd told himself he hadn't taken a lover since the divorce because he'd been too busy. First with fixing up the cabin in Evergreen. Then with his work for Rocky Mountain Search and Rescue. He had a hundred excuses for not pursuing a relationship with some of the women he'd met over the years. For one, he didn't need the headaches that came with having a woman in his life.

But Buzz had always prided himself on being honest. Not only with others, but with himself. As much as he didn't want to admit it, he knew the main reason he hadn't pursued a relationship was because he knew there was no woman who would ever replace what he'd had with Kelly.

No other woman who would ever measure up. Stupidly, he hadn't wanted to settle for anything less.

Damned fool.

Across from him, the woman in question was lying on her sleeping bag. Her knees were up and she had her forearm thrown over her eyes as if trying to block out the rest of the world. Her shirt had ridden up slightly, and he could plainly see the way her jeans hugged her hips and stretched tightly over her flat belly. Even as she lay on her back, he could see the jut of her breasts through her T-shirt. He still remembered the way her nipples had felt against his fingertips. The way the nubs had stiffened through the thin material of her bra....

Buzz had told her two hours of rest, a quick meal, then they would begin searching for Eddie again. How was he supposed to rest when every time he looked at her he got so hot he couldn't stand it?

Angry with himself for having made such a stupid mistake as kissing her, frustrated because he could still feel the hard knot of arousal in his groin, he rose from his sleeping bag and stalked over to his backpack, which he'd hung from a nearby tree branch.

"Where are you going?"

Opening his backpack, he tossed her a protein bar and a small bag of dried fruit, then proceeded to remove the portable shower unit from its case. "I'm going to rinse off some of this dust and sweat," he said. *And make sure the water is damn cold,* a little voice chimed in.

She looked more interested in the shower than the protein bar. Rising, she walked over to him, eyeing the plastic contraption with curiosity. "You brought a *shower?*"

He nodded without meeting her gaze. "It's just a collapsible plastic container with a hose and nozzle."

"I'd kill for some soap and water right now."

"It's going to be cold."

''It's going to feel like a million bucks. How does it work?''

Buzz held up the plastic reservoir. ''This holds about five gallons of water when it's full. Weighs less than a pound when it's empty. All I've got to do is fill it up with water, then hang it from a tree branch.'' He fingered the eighteen-inch hose and nozzle. ''The water flows down this hose and out this little plastic showerhead.''

''All the comforts of home.''

He scowled at her, trying not to think about five gallons of water sluicing over secret places he knew better than to visualize. ''It'll do in a pinch.''

''I suppose this qualifies as a pinch.''

''The casing is black, so in daylight, the sun heats the water.''

The mention of heat conjured images of the kiss. Damn it, everything seemed to make him think of that. When this was all over with, and he got back to civilization, he was going to find himself a woman and work off some of this frustration.

Swearing under his breath, he looked over his shoulder toward the stream. ''I'm going to run down to the river and fill this thing, then shower up. Why don't you go ahead and eat. Make some coffee. I'll let you know when I'm finished. You can shower, and we'll start searching again.''

She nodded, her expression going solemn again at the mention of why they were here in the middle of the wilderness in the middle of the night.

The urge to go to her was strong, but he resisted. He knew what would happen if he went to her now. If he touched her. She'd always driven him just a little bit nuts. Even after three years of marriage he hadn't been able to keep his hands off her. Five years of celibacy wasn't helping matters. Neither was the way those jeans swept over one of the nicest backsides he'd ever laid eyes on.

Turning away from her, he stalked toward the stream, praying an ice-cold shower would keep him from doing something both of them would end up regretting.

Chapter 8

Kelly couldn't believe he'd actually warmed water over the fire for her before funneling it into the bag. Hidden from view by nothing more than the thick darkness and a sleeping bag hung from a branch, she stepped beneath the nozzle and flipped the switch that started the spray. Warm water trickled over her, feeling wonderful against her aching muscles. Not sure how long five gallons of water would last, she soaped up quickly. She knew she would probably regret getting her hair wet, but the need to be clean overrode the prospect of freezing later.

Buzz had already showered and was back at camp. Occasionally, she would hear him blowing the whistle. He'd been on the radio to Rocky Mountain Search and Rescue Headquarters twice in the last couple of hours. There were half a dozen volunteers and Search and Rescue professionals sweeping a ten-square-mile area, but no one had seen her little boy. Aside from the candy wrapper she and Buzz had found earlier, it was almost as if he'd disappeared.

Buzz hadn't mentioned the fire to the north, but she knew the news wasn't good. The winds continued to whip southward. That could only mean the fire was being driven straight at them. She knew Buzz would never tell her that; he didn't want to scare her or cause her to panic. But she saw the truth written on his face as clearly as if someone had printed it in big, bold letters.

She tried hard to stay optimistic. Buzz had taught her a lot about the importance of keeping an optimistic attitude. How important that was to maintain energy and clarity and all the things that would keep her effective and help the search.

At times, though, she felt as if every emotion, every nerve in her body was unraveling. It wouldn't surprise her one bit to find herself reduced to nothing more than a shredded mess of broken pieces on the forest floor. She missed Eddie so much it hurt. She could picture him so perfectly in her mind. The freckles on his nose. The dimple on his chin. The cowlick at his crown that made his hair stick up in the morning. She could hear his sweet voice. Conjure up that ornery look he got in his eye when he challenged her. She could smell his little-boy scent so clearly she felt that if she closed her eyes and reached out he would be there.

At that moment, Kelly would have sold her soul to know he was safe. Even if she couldn't have him with her, she just wanted him to be safe. His well-being was all she cared about. As long as he was safe, she could handle the physical and emotional stress of searching for him. She would search these mountains until she could no longer move. And she wouldn't rest until she held him safe in her arms.

"Please, God, keep him safe for me," she whispered. "Keep him safe until I can get to him. Please."

Realizing she'd used nearly all the water, Kelly rinsed the soap from her hair, then twisted the switch. The water dribbled, then stopped. Cold night air pricked her wet skin. Shivering, she quickly dried with the small towel Buzz had given her, and dressed. By the time she unhooked the empty reservoir from the tree branch, she felt almost human again.

Almost.

Ten yards from the camp she spotted Buzz, sitting on the flat side of a fallen log holding a steaming mug of coffee and wearing a troubled expression. The sight of him sitting alone and obviously deep in thought stopped her in her tracks. For an instant, she just stood there unseen and unnoticed, staring at him, thinking she'd never seen a man look so isolated—or alone.

For a crazy instant, she wanted to go to him, put her arms around him to let him know that wasn't the case at all. She knew it was a crazy idea considering the kiss they'd shared earlier in the day. The kiss that had left her head swimming—and her body remembering how things had once been between them.

The memory of the way his mouth had felt against hers filled her mind, a waterfall of sensation that swamped her senses and drowned out all other thought. She could deny it all she wanted, but her heart knew there was something real and profound left between them. A connection time or miles or hardship hadn't severed. She wanted to believe she'd kissed him back because she was exhausted and over-wrought. But she hadn't been aware of any of those things when his mouth had been fastened to hers and his hands had closed over her breasts.

The memory made her ache with a need she hadn't experienced for a very long time. She'd dated several men since the divorce, even kissed one or two of them. Friendly, tepid dates that had left her wondering why she bothered. Nothing she'd ever experienced in her life could compare to the intimacies she'd shared with Buzz in the years they'd been married. Even though she was only thirty-one years old, she knew nothing like the relationship she'd shared with him would ever happen again.

The thought filled her with a stark sense of loss, a sadness of knowing some of the best years of her life were behind her. Kelly closed her eyes against the memories she kept locked away in that secret place next to her heart. A place that was warm and sweet and *hers*. She didn't like thinking of herself as being vulnerable to him, but deep down inside Kelly knew she was. Today had proven that to her, and she was going to have to be very careful in the coming hours or risk losing a hell of a lot more than her control.

She tried to convince herself that the kiss was nothing more than two people reacting to an intense period of prolonged stress. A man and a woman bound by a child and thrown into a terrible situation. Intellectually, she knew it could never be anything more than that. But her heart had never been quite as logical as her brain, especially when it came to Buzz Malone.

Realizing she was just standing there with her hair dripping water onto her shoulders, she gave herself a quick mental shake and started toward the fire.

Buzz looked up when she approached. Even though he wasn't a cop anymore, he still had that look about him. Back when they'd first met, those sharp, serious eyes of his hadn't bothered her. She'd loved him so much it hadn't mattered that he was too damn brave for his own good. Then he'd been shot, and she'd realized only then that she'd made a terrible mistake by giving him her heart.

"I made coffee," he said.

She jolted at the sound of his voice. She'd been staring at him again. Staring at him and seeing far too much. Feeling her cheeks warm, she handed him the shower apparatus. "Thanks."

He collapsed the reservoir, then stuffed it into a compartment of his backpack. "How are you feeling?"

"Better." Physically, anyway. "The warm water was nice."

He poured steaming water into a cup then handed her the cup. "You're shivering. Coffee will help."

Kelly hadn't even realized she was cold. Unable to meet his gaze for a moment, she accepted the cup then carried it over to her sleeping bag and sat down cross-legged.

The coffee was hot and strong. She sipped, anticipating the zing of caffeine. "What do we do now?"

"If you're feeling up to it, we resume our search."

"Have you heard from RMSAR?" she asked, wondering if he'd called his team while she'd been showering just in case there was bad news.

"Winds are still whipping," he replied. "Twenty-seven homes have been destroyed by the fire just north of Norrie. A dozen more are expected to go if they don't get it controlled."

"Where's Norrie?"

"Two miles north of here."

That meant the fire had gained two miles in just a few hours. The coffee turned sour in her stomach, but she took another sip anyway. She was going to need the caffeine in the coming hours.

"You've got blood coming through your sock."

Surprised by his tone, she glanced over at him to realize he'd spotted the blister that had broken open on the inside of her right foot where her hiking boot had rubbed for the better part of the day. It hurt like the dickens, but she hadn't planned on mentioning it. It didn't seem right for them to take time to treat something as insignificant as a blister when her little boy was huddled somewhere with nothing more than a stuffed animal to keep him company.

"It's nothing," she said.

"It's a blister. You know as well as I do you don't let something like that go. That's Hiking 101 stuff, Kel. Use your head. Blisters get worse if you don't treat them."

She should have known Buzz wouldn't drop it. "Yeah, well, I've got more important things to deal with at the moment."

"You go lame on me and I'll leave you where you fall."

Rolling her eyes, she humphed. "Like *that's* going to happen." She reached for her hiking boots and started to slip them on so the blasted blister would be out of his sight.

Buzz stopped her by tugging the boot from her grasp and tossing it none too gently aside. "For God's sake, Kelly, do you always have to be so damn stubborn?"

"I need to get back on the trail and find my little boy," she snapped.

"He's my son, too. You keep forgetting to mention that." Rising, he stalked over to his backpack, removed the first-aid kit, then tromped back over to her. "Take off your sock."

"Oh, for crying out loud! I don't want to do this!"

"I don't care. Take it off, or I'll hold you down and take the damn thing off for you."

She knew he was right; she was being an idiot about this. She wasn't sure why she was feeling so surly toward him, but she was and she didn't mind letting him know about it. Muttering an oath, she jerked the sock off her foot, and threw it at him.

"It's good to know you can be a mature adult about this," he said.

She called him a very unladylike name.

He knelt a couple of feet away from her. "Give me your foot."

Sighing in annoyance, Kelly leaned back on her elbows and offered up the foot in question. With impersonal efficiency, he set her foot on his lap, trained the flashlight on it and checked the blister.

"That was real smart of you not to tell me about this," he said.

"You didn't ask."

He frowned at her. "By this time tomorrow, you would have been flat on your back."

"I'll have Eddie back by tomorrow at this time," she said fiercely.

Buzz didn't comment. "I've got a bandage and an extra sock you can wear. Should take the pressure off." Reaching into the kit, he removed an individually wrapped alcohol packet and sterilized his hands. He then withdrew a small tube of antibiotic cream and used his index finger to rub it directly into the blister.

His hands were large and dark against her foot. The warmth of his hands felt good against her cold flesh. Kelly didn't want to admit it, but the contact—however impersonal—felt good. The simple kindness of the act fortified her in a way words couldn't. Made her feel somehow connected. Not just to him, but to the rest of the world. And for a few short moments, she didn't feel so terribly alone.

She knew better than to let the rhythmic movement of his fingers relax her. She knew once that happened, exhaustion would follow. She couldn't let that happen. She had to find Eddie. With the fire raging down from the north, they were quickly running out of time.

Still, her eyes grew heavy as she watched him apply the bandage. By the time he finished, her limbs were so heavy, she could barely move. Buzz must have noticed because he reached for the instant coffee, dumped another teaspoon in her cup and poured steaming water into it.

Kelly drank the coffee down, wondering if she'd suddenly built up some kind of an immunity to caffeine because for the life of her she couldn't feel it kicking through her veins.

Despite her fatigue, she slipped on her boots and was on her feet before Buzz could get his backpack loaded and on his shoulders. A glance down at her watch told her it was 4:30 a.m. She wondered if Eddie was asleep somewhere. She wondered if he was warm enough. If he'd rationed his food—or if he was hungry.

Worry gut-punched her so hard it took her breath. Feeling the pain seep into her, she looked around. Nearby, an owl hooted. In the distance, she heard the rush of water over rocks. The moon sat on the treetops, watching them like a staring, white eye.

Shivering, exhausted and more scared than she'd ever been in her life, she followed Buzz into the night.

Buzz put one foot in front of the other and tried not to think about the pain that had been creeping up his spine for the last six hours. Of all the times for the old injury from the shooting to trouble him, why did it have to be now?

Muttering a curse under his breath, Buzz removed two of the prescription anti-inflammatory pills from the pill box he kept in a pocket of his jeans and swallowed them dry.

"Are you all right?"

Buzz looked up to find that Kelly had paused and was looking back at him. "Fine," he grumbled, hoping she hadn't seen him take the pills. He didn't need her running off at the mouth about the injury.

"You're falling behind," she said.

"You're going to wear yourself out if you don't slow down."

"I'm already worn out. I'm just not going to slow down." She lifted the water bottle from her belt and sipped, her eyes scanning the surrounding trees. "Is it your back?"

"My back is goddamn fine."

She handed him the bottle, and he sipped. "I've got some ibuprofen if—"

"I said my back is fine," he snapped.

Buzz wanted to set his backpack down for a few minutes, but his pride wouldn't let him do it with her standing there, waiting for him to double over in pain. Damn his back, and damn her.

"It looks like the terrain gets a little rugged up ahead," she said.

Lifting the whistle from the chain around his neck, Buzz blew three times, trying not to wince when the son of a bitch with the knife slipped it between his vertebrae. He listened for a full minute, but the forest didn't give up any answers.

"It will be dawn in half an hour," he said.

Kelly sighed. "Eddie likes to get up early. He likes to get up and play with his trucks, then he comes in and snuggles with me and we have hot chocolate and cinnamon toast for breakfast. Sometimes we stay in bed and eat Captain Kudos Krunchies."

Abruptly, her face crumpled. A sob escaped her. As if the show of emotion embarrassed her, she lowered her face into her hands. She didn't make another sound, but Buzz saw her shoulders shake as she cried.

It only took him an instant to drop the backpack onto the ground. He crossed the short distance between them in two strides. Then his arms were around her, pulling her soft body against his.

"Easy, Kel," he whispered. "Just…take it easy. It's going to be all right." He stroked the back of her head. Her hair felt like silk against her fingers.

"We've been walking all night," she sobbed. "Buzz, I hurt all over. I'm exhausted. What if we can't find him? Oh, God, what if we don't *ever* find him?"

For the first time since the nightmare had begun, she sobbed freely. Long, wrenching sobs that echoed off the treetops like the cries of a wounded animal. He hated seeing her break like this.

Because he wasn't sure how to reach her or how to comfort her, Buzz just held her against him, trying in vain to ease her trembling, willing to absorb some of her pain because she was breaking his heart.

Concern rippled through him when he felt her sag against him. Kelly wasn't a fainting kind of woman, but he knew even the strongest of people had their breaking points.

"Hey." Shifting away from her slightly, he used his fingertips and brought her gaze to his. "Don't pass out on me."

"I just need to sit down for a moment."

Gently, he eased her to a sitting position on the ground. After pulling it from his backpack, he spread out his sleeping bag. When he turned back to her, she was just sitting with her legs crossed and her face in her hands.

"Sit next to me for a minute," he said.

Without speaking, she scooted over until they were sitting side by side on the mat. Their thighs were touching. She'd stopped crying, but fatigue slumped her shoulders.

"Let me tell you what we're going to do," he began.

When she didn't look at him, he reached for her and turned her to face him. Early dawn cast just enough light for him to see that she was deathly pale. He felt a little guilty for, just a few minutes earlier, being so caught up in his own physical pain. This woman was exhausted. She wouldn't last much longer. Buzz didn't think he was going to be able to talk her into staying put and getting some rest, but he had to try.

"Kel, are you okay?"

She nodded, but the despair in her eyes was so vivid, Buzz had a hard time looking at her.

"Okay," he said. "Chances are, our little guy slept through the night. Maybe he found a cave. Or some brush in a protected area. Maybe he found an area that was protected by rock. Whatever the case, we've got to believe he's okay."

Kelly closed her eyes, squeezing fat tears from beneath her lids. "I believe that."

"In the next hour or so," Buzz continued, "he's going to wake up. He's going to be hungry and scared, so he's going to be listening to his surroundings. He may be yelling for help. We need to be very vocal today, Kel. We need to backtrack and cover all the terrain that we covered last night. I want you to be especially vigilant and keep your eyes open for footprints. For broken branches. Trampled grass. A thread from his clothing. Anything you feel may be out of the ordinary."

"I can do that."

"I want you to keep your ears open in case he's yelling for help."

"Okay."

Seeing clearly that having a solid plan in place was perking her up, Buzz removed two peanut butter protein bars from his backpack and handed one to her. "I need you to tell me if you're holding up," he said carefully. "I need you to tell me the truth. If you need to rest, say it. I don't want to risk your getting hurt on the trail. That's not going to help Eddie. If you're feeling sick or dizzy, I need you to tell me."

She was already shaking her head. "I'm fine. I just needed to sit down for a moment."

Buzz didn't believe her. She didn't look fine. She looked pale and shaken and weak as a kitten. But he knew Kelly Malone didn't have a weak bone in her body. Not only was she physically strong, but he knew first-hand that the force of her will was something to be reckoned with as well.

He'd been bulldozed by that personality a few too many times to let his guard down now.

"I guess I'm going to have to take your word for it," he said.

"I guess you are."

He frowned at her.

She managed a smile. "Good try, but I'm not quitting."

"Neither am I."

Chapter 9

Buzz refused to believe they wouldn't find Eddie. Because of that he knew they were eventually going to have to talk about how they were going to handle their having a son. How that was going to affect their lives—and their relationship. He supposed he'd been putting it off because he still didn't have things straight in his own mind. At first, he'd been too shocked to feel much of anything. The truth of the matter was that he'd never wanted children, never wanted the burden of such a monumental responsibility. He never wanted to hold the fate of something as precious as a child in his hands because he wasn't sure he wouldn't somehow screw it up.

To this day, he couldn't talk about some of the things he'd seen people do to their kids during the years he'd worked the Denver PD's Child Abuse Division. By the time he'd made detective and transferred to homicide, his resolve never to bring a child into the world had become a vow he wouldn't break for anyone.

Not even the woman he'd loved.

Yet at some point in the last two days, Buzz's resolve had been shaken. He'd come to think of Eddie as his son. *His son.* The words shook him inside, conjured up feelings he'd thought he'd never feel. Things he'd thought he wasn't capable of feeling. Things he didn't *want* to feel. And even though he'd never even met the boy, he knew an undeniable connection had been forged between them.

Too bad he didn't have the slightest clue what he was going to do about it.

The sun was just breaking over the treetops to the east when they reached the top of a rise, and they had a clear view of the stream. The water thundered like a white, writhing snake over rocks and boulders to plummet thirty feet into a ravine. To the north, a sheer wall of granite rose up out of a grassy valley. Scraggly juniper topped the cliff like spindly fingers reaching for the sky.

Pausing next to a boulder, Buzz eased the pack from his back and let it drop to the ground. A few feet away, Kelly sank down into the pine needles, leaned back against the trunk of a dead tree and closed her eyes.

"How are we going to handle our having a son?" he asked after a moment.

She opened her eyes and looked at him warily. "I don't know."

"We're going to have to deal with it, Kel."

"We have to find him first."

"We will."

"You never wanted children, Buzz. I don't think that's changed, has it?"

"I'm his father."

"Yes, you are."

"I want to…" Because the words tangled on his tongue, Buzz let them trail. He wasn't even sure what he was trying to say. Did he want to be part of his son's life? Was he qualified?

"Buzz, I'd never keep you from him if that's what you want."

"Come on, Kel, you're moving to Tahoe, for chrissake. That pretty much leaves me out of the picture."

"Eddie can visit you here in Colorado in the summer, on long weekends. You're welcome to come to Tahoe and see him any time."

And watch that son of a bitch Quelhorst worm his way into her life. Into his son's life. Lining himself up as Eddie's father. Drooling all over Kelly and waiting for the chance to make his move. No thanks.

Frustrated and angry, Buzz raked his hand over his stubbly jaw and muttered a curse. It wasn't enough, he realized. He didn't want a little piece of his son's life. He wanted all of it. Wanted to nurture him and guide him and watch him grow. He wanted to love him and protect him from a world that could be as dangerous as it was wonderful.

He sure as hell didn't want to watch his wife fall for some pencil-necked Mr. Corporate America simply because she deserved someone she knew was going to come home alive at the end of the day.

Rising abruptly, Buzz strode over to the edge of the ravine and stared down into the water. He could feel Kelly's eyes on him, but he didn't turn around. He wasn't sure what his expression would reveal, wasn't sure he wanted her to see the expression he knew was etched into his every feature.

Buzz had never had the desire for children. He'd made the decision not to have them at a young age and never questioned it. He'd lived his entire life knowing he would never have to deal with it. But to have a woman he'd trusted jerk the rug out from under him when he'd least expected it made him question everything he'd ever believed about himself.

Needing something to do, anything to keep his mind off the questions pummeling him, he reached for the VHF radio clipped to his belt. "Homer One this is Tango Two Niner, do you read me?"

"We got you loud and clear, Tango."

"What's the twenty on Eagle?" he asked, referring to RMSAR's chopper. "We could really use some help up here."

"She's just south of Norrie, Buzz. Firefighters had to evacuate. They got casualties up there."

Buzz blew out an oath, cursing the fire. "Any chance we can get some more volunteers down here for a grid?"

"Jake Madigan went back out this morning. He checked in a couple of hours ago just south of the campground at Chapman. What's your twenty?"

"I'm about two miles north of there."

The man on the other end of the airwaves hesitated. Buzz felt the hairs at his nape prickle.

"Any sign of the kid?" Dispatch asked.

"Saw a wrapper on the north trail, but negative on the sighting."

"Do you want me to send Madigan up that way?"

"That's affirm."

"Buzz, that entire area is being evaced. The leading edge of the fire is about a mile north of you."

"Send Madigan and anyone else you can find who doesn't have their ass nailed to the ground. Clear." Cursing, he shoved the radio into its sheath. Anger and frustration and a pristine new fear churned inside him. He thought of the innocent child out in the woods all alone and felt the fear take on a new intensity, leaping through him, consuming him much like the flames eating up the forest.

"They've evacuated the entire area?" she asked.

Buzz turned to her, hoping the emotions gripping his chest didn't show on his face. "Yeah."

"Oh, God." She pressed a hand to her stomach. "We're all alone out here? We're the only ones looking?"

"Jake Madigan is looking. He's on horseback. Kel, he's good."

"Just three people? Buzz, that means we don't have much time. If the fire is coming this way—"

"The firefighters evac early, Kel. You know that. They always do. They're cautious. They don't want some diehard holing up in his cabin and deciding he wants to go down with the ship, then changing his mind at the last minute and needing an airlift when they need the chopper on the front line."

She walked to the edge of the ravine and put her hands to her mouth. "Eddie! Where are you, honey?"

Buzz blew the whistle three times, then they stood there and listened. The smell of smoke hung heavy in the air, even though the wind was gusty. He could see it moving like smoky fingers through the treetops. Beyond, a thick haze the color of wet slate sat on the horizon like a curse from hell. It was enough to unnerve even the most seasoned Search and Rescue professional.

Buzz was about as seasoned as they came. And for the first time in his life, he was afraid his worst fear about having children was going to come true. That a child—*his* child—would be snatched away from him by something terrible.

The worst part about it was that there wasn't a damn thing he could do about it.

Kelly wasn't sure how long they walked. It could have been an hour. It could have been two. For all she knew it could have been five. After a while, the dust on the trail, the trees and rock formations started to blend together. The smoke blocked out the sun, like storm clouds filled with violence and rain.

She knew it was important to remain alert. But she was so exhausted she could barely walk. Every inch of her body ached. Her legs felt as if they'd been emptied of bone and muscle and refilled with lead. The kind that would shatter with just the right impact.

Kelly would never admit she'd reached the end of her physical endurance. She wouldn't leave these mountains until she held Eddie in her arms. Or else someone would have to forcibly carry her out.

She prayed to God it didn't come to that.

It was the second time they'd walked this trail. The same trail where they'd found the candy wrapper the evening before. They headed north, where the smoke lay thick and black above the treetops. To her right, the stream slowly dropped away into a gorge. Kelly wasn't sure what prompted her to look down into the gorge at that moment, but the flash of blue amongst the green and brown of the forest stopped her dead in her tracks.

Her heart jolted once hard in her chest, then sprinted into a wild staccato. She squinted, and without even realizing she was moving, her legs took her to the edge of the gorge. "Buzz! I see something! Over there!"

She never took her eyes from the small speck of blue fifty feet down the ravine. "It's blue. Over by that boulder."

Quickly, Buzz worked the backpack from his shoulders, dropped it to the ground and dug out a tiny pair of field binoculars. He put them to his eyes, focused. "Looks like a piece of cloth."

"Let me see."

He passed the glasses to her.

Kelly put them to her eyes, squinted, focused. The sight

hit her like a ramrod to the solar plexus. "Oh, my God. Oh, my *God!*"

"What is it?"

Terror and shock exploded inside her, taking her voice so that she couldn't answer, couldn't speak, couldn't even draw a breath. Her hands began to shake. She lost her focus, struggled with the binoculars to find the speck again.

"Kel." Gently, he took the binoculars from her. "Talk to me, Kel. What is it? What did you see?"

"Oh, God, Buzz. It's Eddie's stuffed animal. His bear. Bunky Bear." Nausea rose into her throat. "How did it get down there?"

"He could have dropped it."

"Please tell me he didn't fall." Abruptly, she pulled away from Buzz. She heard him behind her as she moved closer to the edge of the ravine and looked down. It was steep and chock-full of jagged rock, saplings, boulders the size of Volkswagens and drop-offs not even a mountain goat could scale. At the base, white water churned like ice in a blender.

"Eddie!" she screamed. "Eddie! Honey, answer me!"

Buzz hit the whistle three times. They stood frozen for an interminable minute and listened for a response that never came.

"Honey! It's Mommy!" Struggling against hysteria, she took the field glasses from Buzz and put them to her eyes. She was shaking so badly, she had a hard time focusing at first. Then she caught a glimpse of white, saw a patch of blue denim. A shock of brown hair and a pale, frightened face.

"I see him! Oh, God! It's him! Buzz!" She couldn't stop looking at him. Vaguely, she was aware of Buzz speaking to her, but she didn't understand what he was saying. For an instant, her entire world consisted of tunnel vision, at the end of which was her son.

"Is he moving?" Buzz's voice reached her through that tunnel.

"No. Yes! I just saw him move his leg! He's okay!"

Buzz reached for the binoculars. "Let me have a look."

Kelly handed him the field glasses. Two hundred yards of impossible terrain separated her from her son. Heart pounding, she squinted down at the tiny figure huddled on a boulder the size of an SUV. Elation turned quickly to horror when she realized the boulder was surrounded on all sides by churning white water.

"He's stuck on that boulder," Buzz said.

"How on earth did he get there?"

"Must have fallen into the water at some point. Dragged himself out."

A rush of nausea filled her mouth with bile at the thought of her son in that cold, violent water. "I've got to get down there."

"Wait a minute—"

She swung around to face him, stuck her finger in his face. "Don't even think about trying to stop me."

"I'm not going to let you do something stupid."

Ignoring him, she started for the edge of the cliff. The next thing she knew she was being pushed quickly, but firmly backward. Two strong hands dug into her shoulders. Her body jolted when her back encountered the wall of rock. She fought him, but he shook her hard until she was still.

"Snap out of it!" he growled.

She looked up to find herself pinned by a set of angry gray eyes. Eyes that reminded her of the smoke hovering above, hot and dangerous and violent. She tried to slap his hands off her shoulders, but she might as well have been trying to slap a tree off the side of the mountain. He merely tightened his grip and put his weight into holding her still.

"Don't do this to me," she said.

"Don't get crazy on me now, Kel. Get a hold of yourself."

"I need to get down there." A sound erupted from her throat. A sob or a cough, she couldn't tell. "Please. I want my little boy."

"I'll get him."

"Buzz, he's cold and hungry and scared."

"I'm going down. But I need you to calm down first."

"I'm calm." She said the words, but she didn't think he believed her. She sure didn't.

"I need your help. I can't get down there without it."

"Okay." She gulped air. "I'm...okay."

Slowly, as if half expecting her to bolt, he released her, then stepped away.

Kelly drew a deep, calming breath. The jolt of adrenaline had eradicated the exhaustion, but her limbs felt shaky, her mind foggy, as if she were watching the scene unfold from inside a bottle. Bending at the waist, she put her hands on her knees and breathed in deeply, forcing back nausea, trying to clear her head.

"I'm going to rappel down there," Buzz said after a moment. "I don't have a full harness—just the light rig in my pack—so I've got to rig something. I need you to spot me from up here. Watch the rope for me. Can you do that?"

"Yeah." She looked up to see him pulling a coiled length of yellow nylon rope from his backpack. Suddenly, a new fear rippled through her. A fear that didn't have anything to do with her lost child, but for the man who was about to risk his life to save him.

Her legs shook when she crossed to him. "Are you sure you can get down there?"

"I'm sure." He didn't even look at her, but concentrated fully on knotting the end of the rope, then quickly stepping into the harness.

"Buzz, the bullet in your back…"

"Shut up, Kel."

"I can rappel down," she said. "I know how to do it. I'm in good shape."

"There's no way you can get him back up the cliff. You may be in good shape, but you're not strong enough." When she didn't say anything, he cut her a sharp look. "I can do this, damn it."

She stared at him, her heart beating hard and fast in her chest. For the first time in her life, she understood him. She understood why men like him did the things they did. Why they devoted their lives to saving others. The realization came to her like the white flash of a bomb inside her head. And it shamed her that she'd never understood until now. It made her feel shallow and small and petty because she hadn't supported him. She hadn't been strong enough to let him do what he did best, what he loved. And it hurt that it had taken this—her son's life—for her to understand what she should have understood all along.

He stalked over to the edge of the ravine, turned and spotted a sturdy sapling, then crossed to it and looped the rope several times around the base. "This will help take some of the stress off you," he said. "I want you to feed the rope and lower me down. A foot at a time. Nice and slow."

"How are you going to get across the water?" she asked.

"I don't know. But I need to get closer to see what's on the other side of that boulder. Maybe I can get to him." He grimaced. "If I need the rope, I'll yell for you to untie it and toss it down to me."

"How will you get back up if I toss the rope down to you?"

"Chances are I won't need it. But if I do…" He shrugged. "I'll have to figure something out if it comes to that. Right now, I just want to get that boy away from the water. He's in a very dangerous position.''

She nodded.

''Once I get him, and we're ready to come back up, I want you to loop the rope a couple of times around this sapling, and keep it taut.''

''I can handle that.''

''I don't have any gloves for you. I need them myself this time.''

''That's okay. I can do it.''

''I know you can.''

She flinched when he reached out and thumbed a tear off her cheek. It surprised her because she hadn't even realized she was crying.

''We're going to be fine,'' he said.

''I know.'' She knew the quick smile was for her benefit, but she appreciated it nonetheless. ''Be careful.''

''Hey, jumping off cliffs is my specialty, remember?''

She choked out a laugh. ''Yeah, and you stop bullets, too.''

''That's my girl.'' He tested the rope, checked the harness around his hips. ''Whatever you do, don't let go of that rope.''

''Don't worry. I won't.''

Abruptly, he leaned forward and crushed his mouth to hers. She hadn't been expecting him to kiss her and the power of it nearly took her feet out from under her. He kissed her hard, desperately, hungrily. She opened to him, and their tongues touched briefly. She tasted hope and fear and determination on his lips. Desire tugged sharply, followed by a pang of emotion so powerful it took her breath. She wanted to close her eyes and hang onto him, but the moment ended and he pulled away.

He grinned at her. ''You never forgot how to kiss.''

She smiled back at him even though she was shaking inside. "Neither did you."

"Hold that thought." And with a wave of his hand, he shoved off into space and disappeared over the edge of the cliff.

Buzz knew he was in trouble before ever reaching the bottom of the gorge. His back had gone into spasms halfway down, a knifing pain that started at the small of his back and shot down his right buttock all the way to his little toe. It wasn't the first time he'd had problems with the sciatic nerve, but it sure couldn't have come at a worse time.

Ignoring the pain as best he could, he paused long enough to down a couple more pills, then turned his head to get his bearings. White water roared like an earthquake below. The terrain was rugged as hell and consisted of gnarled juniper, moss-covered boulders and loose rock that made for precarious footing. The hovering smoke lent a surreal aspect to the scene.

He pushed off with his feet and swung back, but still couldn't see the boy from where he hung. The harness cut uncomfortably into the backs of his thighs, but the discomfort was minor compared to the ice-pick jabs in his back. Damn, he was getting too old for this crap.

He could still see Kelly above him. Even from ten yards away, he could see the sharp-edged worry in her eyes. He prayed to God she didn't get some crazy idea about climbing down to help. When it came to her son, she was as protective—and courageous—as a lioness. He admired her strength, her tenacity—and tried not to think about all the other things he admired her for.

Raising his hand he waved to let her know everything was all right. She waved back.

Buzz started downward again. He shoved off into space,

let the rope slide through the gloves, and landed four feet down the side of the ravine. The rope groaned against his weight. Loose rock gave way under his feet, and he slipped, but he didn't stop.

A few minutes later, he reached the bottom of the ravine. The narrow bank was rocky, nearly impossible to walk upon and only a couple of feet wide. Climbing onto a huge boulder, Buzz pulled himself upright and scanned the area. Twenty feet away—nearly on the other side of the stream— Eddie jumped up and down, waving his hands. Buzz could see that he was crying, and his heart pinged hard against his ribs.

"Eddie, I'm going to come get you!" he shouted. "I want you to stay put! Everything's okay, but you need to stay where you are!"

The boy said something, but Buzz couldn't hear him over the roar of the water. Damn, the way the kid was jumping up and down worried him. One wrong move and he'd tumble headlong into the churning water.

Because he wasn't sure if the boy could hear him over the roar of the water, Buzz motioned as best he could with his hands.

The boy edged closer, crying, holding out his hands. Buzz could see his mouth moving, but he couldn't hear him over the water. The initial zing of fear went through him. "Son, I want you to sit down!" he shouted. "Stay put! I'm coming over for you, okay? Just stay where you are."

Cursing beneath his breath, he looked frantically around for a way to get to the boy. He was in the process of sliding off a boulder when the unthinkable happened. One minute his son was perched on the edge of his rock island. In the next instant, his sneakers slipped out from under him. In a blur of white T-shirt and blue jeans he tumbled down, and the water swept him away.

Chapter 10

"Eddie!"

Terror ripped through Kelly as she watched the churning white water swallow her son. Panic pulled her in a thousand different directions. Her first instinct was to run after him, to fling herself down the ravine, brave the icy, turbulent water and forget about everything but saving her son.

But the voice of reason stopped her. Rescuing her son from a raging white-water rapid wasn't going to be an easy task. And while panic threatened to drag her down the into the abyss of hysteria, the knowledge that Buzz was only a few yards away from her son gave her the strength she needed to keep her head—at least long enough to realize she was going to need the rope.

She looked down in time to see the rope go taut in her hand. An instant later, several feet of it was yanked through her palms. Pain zinged where the rope burned her, but still she closed her hands around it, just in time to keep the end from whipping out of her grasp. Realizing she didn't have the strength to hold it for long, she looped it quickly around the nub of a broken trunk, then snatched up the field glasses that hung around her neck.

Through the glasses, she caught a glimpse of Buzz, in the water, fighting the rope from his body. An instant later, he freed himself from the rope and the water swallowed him.

Another wave of fear rocked her. Fear that Buzz wouldn't be able to reach her son. Fear that the water would take not only her son, but the man who had fathered him.

Operating on autopilot, she worked furiously to yank the rope up from the ravine and coil it around one shoulder. Simultaneously, she began running in the direction the current carried Buzz and her son. She tore through brush, barely feeling the branches tearing at her face and clothes. Gasping breaths tore from her lungs as she pushed her body to the limit and ran as fast as her legs would carry her. All the while, her hands worked quickly to coil the length of rope that now trailed along behind her.

Twenty yards down stream she lost sight of Eddie. "Eddie!" She knew he couldn't hear her over the roar of the water. But she couldn't keep herself from crying out his name. She needed to say it. Needed to hear it.

Please, God, let them be all right.

Another ten yards and the terrain sloped dangerously. Using the myriad saplings and low-growing branches to keep her balance, Kelly hurled herself down the incline toward the water. She covered the ground at a reckless pace, hurdling fallen trees, stumbling over rocks, skidding over loose earth that gave way beneath her pounding boots.

A moment later, the woods opened up to a rocky sandbar. The roar of the water deafened her. She looked down at her hands, realized she now held the entire length of rope. Dully, she noticed the blood, too, but it didn't register in her mind that it might be hers.

Scrambling over rocks slick with moss, she jumped into a still pool of backwater that was knee-deep. A few feet away, white water pounded giant boulders, forming a whirlpool large enough to suck down an automobile. Twenty yards upstream, she caught sight of two dark heads bobbing in the white waves. Buzz had one armed wrapped around her child. She could hear Eddie crying.

"Buzz! Hold on to him!" she cried.

Wondering how to stop them, how to keep them from being carried down stream and into the whirlpool, Kelly looked wildly around. Spotting the two boulders on the other side of the stream, she realized what she had to do.

Picking up a broken branch the size of a baseball bat, she quickly tied the rope to its center point. No time to test the strength of the knot. No time to aim. She threw the stick like a spear up and over the boulders, praying it would wedge between the two rocks. Out of the corner of her eye, she could see that Buzz and Eddie were being swept toward her at an astounding speed. She tugged hard on the rope, closed her eyes in a silent prayer when it held.

There was no time to think, only time to act. Kelly quickly fed the rope until it lay in a bright yellow line across the raging surface of the water.

"Grab onto the rope!" she shouted.

She didn't have to say it twice. Having seen the rope, Buzz raised one of his arms straight up out of the water. The other arm was wrapped around the small, dark-haired form of her son. An instant later, the rope caught him at his armpit. The rope jerked taut, stopping Buzz and Eddie dead in the water. Kelly let out a yelp when the rope held. But her newfound relief turned quickly to horror when the furious current swept over them with such force that it sent a rooster tail of water spraying two feet into the air.

Knowing Buzz couldn't hold on for long with only one arm, she quickly tied her end of the rope onto the base of a stump, grabbed onto the rope and waded out as far as she dared. The current swirled with dangerous power around her ankles. "Hold on!" she cried.

She had no idea how Buzz managed, but with Eddie wrapped in one arm, he used the other to work his way along the rope until he was close enough to the bank to get his feet under him. Gripping the rope so hard her nails cut into her palms, Kelly waded deeper into the swift current, and held out one arm to her son.

"Eddie! Sweetheart. Come to me. Come to Mommy."

As if with the last of his strength, Buzz shoved the boy toward her. Not daring to let go of the rope just yet, she wrapped one arm around him. "I've got you, sweetheart."

"Mommy," he cried. "Mommy."

Emotion ripped through her at the sound of his sweet voice. That tiny voice she loved with every cell in her body. "Honey, are you okay?"

"I-I'm c-cold."

"Are you hurt, sweetheart? Does anything hurt?"

"My knee hurts." He started to cry. "And I'm scared."

Closing her eyes, she put her hands on his face and kissed his forehead. His pink cheeks. His wet eyes. The top of his very wet head. "Don't be scared, honey. Everything's okay. You're safe now." She wanted to say more, wanted to reassure him, but her throat locked up tight as a drum.

Kelly didn't remember picking him up and carrying him over the sandbar near the rocky shore. She didn't remember crying his name over and over again as she laid him down on a bed of pine needles at the base of the cliff. When he looked up at her with the sweet eyes she had feared she would never again look into, all the bottled emotions inside her fractured. Hugging him to her breast as tightly as she dared, she bowed her head long enough to thank God, and then she wept.

* * *

Buzz lay face-down on the rocky sandbar for what seemed like a long time. Water soaked his clothes, the cold seeming to sink through his skin and go all the way to his bones. Rocks dug uncomfortably into his face and stomach and thighs, but he didn't move. His back ached as if he'd been run over by a bulldozer, but he didn't have the energy even to groan, so he just lay there and tried not to think about what had almost happened—or how damn lucky they were to be alive.

Over the roar of the water, he was vaguely aware of Kelly crying. Of the little boy crying. The sound of their voices—the fact that they were alive—made him smile. It didn't matter that he felt like death warmed over. Or that he didn't have the slightest idea how close the fire was. Or how the holy hell they were going to get back to the campground. All that mattered at the moment was that they were alive.

"Buzz? Are you okay?"

He raised his head and looked at Kelly. "Peachy," he growled.

Blinking back tears, smiling tremulously and cradling her son—their son—in her arms, she mouthed the words "thank you."

Several minutes passed before he was able to drag himself to his knees, then get unsteadily to his feet. His boots sloshed when he crossed the sandbar to where Kelly and her son—his son—were huddled against the base of the cliff. Buzz looked down at them, felt something vital shift, then freefall in his chest. The quick rise of emotions, the need to protect what was his stunned him.

He stared at the woman he'd once loved more than life itself. Her head was bowed, her cheek pressed hard against her child's head. She held the little boy so tightly he wondered if the kid could draw a breath.

The child shivered in her arms. Even from where he stood, Buzz could hear his little teeth chattering. Though it was soaked, he could see that Eddie's hair was the same pretty brown as his mother's. In the moments he'd held him in his arms as they were being swept down the river, when he'd looked into his son's eyes for the first time, he'd noticed a hundred things about him. The small, angular body. The sweet scent of child. A freckled nose. Eyes that were the same stormy gray as his own. Eyes that had been filled with a child's trust.

For a moment, Buzz couldn't speak, just stood there like an idiot, staring at them, aware that his heart was beating a hard tattoo against his ribs. He couldn't believe this perfect little child was his. A precious life he and Kelly had created. A little boy he would gladly give up his own life to protect.

A little boy without a father.

The repercussions struck him with the force of a sledgehammer. His knees went weak. Nausea roiled in his stomach. He felt as if someone had just punched him right between the eyes. If he didn't know better, he might have thought he was having some kind of damn anxiety attack.

Buzz had been involved in dozens of life-and-death situations in the years he'd been a cop. He'd participated in a hundred or more rescues in the course of his career with RMSAR. None of those events had ever made him feel like this.

He jolted when a gentle hand touched his forearm. "Hey, are you hurt? What's wrong?"

He hadn't noticed that Kelly had risen, and was now looking at him with concerned brown eyes. "Buzz?"

He stared back at her, shaking inside, wondering why this particular rescue had affected him that way. "I'm fine," he said.

A tentative smile touched her mouth. "You wouldn't lie to me, would you?"

"Probably."

"You saved his life."

"You're the one who threw the rope."

"Buzz…for God's sake, don't argue." Her voice broke. "Just…thank you."

Because he didn't trust his voice not to betray him, Buzz looked away, turned his attention to his son. Eddie was sitting on the ground, shivering, holding onto his mother's leg. Buzz knelt so that he was eye-level with the little boy. "You okay, tough guy?" he asked.

The child blinked at him, sniffed hard once, then looked up at his mother. "I-m c-cold. I w-want to go home."

"We're going to take you home," Buzz said. "Are you hurt anywhere?"

Another sniff, then Eddie used the back of his wet sleeve to wipe his runny nose. "My knee hurts."

"Well, we'll just have to check it out, then, won't we?"

Eddie threw a questioning look at his mommy, held her leg tighter.

"My name's Buzz."

"That's a funny name."

"Yeah, it is, isn't it?"

Eddie nodded, sniffed.

"I'm a Search and Rescue medic. Do you know what that is?"

"Kinda."

"Then you know I rescue people when they get into trouble."

"Like you did me?"

Buzz smiled. "That's right. I'm trained to treat injuries that happen out on the trail, too."

"Like a doctor?"

"Sort of." Buzz glanced over when Kelly knelt beside him. "Do you mind if I have a look at your sore knee?"

Eddie looked over at Kelly, and she nodded. "Show him where it hurts, honey."

Eddie stuck out his right leg then proceeded to roll up his pants. Buzz noticed Kelly's hands were still shaking when she reached out to help him.

Buzz wasn't an emotional man. But to look into that innocent face, into those little eyes and see his own reflected back was almost too much to bear. The knowledge that this child was his overwhelmed him. Emotions he'd sworn he'd never feel threatened to tear down his defenses, rip him open, make him doubt the beliefs he'd held close his entire adult life. Awe mixed with anger, love with a sense of betrayal, and cut him as deeply as any knife. The power of those emotions struck him over and over again until he felt as battered emotionally as he was physically.

Holding onto his composure by a thread, Buzz reached out and prodded the small knee. "He's bruised, but nothing's broken," he said, relieved. "We need to get him dry and get some food into him."

Kelly nodded. "Your pack is still up on the trail where we left it."

Buzz rose and scanned the steep incline Kelly had come down to reach the water. "I want you and Eddie to wait here. I'll hike back up to the trail, pick up my pack and the radio and meet you back here."

"Okay."

"I'll radio RMSAR headquarters, have them notify your family and see if we can get the chopper out here for a swoop and scoop."

She nodded.

Buzz looked up at the treetops. "If anyone can fly a chopper in these winds, it's Flyboy. I'll know more when I get back."

She looked as though she wanted to say more, but Buzz didn't give her the chance. He didn't like the way he was reacting to her, didn't like the way he was reacting to Eddie. Most of all, he didn't like the way he was starting to feel. He didn't want to feel anything, because he knew in a few days it wouldn't matter.

"Homer One this is Tango Two Niner, do you read?"

"Homer reads you Tango. What's up, Buzz?"

Easing his backpack onto his shoulders, Buzz spoke into the radio as he started back down the trail. "I've got the missing child. You can call off the search."

Dispatch let out an ear-splitting whoop. "Hot damn! What's your twenty?"

"I'm half a mile north of the Panther Creek Blue River fork. What are the chances of getting Eagle out here for a swoop and scoop?"

"Negative. Flyboy got recalled to base. Winds are at fifty knots and we got thermals all over the place." He paused. "You got injuries?"

"Negative, but we got a tired and hungry four-year-old kid."

"Winds are supposed to die down overnight."

Buzz cursed. "What about the fire? They got it contained?"

"Not yet. Smoke jumpers are out in force. A bunch of guys came down from Yellowstone. That makes about two hundred men working on it. Damn winds are feeding it."

"We've got smoke here. Are we going to be all right?"

"You'll be fine overnight. Flyboy should be able to make it out first light."

"Tell Flyboy to get on the horn at 0400 with a pick-up point."

"Roger that, Tango."

"Over and out."

Buzz didn't relish the idea of spending another night in the mountains. He wanted to believe the dread curling through him was because that poor child had had a couple of very tough days and needed to get back home. Or maybe because he himself was tired and cold and hungry and needed a hot meal and his own bed.

But Buzz was honest enough with himself to acknowledge that the primary reason for his dread was because he didn't want to spend any more time with Kelly. He knew that was selfish—perhaps even cowardly—but until he figured out how he felt about all this, he just didn't want to get any closer to either of them.

He and Kelly had been so immersed in the search, they hadn't yet properly discussed what kind of role—if any—Buzz would play in Eddie's life. He hadn't had time to think about it; hadn't had time to sort out his feelings or decide a damn thing.

For the first time since finding out about Eddie, he felt trapped. How in God's name was he going to handle this?

He couldn't think of a worse situation for a man like him. A man who didn't like to feel anything at all suddenly feeling too damn much. Not only for the boy, he realized, but for the woman who'd given him that child.

The situation nagged him as Buzz made his way down the steep trail toward where he'd left Kelly and Eddie. He tried to focus on the dull ache in his back, on the discomfort of being wet and cold and exhausted. Instead, all he could think about were the woman and child waiting for him and the fact that he didn't have the slightest clue what he was going to do about either of them.

Chapter 11

They made camp at dusk in a small clearing at the base of a rocky slope that protected them from the winds driving in from the north. Buzz set to work digging a shallow pit for the fire. Kelly opted to gather some dry kindling. Since Eddie was wearing only her flannel shirt and an extra pair of socks while his clothes hung to dry, he had to stay at camp with Buzz. Of course, her awestruck son wasn't complaining about that.

Kelly didn't stray far from where Eddie and Buzz were working on the pit. She'd never considered herself an overprotective mom, but she was having a hard time letting her son out of her sight. Every instinct she possessed screamed for her to gather his forty-two-pound body into her arms, hold him tight and never let him go.

Of course, her son had other ideas.

Eddie liked to talk and wasn't a bit shy about talking to strangers. Not that the man who'd saved his life was a stranger, exactly; they'd been hiking the trail most of the

day. Kelly had watched father and son with an odd mix of
pain and amusement. One minute they would have her
smiling. The next, the pain, the sense of all the time they
had lost was so intense, she nearly doubled over with it.

Early on, Buzz had done his best to ignore the little boy
and his nonstop chatter. But as afternoon stretched into evening, Eddie had managed to draft him into several conver-
sations.

"So what happened next?" Eddie asked excitedly about
a rescue story Buzz had mentioned.

Buzz made a neat circle of river rock around the perim-
eter of the shallow pit. "The medic jumped out while the
chopper hovered," he said. "Wind from the rotors kicked
up snow and debris, but we winched him down anyway."

"What's winched?"

"A winch is a long steel cable with which the medic is
lowered down to the ground."

"You mean he jumped out of the chopter! Wowwee! I
wish I coulda seen it! I'll bet that was cool."

Kelly watched father and son, mesmerized by the picture
they made. It was a picture she'd seen a thousand times in
her dreams, but had known reality would never yield.

Buzz re-hung Eddie's wet clothes from a tree branch
above the campfire pit. Eddie sat on a log, kicking out his
feet, and watched every move the big man made, a combination of curiosity and awe showing plainly in his young
eyes.

"Was the lady hurt?" Eddie asked after a moment.

"We treated her for hypothermia."

"What's that?"

"That's when you get really cold."

"I got frosted on my big toe once when I was ice-
skating."

Buzz looked up from his work. "You mean frostbite?"

Eddie nodded. "That, too. Mommy had to take me to the doctor."

"Is that so?"

"Yeah, but it was okay. I'll bet I had hippo terma today. I was really cold."

"You mean hypothermia."

"Yeah. Hippo terma."

Buzz rubbed his hand over his jaw, obviously trying to hide a smile.

"Do we get to ride in the chopter tomorrow, Buzz?"

"Sure do."

"Do I get to ride on the winch?"

"That depends on where they pick us up. Chances are the pilot will land at a pre-designated point and we won't have to use the winch."

"Are you going to come with us?"

Buzz reached down and mussed his hair. "Yeah, kiddo, I'll be there."

Kelly wasn't sure why the casual gesture of affection got to her, but it did. Like a hand reaching into her chest and giving her heart a single hard squeeze. She knew it was silly for her to be getting all emotional now that they were safe. She knew her emotions were riding high because she'd come so close to losing her son. And because the man she'd tried so desperately to exorcise from her life— from her heart—kept finding his way back to both.

Why did things always have to be so complicated?

Of all the men on this earth that she could have fallen in love with all those years ago, why did it have to be Buzz? A man who was everything she didn't need, everything she didn't want—everything she longed for.

For three years she'd loved him with every fiber of her heart. It hadn't been enough. Experience told her he would eventually hurt her, hurt her again. Only this time, he would hurt her son, too. She couldn't let that happen no matter how she felt about him.

Buzz Malone might be a good man, he might be courageous and daring and kind, but it took so much more to be a good father. Her own father had been a good man. Jack McKee had been kind and courageous and daring. But he'd also been a risk taker. He'd put his family through hell. When Kyle followed in his footsteps and they'd perished in that fiery crash, Kelly had lost the only two men she'd ever loved. Her life had been forever changed.

She'd grieved for months. But she'd also been angry with them. Angry that two men she'd loved had chosen their dangerous profession over their family. Over her.

In a small corner of her heart, she knew that was selfish. She knew that if it wasn't for the brave men and women who put their lives on the line every day—police officers and firefighters and a dozen other nameless professions—countless innocent people would die. Still, right or wrong, Kelly had never been able to forgive.

No matter how powerful her feelings for Buzz, she could never give in to them. She could never open her heart to him, could never let him get too close to her son. If she did, she would not only risk her own heart, but her son's, and she swore that was the one thing she would never do.

Realizing she was just standing there in the shadows of the trees holding an armload of kindling and watching them, Kelly shook the thoughts from her head and started toward the clearing where Buzz and Eddie were embroiled in yet another conversation.

"What does R-M-S-A-R stand for?" Eddie asked, referring to the letters emblazoned on the cap Buzz wore.

Buzz repositioned a tiny pair of jeans over a branch and looked down at Eddie. "Rocky Mountain Search and Rescue."

"My mommy's a tour guide."

"I know."

"How do you know?"

For a moment, Buzz looked flustered. "Your mommy and I are friends. She told me."

"We're going to move to Lake Tahoe. It snows a lot there."

"I know that, too."

"You ever been there?"

"Can't say I have."

"Then how do you know it snows a lot?"

"I just do."

Feeling guilty for eavesdropping, Kelly cleared her throat and stepped into the clearing. "I found plenty of kindling," she said, dropping her armload of wood a few feet away from the fire.

"Mommy!" Jumping up from the log he'd been sitting on, Eddie ran over to her, dried leaves and pine needles sticking to the bottoms of his socks. "Buzz was just telling me about a R-M-S-A-R guy who jumped out of a helicopter and rescued a lady from the side of a mountain!"

Because she couldn't resist, she knelt and pulled him into her arms. "Sounds like the same guy that fished you out of the river today, puppy face."

He giggled. "I'm *not* a puppy face."

God, she loved it when he smiled like that. She loved everything about this beautiful child, and she felt like the luckiest woman in the world every time she held him in her arms. "You'll always be my little puppy face."

"Even when I'm a hundred years old?"

"Especially when you're a hundred years old."

Pulling away from her, he mimicked the sound of a helicopter and circled around her, his arms stretched out like wings. "I'm going to learn how to fly a chopter!" He flew over to Buzz. "I'm going to be just like Buzz when I grow up!"

Kelly felt herself recoil. She knew he was just a little boy sounding off, but the words hit close to home, made her think of another little boy with a bad case of hero worship who hadn't lived to see his twenty-first birthday.

"I set up the tent for you and Eddie."

Buzz's voice jerked her from her reverie. Kelly felt herself flush, then looked down at her hands. "Oh. Good. Thank you."

"It's a one-man tent. Pretty small, but the two of you ought to be able to sleep comf—" His voice cut off abruptly. The next thing she knew he was staring at her hands, reaching for her. "What happened to your hands?" he demanded.

Kelly looked dumbly down at her raw and oozing palms. "I was holding the rope when you slid down the ravine. It slipped through my hands. The rope must have burned me."

He turned her hands over and grimaced. "Those are serious rope burns. Why didn't you tell me about this earlier?"

This was the closest she'd been to him all day, and she was keenly aware of her heart beating too fast. Even though it was chilly, sweat broke out on the back of her neck. "I was just…preoccupied with Eddie." She didn't think it was a very good idea to tell him she'd been avoiding getting too close because she didn't like the way she was reacting to him. There were too many complicated emotions zinging between them. Too many topics left undiscussed, and every single one of them was as volatile as a land mine—and twice as dangerous.

"Sit down," he said. "I'll get those burns cleaned and some antibiotic ointment on them."

"Wait, Buzz."

He stopped, then turned and looked at her over his shoulder.

"I'd like to get Eddie fed and bedded down for the night first," she said. "He's exhausted and hungry."

He nodded. "I've got some jerky and a few protein bars." He walked over to his backpack and pulled out several individually wrapped packages. "It's not much, but it'll hold us over until morning."

"I don't need anything," Kelly began, "I just want Eddie—"

"Kel, there's plenty for all three of us."

Feeling awkward, she walked over to one of the logs Buzz had placed near the fire and sat. He joined her a moment later with the first-aid kit in one hand, the packages of food in the other.

She glanced over at Eddie who was amusing himself by swinging a length of kindling through the air. "Eddie, honey, come on over here and have something to eat."

Eddie trotted over to where Kelly was sitting. "I'm starved," he said, eyeing the packages in her hand.

"Jerky first, then you can have one of these protein bars."

"Aw, Mom..."

"No arguments." She unwrapped a small package of jerky and handed it to him. "Peanut butter or chocolate chip?"

Eddie considered the question with the seriousness of a doctor choosing a surgical instrument. "Chocolate chip."

She handed him one of the bars. "And be sure to thank Mr. Malone."

"He said I could call him Buzz."

Kelly felt Buzz's eyes on her, but she didn't look up. Instead she concentrated on opening her own package of jerky, praying the subject of Buzz's relationship with Eddie didn't come up. She didn't know what to say. Exhaustion had a way of magnifying emotions, and she was feeling downright fragile inside at the moment. "Just make sure you thank him for the food, all right?"

Grinning at Buzz with adoration in his eyes, Eddie bit into the jerky and tore off a piece with his straight little teeth. "Thanks."

Buzz smiled. "You're welcome."

"This'll make me strong, won't it, Buzz?"

"As long as you eat the jerky first." Walking over to his backpack, he bent. "I almost forgot to give this to you, Eddie."

Kelly tried not to notice the way he said her son's name. The way he looked at him, with a combination of wonder and amusement and pleasure. She tried not to notice the way he walked. The way those jeans hugged his lean hips and long, muscular legs. He was the only man in the world who could affect her just by the way he moved. Buzz Malone didn't just walk, he strutted.

He straightened a moment later, then turned, a small teddy bear in his hand. "I guess you must have dropped this when you fell into the ravine."

Eddie stood transfixed, his mouth open, his gray eyes wide with surprise. "Bunky Bear! Wow! You found him!"

"Hey, that's why they call us Search and Rescue guys."

The little boy darted forward, grabbed the stuffed bear, then threw his arms around Buzz's hips. "Thanks, Buzz!"

Kelly's heart turned over in her chest at the sight of her son hugging Buzz. She'd dreamed of it a hundred times in the last four years, but never thought it would really happen. That the situation was so impossible to resolve broke her heart.

"Sweetheart, it's bedtime," she said, hating it that her voice was shaky.

"Mommy, I'm not sleepy yet."

"Do as your mother says, tough guy," Buzz said easily.

Eddie eyed Buzz for a moment as if considering chal-

lenging him, then hung his head and started toward the tent.
If Kelly's heart still hadn't been in her throat, she might
have smiled or made a joke, but her emotions were strung
so tightly, she didn't trust herself to do either.

"I forgot to say g'night to Buzz."

Kelly looked over at Buzz to see him nod. "Make it
quick, kiddo."

Grinning from ear to ear, Eddie charged the big man and
without warning flung himself into his arms.

The momentum sent Buzz back a step, but he still managed to catch the little boy. "Whoa there, partner!"

"G'night," Eddie said and planted a sloppy kiss on
Buzz's stubbled jaw.

Kelly saw Buzz wince, and her heart stumbled in her
chest. Leave it to an innocent to show the adults how infinitely easy simple affection could be, she thought, and
had to turn away to blink back tears.

A moment later, Eddie wriggled free of Buzz's arms and
darted toward the tent. "Come on, Mommy! Let's check
out the tent!"

Kelly couldn't bring herself to look at Buzz, couldn't
bear for him to see the uncertainty she knew was etched in
her expression. She didn't want him to know how seeing
them together was affecting her. Putting crazy notions in
her head. Making her want things that could never be.

And long for a future they could never have.

Buzz lay a few feet from the fire with his hands laced
behind his head and stared up at the swaying treetops and
patches of night sky beyond. Smoke from the forest fire to
the north scented the air and skittered like low clouds over
a yellow moon that sat on the horizon like a heavy-lidded
eye. He should have been exhausted considering he'd had
no rest, and very little sleep and food in the last two days.

But his mind was troubled, his heart heavy, and he knew from experience that sleep wouldn't come any time soon.

He'd relived the rescue a hundred times in his mind since it had happened. The first moment when he'd touched his son. The instant he'd put his arms around his small, cold body. The wave of emotion that had swept through him every bit as powerfully—and dangerously—as the churning water.

He'd tried hard not to let Eddie get to him. Buzz knew better than to get emotionally involved with this child who'd been thrust into his life. He knew all too well that the child could be swept out of his life just as swiftly. And Buzz would have very little say in the matter. He tried to convince himself he didn't care one way or another. Buzz didn't want children. Damn it, he didn't. He was *not* father material. He hadn't even made a very good husband, for God's sake. And not a damn thing had changed.

Only it had. Everything had changed. His entire world had come crashing down around him, and Buzz was honest enough with himself to admit it.

A *child*, a young life of his own creation, a life he was responsible for guiding and shaping and, God forbid—*loving*—wasn't something a man walked away from. He didn't have the faintest idea how he was going to handle this, but it wasn't going to be by running away. He'd never run away from anything in his life, and he didn't intend to start now.

More than anything, Buzz needed to talk with Kelly. Away from Eddie's sensitive ears because he had a feeling the conversation wasn't going to be pleasant. He hoped they could agree on a mutually acceptable resolution. Do what was best for the child, because his well-being and security were what counted most. Buzz and Kelly hadn't agreed on much in the years they'd been married, but Buzz knew her well enough to know she would put all of it aside to do what was best for their son.

Raising his head slightly, he glanced over at the tent. She'd been inside with Eddie for nearly an hour. Buzz had thought she would come out after the boy fell asleep so they could talk and get a few things straightened out. Not that the situation could be straightened out with a simple conversation, but it was a start.

Hell, what a mess.

Restless, he turned onto his side and faced the fire. He didn't know what to say to her even if she *did* have the guts to come out and face him. What was he going to say? I want to be part of my son's life? A part-time dad who takes him fishing twice a year and sees him at Christmas time? Watch him grow up through the photographs you send me from Lake Tahoe?

Frustrated and angry, Buzz shifted again and resigned himself to a long, cold and sleepless night. His back ached dully. He was hungry. Cold. The bruises he'd sustained while bouncing off boulders in the water throbbed with every beat of his heart.

"Are you awake?"

He sat bolt upright at the sound of Kelly's voice. She stood a few feet away, her arms folded protectively in front of her, watching him. He hadn't heard her unzip the tent flap and come out, and he felt a moment of panic because he didn't have a clue what he was going to say to her.

His heart did a slow roll at the sight of her, then moved into a quick, unsteady cadence. "I'm awake," he managed.

Hesitantly, she approached him. Firelight illuminated her features. Dark, serious eyes filled with the caution of prey approaching predator. Her hair was pulled back in a ponytail. Her face was smooth and pale within the dark frame of hair. She'd taken off her flannel shirt. The T-shirt and jeans she wore hugged her narrow waist and the curve of her hips.

"You want some company?" she asked.

He wasn't sure how he was supposed to answer that, so he didn't. The last thing he wanted to do was admit just how badly he'd wanted her to come out of that tent and talk to him. He wanted to believe it was because they had so much to discuss, but he knew at least part of that need wasn't so cut and dried.

"How's Eddie?" he asked.

"Poor little guy. He went out like a light."

"He's been through a lot."

"We all have." On reaching the fire, she stuck out her hands as if to warm them.

Buzz wondered why she wouldn't look at him. "You've done a good job with him," he said after a moment. "He's smart as a whip and seems happy."

She looked at him then, and he didn't miss the quick flash of pride—of love—in her eyes. "Thank you. He's an incredible little boy."

"Why don't you let me have a look at your palms now?" he asked.

As if remembering the abrasions on her hands, she looked down at them. "Oh. Okay." She laughed. "They're starting to hurt."

Leaning over, Buzz rummaged in his backpack for the first-aid kit, set it on his lap and opened the lid. "Have a seat."

Kelly lowered herself onto the log next to him and turned toward him.

"Give me one of your hands."

He didn't miss the hesitation when she held out her hand. As impersonally as possible, Buzz took it in his and turned her palm up so he could look at the wound. "This must have hurt like the dickens."

"I barely noticed when it first happened, but it hurts now."

He risked a look at her. "You did good today, Kel. Throwing the rope the way you did was a smart thing to do. You stayed calm. You kept your head."

She smiled wryly. "Are you trying to tell me I saved your life?"

"Not just mine."

She looked away, blinking rapidly. "Don't give me too much credit, Buzz. I know you wouldn't have let go of him. No matter what might have happened, I know you wouldn't have let go of him."

About that, he thought, she was right.

"This is going to sting a little bit." Opening a small container of peroxide, he saturated a gauze pad and drizzled it liberally over her abraded palm. Kelly didn't so much as wince. Her hand was small and cold within his. Her knuckles were scraped. One of her nails was turning purple.

"Feel okay?" he asked.

"It hurts like hell, but I'm too damn tired to scream."

He smiled a little at that, but didn't look over at her. He could feel her gaze on him, but he didn't take his eyes off her palm. He didn't want to make eye contact with her when he was this close to her. They might have failed as husband and wife, but it hadn't been for lack of chemistry.

"Today must have been…hard for you," she said after a moment.

"I'm not sure *hard* is the right word."

She winced, but Buzz didn't acknowledge it. "I don't know how to handle this, Kel," he said. "You walked out on me five years ago. Now suddenly you're back. Only now I have a four-year-old son. That's a lot for a man to absorb in just a couple of days."

"I don't know if it makes any difference now, but I'm sorry. It was wrong of me not to tell you."

Buzz finished with her right hand, then started on the left. He was very thankful he had something to do with his hands, something to look at besides her eyes.

"It makes a difference." He looked up at her, felt the impact of her like the front end of a truck traveling at a hundred miles an hour. "But it doesn't change the situation. We're the same people we were before the divorce. The same problems are there. Only this time, when all is said and done, I can't just forget I have a son."

"I wouldn't ask you to do that."

"I don't know how to be a father." He remembered the way he'd felt when that little boy had wrapped his arms around him and kissed him with such open affection and felt a knot of emotion form in his chest. "I'm not sure I'm cut out for that. But I'm not going to walk away."

"I won't keep you from him," she said.

"It's going to be a tad difficult for me to be involved in his life when you're in Tahoe."

"That's a twelve-hour drive from Denver. A couple of hours if you fly."

"You've put me in an impossible situation."

"I don't expect anything from you, Buzz," she said quickly. "I don't expect money. I don't expect you to love him. I don't expect you to forgive me."

Anger rumbled like thunder in his chest, and he held onto it like a lifeline. It was better than the other emotions pounding through him—and a hell of a lot safer. Any emotion was better than the sharp-edged need, the stark sense of loss, of betrayal that cut him every time he thought about what she'd done. Not only to him, but to their son. An innocent child who might never know his father because she hadn't seen fit to tell the truth.

"You may not want anything from me, Kel," he began. "But I'd like a few things from you."

Her hand jolted within his. Her gaze fixed on his, and in

their brown depths Buzz saw emotions he didn't want to
see, didn't want to confront. He felt those same emotions
tangle and snap inside him.

"I'd like some answers," he said. "I'd like to know why
this happened. Then I think we need to figure out what the
hell we're going to do about it."

Chapter 12

Kelly had dreaded this moment for five unbearable years. She'd known all along that eventually she would have to face him. Buzz would somehow find out about Eddie and she would have to own up to what she'd done, confront the man she'd lied to. The man she'd betrayed and cheated and hurt.

The man she'd once loved more than life itself.

Heart pounding, she sat silent and still and watched him, unseeing, as he treated the rope burns on her palm, wondering how he could function, how his hands could be so steady when the world around them crumbled and shook. She could feel the tension coming off him, like steam off a geyser in the seconds before it blew. Her own emotions trembled inside her, locked in her chest, ready to explode outward at the slightest touch.

Because she was shaking, she waited until he was finished treating the abrasions before attempting to speak, using those few precious moments to gather her courage and shore up defenses that were far too battered to do her any good now.

Easing her hand from his, she forced a gulp of air into her lungs then let it shudder out. "You made it clear when we were married that you never wanted children. You were adamant about it."

"I might be able to accept that if I didn't know you so well."

She arched a brow, trying to look cool and amused when in reality her heart was beating out of control. "Why do you say that?"

"You're too logical a woman not to realize you could come to me with this. That's how I know there's more going on than you want to say."

"You're a responsible man, Buzz. I didn't want you to feel trapped. I didn't want you to feel obligated."

"I guess you figured keeping me in the dark was better?"

"I figured all of us would be better off if you and I split cleanly and amicably."

"This has been real clean and amicable, hasn't it?"

"Life doesn't always cooperate." She sighed. "Look, I didn't plan on getting pregnant."

His gaze turned glacial, boring into hers like an awl through ice. "It *was* an accident, wasn't it, Kel?"

"You know damn good and well it was," she snapped. "How dare you accuse me of using you for something like that."

"I never thought you'd keep the fact that I had a child from me either, but you did."

Aware that anger had joined the chorus of emotions screaming through her, she worked hard to keep her voice steady. "You're entitled to decide whether or not you want to have children, Buzz. But it would have saved us both a lot of heartache if you had told me how you felt *before* we got married.''

''What are you saying, Kel?'' he asked nastily. ''That you would have turned me down?''

''Yes,'' she said, but they both knew it was a bald-faced lie. The night he'd proposed to her they'd been so crazy in love a war of the worlds couldn't have kept them apart.

''I wasn't thinking about kids when we met. Neither were you.''

''You should have told me how you felt about having a family.''

''It never came up.''

''You avoided the topic because you didn't want me to know *why* you feel the way you do.''

He laughed, but the sound was stark and bitter. ''Oh, for pity's sake, don't start psychoanalyzing me!''

''It took you almost two years before you told me about your father. About what he did to you.''

Buzz flushed, his hands clenching into fists at his sides, and Kelly knew she'd hit a nerve. She knew that nerve was alive and exposed and painful as hell when exposed. And she knew he would fight her tooth and nail to keep it buried.

''Damn it, Kel, that's ancient history.''

''It's exactly that kind of history that molded us into the people we became. You didn't want me to know your own father abused you. That you were taken away from him by Child Protective Services when you were a teenager. To this day you've never told anyone what he did to you.''

''That's enough,'' he said in a dangerously calm voice.

''Not all people are as cruel as your father.''

''There are a hundred other reasons why I never wanted kids. My father was just one of them.''

''When we were married, I was stupid and naive enough to think I could change you. That I could change your mind. I thought our love was so strong we could overcome any problem, any disagreement. We had something beautiful, and I wanted so badly to make it complete. I wanted a family. Then you took the job in the Child Abuse Division and everything changed.''

His expression closed up, the way it always did when she brought up the dark years he'd spent working the CA Division of the Denver PD. ''I saw first-hand the things people do to their children,'' he said. ''The things they do to other people's children. The things I saw, the things I learned when I worked CAD made me realize I did not want to bring anything as innocent as a child into this world. I won't apologize for that.''

''You never considered my feelings, Buzz.''

''In your eyes, considering your feelings would have meant doing something I didn't want to do.''

''God forbid you might have to compromise,'' she snapped. ''That word isn't part of your vocabulary, is it?''

''How in the hell do you compromise when one of us wanted children and the other did not?''

''You didn't want children because you were afraid,'' she said. ''In my mind, that's not good enough. I never accepted that. Not from you.''

''Is that why you asked for a divorce?''

She hated the way he was looking at her. With hurt and fury and a newfound coldness she'd never seen in his eyes before. ''You know why I filed for divorce. You know it was a hell of a lot more complicated than that.''

''Maybe you filed for divorce because you knew you could get what you needed from me even if we weren't married. I mean, come on, we both know sex was the one thing we never argued about. The one thing we could never resist no matter how angry we were at each other.''

The anger struck her with such force that for a moment she wanted to strike him. She'd never hit anyone in her life, but the urge to do so now was so strong she could barely hold herself back. "How dare you accuse me of something so despicable."

"What do you expect me to think? How do you think this looks to me? If Eddie hadn't gotten lost in those woods, I *never* would have known about him, would I?"

"You never wanted a child. Damn it, Buzz, you never even wanted a wife. Sure, you went through the motions. But the whole time we were married, you did what *you* wanted to do—even if that meant risking your life—and all the people who loved you could just be damned."

"I may not deserve a husband of the year award," he said. "But I damn well didn't deserve to be treated the way I was."

"We were already divorced when I got pregnant."

"That divorce was a farce," he snarled.

"Our marriage was a farce!" she shot back.

"You took care of that, though, didn't you?"

"I did what I had to do to keep from becoming a widow! At the rate you were going that would have happened sooner or later. I ended our marriage because I refused to live in fear of getting that phone call in the middle of the night, telling me my husband wouldn't be coming home ever again."

"You knew who and what I was when you married me."

"And it took me three years to realize marrying you was the biggest mistake of my life!"

Cursing, Buzz rose abruptly and paced to the edge of the clearing and stood there with his back to her.

Kelly sat there for a moment, struggling to get herself under control. She'd seen him upset before. Many times, in fact, and most of those times she was the cause. She'd seen him rant and rave and cuss the world. But in all the years she'd known him, she'd never seen him like this. She'd never seen him so angry he shook.

"You almost died the night you were shot, Buzz," she

whispered. "That was when I knew it wasn't going to work. No matter how...powerful things were between us, no matter how much I cared for you, I knew it wasn't enough."

"But I didn't die, Kel, did I?"

"If the bullet had been a fraction of an inch in the other direction, you would have been paralyzed for the rest of your life."

"You can't live your life based on ifs," he snapped. "It didn't happen."

"When you came home from the hospital and told me you were going to be retiring from the PD, I was so happy. When that corporate security job came up, I thought our problems were over. I thought I would never have to worry about you getting shot in some back alley or warehouse. I begged you to take that job. You were barely out of the wheelchair when you announced you were going to take the team leader position with Rocky Mountain Search and Rescue."

"Search and Rescue work is not the same as being a cop. Not even close."

"Jumping out of helicopters, skiing into avalanche-prone areas in winter, rappelling down sheer cliffs. Don't tell me you're not an adrenaline junkie."

He stared hard at her, his jaw flexing.

"You made a choice that day, Buzz. You chose living on the edge over our marriage. Over me and any future we might have had together."

"I am who I am, Kel. Nothing will ever change that. Not you. Not whatever job I take." Turning abruptly, he paced back over to her.

"That's why we're not together, Buzz. That's why our marriage didn't last."

He stared at her long enough to make her want to squirm. "When did we...when did you get pregnant?" he asked.

She didn't want to talk about the lonely weeks following the divorce. The countless nights she'd lain awake, unable to sleep because she'd missed him so desperately. Because she'd hurt him so deeply. She knew he would never admit it—not big, strong, I-don't-need-anyone Buzz Malone—but she'd hurt him as badly as a man could be hurt by a woman. She knew that now, had known it then, and she had learned to live with it, accept it because she knew what the alternative was.

"You came to me several times after you moved out, Buzz. After the divorce."

Choking out a humorless laugh, he lowered his head and pinched the bridge of his nose. "Jesus."

Responsibility for what she'd done pressed down on her. Kelly had never been irresponsible or impulsive or even prone to lapses in judgment, though she had made more than a few mistakes in her lifetime—most of them involving the man standing before her. After their breakup, she'd been desperate to make a clean break, even if that had meant doing something irrevocable.

"You didn't waste any time going off the pill. You sure as hell didn't bother to tell me you had."

"I know it wasn't the smartest thing to do, but, for God's sake, Buzz, the fact that I still needed those pills was just one more tie to you that needed to be severed. I mean, it wasn't like I was going to be with anyone else. In my mind, I no longer needed birth control."

Remembering more than was wise at the moment, she raised her gaze to his. He lifted his head to look at her and his jaw flexed. She instinctively knew he was remembering that last night. He'd come to her the night he received the divorce papers in the mail. It had been a night of angry words, of unbearable heartbreak, and finally, of pain-numbing passion. When she'd wakened in the morning he'd been gone, and she'd known he would never come back.

"Now that I've had time to think about it, I believe my going off the pill was more symbolic than anything else."

Buzz groaned. "Oh, Kel. Jesus."

"It's not like we planned to end up in bed. It's not like either of us kept condoms on hand. I mean, we were married for three years."

"Kel, why didn't you say something?"

"Don't tell me cold, hard knowledge would have stopped us that night. You know as well as I do that nothing could have stopped what happened between us." The thought of everything they'd done the night Eddie was conceived sent a hot blush to her cheeks. Even though they'd been divorced and hurting, their hearts in turmoil, their lovemaking had been one of the most erotic experiences of her entire life. It was as if for a few short hours, they'd transformed pain into passion and made magic one final time.

"Two months later my doctor confirmed I was pregnant."

"You haven't been with anyone else?"

She wanted to tell him to go to hell, but she held her tongue. He deserved the truth. "No."

"Why didn't you call me? For chrissake, you could have sent me a letter."

"Because I wanted...I wanted...us to be over." That wasn't exactly true, but the words came out in a flood. She hadn't wanted it to be over. Not really. She'd just wanted the pain to stop.

"If I had told you," she continued, "nothing would have changed. You would have kept coming around, and I would have continued letting you. I couldn't go on like that. I couldn't." Her eyes heated and to her horror, she felt on the verge of tears.

"Why didn't you tell me about my son?"

"Because you never wanted him. You never wanted me."

"I deserved to know, damn it."

"I didn't want him hurt!" She hadn't meant to say it, but now that it was out in the open, she wasn't going to take it back.

He shot her a narrow-eyed look. "You know damn good and well I would never hurt a child. Any child."

"Not maliciously. Not on purpose. But I know what kind of man you are, Buzz. And I just happen to know from experience that you're exactly the kind of man who would end up hurting him."

He started toward her. "How can you possibly believe Eddie's better off without a father?"

"He needs a man who's going to be there for him. A man he can count on. Not some superhero he'll never be able to measure up to."

"Like your Mr. Corporate America, huh?"

She gaped at him, shocked that he would bring up Taylor Quelhorst at a time like this. "I am *not* involved with Taylor."

"You might want to clue him in on that because I've seen the way he looks at you. And you can bet your next paycheck once he gets you to Tahoe things are going to change."

"Taylor has nothing to do with any of this!"

"Don't lie to me, Kel. Don't tell me you haven't thought about getting involved with him. I know *he* has. He can't keep his goddamn eyes off you. He can barely keep his tongue in his mouth when he looks at you."

"That's not true!"

"Or maybe you're willing to sell yourself out to land a good father for Eddie, is that it? Someone who doesn't spend his days jumping out of helicopters and skiing in avalanche season.''

''Go to hell!'' She whirled away from him, but he caught her arm and stopped her.

''Don't turn away from me,'' he growled.

''Let go of me!

''We're not finished.''

''We've been finished for a very long time!''

''Why don't you tell me the real reason you didn't tell me about Eddie?'' he snarled.

Kelly gaped at him. Anxiety clenched her stomach so hard she was nauseous. ''I don't know what you're talking about.''

''You knew if you told me about Eddie that I would want to be part of his life, didn't you?''

She tried to shove away from him, but he now gripped both biceps tightly. ''No!''

''You knew you'd have to deal with me. That I would be not only part of Eddie's life, but yours too. Isn't that the real reason you never told me?''

''Buzz, please, just stop it.''

''You don't have the guts to deal with me, Kel, do you? You don't have the guts to deal with a man who's willing to put his life on the line for what he believes in or for what he loves. You just can't handle that can you?''

''That's not true.''

''It's true and you know it. Your father was that kind of man, wasn't he? And your brother Kyle followed in his old man's footsteps, didn't he?''

The mention of her brother's name went through her like a straight razor. ''My brother and father have nothing to do with this.''

''That's where you're wrong, Kel. They have everything to do with this. That's why you're not being truthful with me. That's why you're not even being truthful to yourself.''

She succeeded in twisting away. "Stay away from me."

"I'm nothing like your father."

Raising her hands, she took a step back. "You're exactly like him. And sooner or later you're going to get yourself killed." She put a trembling hand over her mouth. "I couldn't bear it, Buzz. I swear, I couldn't bear losing you that way."

Her own words horrified her. She hadn't meant to say them, hadn't mean to crack open her heart that way.

"Jack was an adrenaline freak, Kel. I'm not. I might have a job you consider dangerous, but I sure don't have a death wish."

"You keep forgetting, Buzz, I'm the one who sat in the intensive care unit at the hospital going slowly insane until the surgeon came out and told me you were going to make it through the night. I won't live my life that way, and I won't put my son through losing his father."

"I'm not a cop anymore."

"Search and Rescue is dangerous work."

"It's important work, but not nearly as dangerous as most people think." He sighed. "Maybe it's not me you're worried about. Maybe it's Eddie."

She stared at him, keenly aware of her heart rapping a hard tattoo against her ribs. And for the first time, she knew he understood. And for the first time she understood clearly herself.

"You saw the way Eddie looks at you," she said. "He's only four years old. His mind is impressionable. He's only known you for a few hours and already he looks at you like you're some kind of hero."

He blinked at her as if momentarily stunned, but that didn't keep him from stepping toward her. She took another step back. "He looks at you the same way Kyle looked at Dad. Look what happened to Kyle. No matter what, I won't let that happen to my child."

Understanding struck him like a wrecking ball slamming into a building. For the first time, the divorce, the secret pregnancy, the child she'd hidden from him made perfect, terrible sense.

He looks at you the same way Kyle looked at Dad.

Buzz had seen the parallel before, but he'd never imagined that the deaths of her father and brother had affected her so profoundly. The implications astounded him. She hadn't asked for a divorce because she didn't love him or because he didn't want children or because he couldn't handle sitting behind a desk. She'd asked for a divorce because she couldn't live with losing him. She hadn't told him about the baby because she couldn't bear the thought of losing her son the same way she'd lost her brother.

Buzz almost couldn't believe it. For a full minute he just stood there feeling waylaid while his heart beat out a wild staccato in his chest. He wasn't sure who moved first, but in the next instant he had her backed up against the face of a smooth granite boulder. A surprised gasp escaped her when his body came full length against hers. He raised his hands to cup her face, then tilted her head closer.

"You have no idea what that divorce did to me," he ground out. "You walked out on me. That hurt, Kel."

He could feel the rise and fall of her breasts against him. Hear her quickened breaths. He could smell panic, knew she was on the verge of bolting, but he didn't let her go. Wasn't sure if he could even if he wanted to.

"I know," she said. "It hurt too much to love you."

"A divorce doesn't magically make someone stop loving."

"I couldn't live with you. I can't ever live with you."

"I'm not going to hurt you. I'm not going to hurt Eddie. And I'm sure not going to get myself killed."

"He's just like you, Buzz. He's fearless and daring with

a never-ending sense of adventure. Those things scare me because I know where they can lead."

"You're wrong about me," he said. "You're wrong about all of this."

He didn't intend to kiss her. Now wasn't the time to test his control. It sure as hell wasn't the place. But the chemistry between them had never relied on anything as reasonable as timing or simple right and wrong. The pull was too strong to resist, so he went with it and lowered his mouth to hers.

Her lips yielded softly to his. She tasted as sweet and mysterious as dark chocolate. The familiarity of her scent taunted him, tested his restraint, broke it. Crazy thoughts rushed through his brain like flashes, unleashing a hunger he'd kept buried for five long years. He knew it was insane to want her like this, to hope for something that could never be, but the taste of her mouth intoxicated him, made him believe in impossible dreams.

"Don't do this to me." But even as she said the words, her head lolled back and she offered the tender flesh of her throat.

Buzz kissed her neck, tasting her, remembering, savoring the sweetness of her flesh. Arousal flowed hotly through his veins. Pleasure zinged through his brain like a shot of whiskey on an empty stomach. She was the only woman in the world who could make him shake with need. The only woman he could hate and love at the same time and know fully he would never reconcile the two.

He kissed her throat, her jaw, her temple, then worked his way back down to her mouth. Something primal broke free inside him when she opened to him. He used his tongue, and she accepted him, welcomed him in with a small sound of pleasure at the back of her throat.

Buzz knew kissing her like this was a mistake. He knew it would do nothing but hurt him in the long run. The conversation they'd just had hadn't solved a damn thing. And if he let this go any further it would complicate an already complicated situation exponentially.

But control had never been his strong suit when it came to Kelly. She could topple that stone-and-steel structure with nothing more than a look or a sigh…or a single, earth-shattering kiss.

Five years of need and hurt tangled inside him, a rope drawing ever tighter around him until he felt as if he couldn't breathe. A hundred memories of how it had once been between them joined the melee. Caution sparked, a tiny light in a raging sea, but was quickly doused by the rush of heat that flamed over him like the afterburners of a jet engine.

Buzz knew all too well what it was like to want. He'd learned to live with it, learned to live with a lot of things in the last few years. He'd told himself a thousand times he didn't miss her. He didn't dream about her. He didn't fantasize about her. Or want her. Or think about having a future he knew could never be.

But when she moved tentatively against him, all that need exploded, shattering boundaries he'd sworn he would never breach. She gasped when he pressed his hard length against her. Then, taking her hands in his, he slid them above her head and moved against her.

"Some things never change," he said breathlessly. "This hasn't changed."

"We're going to hurt each other," she said.

"The way you feel against me…Kel, maybe it will be worth it."

"Nothing's worth that kind of pain." But she didn't ask him to stop.

Moonlight poured over her, turning her hair to silk, her features pearlescent. He looked down at her, breathing in her scent, putting it to memory, knowing that no matter what happened in the coming days, he would always have this moment.

"You're beautiful," he whispered.

She tried to look away, but he cupped her chin and forced her eyes back to his. "I mean that, Kel. You're beautiful. Inside and out and every place in between. Whatever happens after tonight, I want you always to know I feel that way about you."

A small, embarrassed smile curved her mouth. "You know better than to say something like that to me at a moment like this."

"Why?"

"Because we both know we're about an inch away from making a very big mistake."

"We're pretty good at that, aren't we?"

"We're good at a lot of things."

Lust and need and something else he didn't want to name coiled deep in his chest. Vaguely, he was aware of his own heavy breathing. The pounding of desire in his groin. The wild flutter of his heart. "If you want to stop this, I suggest you say so in the next thirty seconds," he said.

"Being with you like this won't solve anything. I think we both know it will only make everything worse."

He knew she was right, but he wasn't a good enough man to admit it. And he sure wasn't a good enough man to stop. Instead, he bucked logic and kissed her again. Hard and without the finesse she deserved. For an instant, he thought she would turn away, turn him away. Instead, she melted in his arms, opened to him. Her arms went around his neck. He groaned when she moved against him.

Her softness met his hardness with a silent crash, and Buzz saw stars. He skimmed his hands down her sides, pausing at her breasts. It had been so long since he'd touched her like this, since he'd touched any woman, but his hands hadn't forgotten the sheer perfection of her. She shivered when he skimmed his thumbs over her breasts. The hardened peaks of her nipples teased his palms through the silk of her bra. Cupping her, he molded the soft flesh. She arched into him, trusting him, giving him full access. Her nipples were larger than they'd been the last time they'd been together and he marveled at the ways pregnancy had changed her body, a body he'd once known intimately.

A body he desperately wanted to know again.

A new urgency burned through him. Lifting her T-shirt, he tugged it over her head. Her hair tumbled wildly over her shoulders. Her bra shimmered white in the moonlight. He could see the peaks of her nipples through the material, the frosting of lace against her flesh. Never taking his eyes from hers, he reached behind her and unfastened the tiny hooks. The scrap of material dropped to the ground.

The sight of her awed him, made him realize just how long it had been, just how desperately he'd missed this, how desperately he'd missed her. "Having a baby made you even more beautiful," he whispered.

She laughed, but it was a nervous laugh. "I sort of looked like a basketball when I was pregnant."

He smiled, trying to imagine her body rounded with child, and felt a sudden, stark sense of loss. He didn't want to feel that. Not now. All he wanted at the moment, all he needed was the pleasure he knew only she could give him.

"I've thought of you a thousand times in the last five years," he said. "Touching you like this."

"I've thought of you, too." She closed her eyes for a moment, then looked at him. "Buzz..."

Her voice trailed when he skimmed his fingertips gently over her. "Like this?" he asked.

She shivered. "Yes."

The word ended in a gasp when he bent his head and took her nipple into his mouth. She cried out softly, arching and throwing her head back as he laved the hardened peak with his tongue. He suckled her, nipping and tonguing, first one breast and then the other. She writhed beneath his manipulations, her cries of delight echoing amongst the rocks to be lost at the treetops and fading into the night.

He tried not to think about how far this might go or where it would lead them. All he knew was that he wanted her, he wanted to take it to the limit just one more time. Logic told him they should stop before things got crazy. But Buzz knew the situation had passed that point the moment he'd touched her.

His mouth left her breast, his tongue leaving a wet trail to her neck. He kissed her mouth. She tensed slightly when his hands went to the snap of her jeans, but she didn't stop him. He knew what she was thinking. He sensed the war raging inside her. The war between sanity and lust, emotion and logic, right and wrong. The very same war raged within him.

The snap at the front of her jeans opened easily. Lowering the zipper, he set his hand over her flat belly. Warm, taut flesh met his palm. He barely heard her whisper his name over the jackhammer of blood in his ears. His fingers met the silk of her panties, then the crisp curls of her mound.

Vaguely, he was aware of her trembling. He heard labored breaths, but for the life of him he couldn't tell if they were hers or his. A sound escaped her when his fingers found her most intimate place. She squirmed in his arms, opening to him, her body melting around him like hot wax. His heart pounded like a locomotive, laboring up a hill with a heavy load. He slipped two fingers inside her and she went rigid in his arms. A cry bubbled up from within her, but he swallowed the sound with a kiss. He made love to her mouth, all the while his fingers moved rhythmically inside her. He felt the rise of high-wire tension coming through her body and into his, but he didn't stop, refused to give her a reprieve. Not until she gave him what he wanted, what he needed.

"Climax for me," he whispered, stroking her, stroking.

She came apart in his arms, like a bomb exploding in slow motion, pelting him with sensation. He felt her body spasm. Her legs buckled. She cried out, but his name came out in only a whisper because her breaths were coming in short, labored gasps.

Gentling the kiss, Buzz closed his eyes against the burst of emotion and held onto his control by the force of sheer will. He held her tightly, aware that he was still touching her intimately, and tried not to think about what he'd just done and what it would mean in terms of their relationship or where they went from here.

The discipline cost him, but he held her gently as she slowly came back down to earth. Kissing her, never taking his eyes from hers, he swept her into his arms. On shaking legs, he carried her over to his sleeping bag and settled her onto it.

"What are you doing?" she asked.

"I'm going to make love to my ex-wife."

Her cheeks were flushed and moist with a sheen of perspiration. Buzz had never seen any woman look as beautiful as she did at that moment. She glanced over at the tent, realized belatedly that she was concerned about waking Eddie.

"Is he a sound sleeper?" Buzz asked.

"I need to check on him," she whispered, moving to rise.

Buzz put his hand gently on her shoulder, pressing her down. "Let me."

Rising to his full height, resisting the urge to rearrange himself, he strode over to the one-man tent, unzipped the flap and peered inside. The smell of little boy and laundry detergent and the scent of Kelly's shampoo lingered. It was a few degrees warmer in the tent. Anxious to get back to Kelly, he looked around as his eyes adjusted to the darkness. The sight of his son stopped him, the barrage of emotions that followed froze him in place.

The little boy was sleeping soundly with one arm draped protectively over the ratty stuffed bear he'd been carrying around with him. Buzz stared, aware of the uneven tempo of his breathing, the strum of his heart, the sharp pang of an emotion he didn't want to identify punching through him. For a moment he was moved so profoundly that tears burned at the backs of his eyes. Awe and disbelief that such a beautiful child could be his flowed through him in a torrent.

Moving into the tent, he raised the sleeping bag higher on Eddie's thin shoulders and covered him. Without realizing he was going to, Buzz leaned forward and kissed the little boy's soft cheek. "Night, son."

He closed his eyes tightly, determined not to let this get to him. Struggling to get a handle on his emotions, he backed from the tent, then sat back on his heels and pulled in a long breath.

He knew it was stupid to get emotional over something as simple as kissing his son good night, but for the first time in too many years to count, Buzz was having a hard time keeping it together. He could already feel the losses piling up around him. Soon it seemed the ground would open its hungry mouth, and everything he'd ever wanted would be gone.

Chapter 13

Kelly told herself she could handle this. She could keep a handle on her emotions. Keep her heart in check. Not let him get to her with those intense gray eyes and those hands that knew just where to touch her.

He was the only man in the world who could make her lose control. The only man who could offer her a mistake and make her think it was heaven. But she knew he could, indeed, offer her a little slice of heaven. At least for a little while. Because in the moments she'd been wrapped in his arms, she *had* been in heaven. The down side was that at some point she would have to leave his embrace and the reality of what she'd done would come crashing down on top of her.

"You look like a woman faced with the firing squad instead of a roll in the hay with her ex-husband."

She jolted hard at the sound of Buzz's voice. Because she didn't want to comment on what he'd said, she asked about her son. "How is he?"

"Sound asleep." He made no attempt to lie down on the sleeping bag with her. "I covered him up."

"Thanks. It's cool tonight."

"Yeah." He shifted his weight from one foot to the other.

Kelly knew better than to give her eyes free rein, but they took on a life of their own and swept over him. His jeans were snug enough that she could see the hard ridge of his arousal just behind his zipper. The realization that he'd given her so much pleasure, and she was already having second thoughts about going through with this made her feel guilty. It was a silly thing to feel because even when they'd been married Buzz had never been selfish that way. Of course, back when they'd been married she'd never told him no....

Making love with Buzz was like stepping into a swirling whirlpool. She knew once she did—if she did—she would be tumbled around and swept away. Maybe for good.

"You're having second thoughts," he said after a moment.

"I'm sorry."

"It's okay. We don't have to do this."

It hurt to hear the words because the ache to have him close was so intense she could barely take a breath. She hadn't put her clothes back on and her body still throbbed where he'd touched her earlier. She could still feel the wetness between her thighs. The heaviness of her breasts. The stab of need in her womb.

Guilt and need and a dozen other emotions thrashed inside her, pulling her in different directions. God, how she wanted to go to him, touch him, kiss him the way she had a thousand times before. But caution refused to let her move, refused to let her put so much of herself on the line for a man who would do nothing but hurt her, hurt her son.

"I don't know what to do," she whispered.

"You know what you want," he answered in a rough voice.

"I can't get involved with you."

"You already are."

"We've been down that road before, Buzz."

"If I remember correctly, it was a pretty damn good ride."

"It was a mistake."

"Some mistakes are worth making, Kel." He knelt on the sleeping bag next to her.

"Some just hurt."

"I won't hurt you."

You already have, she wanted to say, but it was too late. Her voice locked up. He was so close she could feel the warmth coming off him. She could smell the faint remnants of his aftershave and the all-too-familiar scent that was uniquely his. Need coiled like a spring inside her, tighter and tighter until she felt she would explode. Her heart pounded. Her breaths quickened and she could see the faint white puffs in the cool night air between them. No one else had ever done that to her—make her feel as if she'd run a ten-mile marathon, when he hadn't even touched her yet.

"I want you, Kel," he said. "I want you more than my next breath. I've never stopped wanting you."

The words shocked her brain, battered her defenses. She told herself he was talking about physical need. He was a man, after all. But she knew that wasn't what he meant and nothing else he could have said would have shocked her more.

She stared at him, wanting him so desperately the need was an ache. But the knowledge that loving him tonight would only hurt her tomorrow and bring to her heart a pain she was all too familiar with stopped her.

He sat back on his heels. "Come here."

Indecision hammered at her. A moment of heaven for a

lifetime of hell. She'd never been more at odds with herself. Body and mind. Heart and soul.

Buzz took the decision away from her. One moment he was gazing at her with the cool indifference of a man who was the epitome of control. The next he reached for her, grasping her biceps and pulled her toward him.

He didn't ask for permission to kiss her. His mouth came down on hers like a bird of prey swooping down for a kill. The fierceness of the kiss took her breath. For an instant, he possessed her, and despite her resolve not to make a mistake, she reveled in the sensation. Her brain ordered her to pull back, but the hot desire coursing through her body banked the order with military precision. Instead she opened to him, and he went in deep. Sensation streaked through her body like electricity and exploded in her brain like a bomb. The sleeping bag she'd been wrapped in fell away from her. Vaguely, she was aware of the cool night air on her back. She gasped when his hands went to her breasts. He molded her and her body jolted with pleasure, arching against him and all she could think was that she wanted more.

He tore at his clothes as he kissed her. Desperate to feel his bare flesh against hers, she reached for the snap of his jeans, but her brain was so overwhelmed she couldn't manage. When he pulled away to work off his shirt, Kelly opened her eyes, found herself looking at his bare chest. He was leaner than she remembered, but his muscles were more defined. A dark blanket of hair covered his chest and ran in a thin line down to the waistband of his low-rise jeans.

He never took his eyes from her as he worked the jeans over his narrow hips. She watched him undress, mesmerized by the stark male beauty of his body. The sensuality of the moment overwhelmed her. She felt as if someone had doused her with gasoline and set her aflame. She was burning from the inside out, and the sensation was only increased by the desperate knowledge that this would be their last time together.

When he leaned forward and kissed her it was with a gentleness that brought tears to her eyes. That a man like Buzz could be so gentle with her was profound and it moved her as nothing else could have. Kelly wasn't much of a crier, but a muffled sob escaped her. She felt Buzz stiffen. Then he pulled away slightly and looked at her with a puzzled look.

"Don't stop," she whispered.

"Kel, if you don't want to do this—"

"I do. I want this...too much."

"Why are you crying?"

"I'm not."

"Kel...for Pete's sake, yes you are."

"Because I want this. Because it's a mistake, but I want this anyway."

She could feel him shaking with tension and restraint and uncertainty. She could feel that same tension zinging through her own body. He stared at her, his expression cautious and puzzled. Because she knew he wouldn't proceed without some kind of encouragement from her, she leaned forward and brushed her lips across his.

That was all it took. In one smooth movement, he unzipped the sleeping bag and slid in beside her. The hard length of his body against hers shocked her. He felt solid and warm and strong beside her. It had been so long since she'd been with a man—since she'd been with Buzz—she'd forgotten what it was like. But her body remembered. Oh, yes, her body remembered.

When he moved over her, she opened to him. He looked down at her and she wanted to cry out with the joy of holding him close. She tried not to think about tomorrow or next week or next month. She tried not to think about what it would be like to walk away from him for the last time.

"I haven't been with anyone since that last night," he said.

The words shocked her. She'd assumed he'd moved on with his life. Over the years, she'd thought of him often, wondering if he'd found someone special, never letting herself examine too closely how that made her feel.

"That's a long time," she said.

"Some things are worth waiting for."

His kiss devastated her, shook her all the way to her core. He worked her mouth with his, nipping at her lips, their tongues sparring. She moved restlessly beneath him, arousal burning her, making her impatient.

"Please," she said, breaking the kiss.

"Not yet."

She withheld a cry when he took her nipple into his mouth. Buzz had always been a patient lover. But she felt feverish. Unzipping the bag slightly, he moved lower, kissing the heated flesh of her belly, dipping his tongue into her navel, leaving a wet trail as he worked his way lower.

Her control left her when his lips brushed over the crisp curls at her V. She knew what he was going to do next. While the part of her she needed to protect cried out against the intimacy of the act, another side of her pleaded for him to continue, for him to touch her in the most intimate way a man could touch a woman.

"Don't be afraid," he whispered. "I won't hurt you."

But she knew he would. She was about to speak, but when his mouth touched her there, her thoughts exploded into chaos.

He kissed her deeply, and she closed her eyes against the blinding burst of ecstasy. In the back of her mind, she wondered how a man could make love to her like this and at the same time know they couldn't be together forever.

Pain clashed with pleasure, tearing at her like violent waves against the fragile shore.

Opening her, he stroked her and Kelly lost control. Her senses exploded, overloading her system, then shut down one by one until she was aware of nothing except the moment between them.

She was still trembling when he moved over her. She could feel him shaking, too. Bracing his arms on either side of her, he looked down at her. She'd never been able to read Buzz fully—that was one of the things that had always driven her nuts when they were married. She'd never known what he was thinking. But in that moment, she could see all the way into his soul through his eyes. And she saw all the things she felt in her own heart. Things she didn't want to see. Emotions that would make their eventual parting even more difficult.

"Easy, honey." He kissed her cheek, her temples, the tip of her nose. "You're shaking."

"You've always made me shake."

"Is that good or bad?"

"Very, very good."

The lines of his face were taut when he looked down at her. Never losing eye contact, she opened to him. They didn't speak, but in that instant, they didn't need words.

Her vision blurred when he entered her. There was a moment of discomfort and then an electric shock of pleasure. She would have cried out, but he stole her voice with a kiss. The world shook when he began to move within her. Long, steady strokes that made her feel wild and out of control. Her body bucked beneath his, taking him deeply within her. She heard a heartbeat racing out of control, heard his name, realized she was saying it over and over again, only he was kissing her and her cries were little more than moans of delight.

Emotion and physical sensation melded. Kelly felt the

war in the deepest reaches of her heart. And while her body surrendered, her emotions refused to submit, and she knew there would be no victor.

All the while, Buzz kissed her as if knowing these would be their last moments together. Kelly felt the same desperation egging her on. She kissed him back with every emotion exploding inside her. Regret. Fear. The tattered remnants of her love for him.

Violent waves built deep inside her, pounding her like a relentless sea. Kelly rode the waves, letting them tumble and shake her until she didn't know up from down. Pleasure streaked through her like a scream echoing in a cave. The intensity of it took her breath and jumbled her thoughts until all she was aware of was his body moving within hers, stretching her and filling her and driving her to slow, inescapable madness.

Completion crashed over her like a tidal wave. She heard her name, realizing he'd uttered it aloud. Once. Twice. He shuddered above her, his body going rigid. She whispered his name and accepted him without question, without hesitation.

And she knew neither of them would ever be the same, and that the mistake she had just made would cost her something she would never be able to get back.

Buzz lay awake in the sleeping bag, his body aching with exhaustion, his heart heavy with the knowledge that he'd just made the worst mistake of his life. It had taken him five long years to learn to live without Kelly, to convince himself he was better off alone. While he might not have managed to make himself believe it, he had managed to accept it, to live with the decision they'd made.

Tonight, he'd proven to himself just how wrong a man could be when it came to denial.

Around him the night throbbed with life. An owl

screeched from a nearby branch as it dove for a scampering field mouse. The treetops whispered like recalcitrant children as the winds continued to whip down from the north.

Buzz stared up at the sky and tried to turn off his thoughts. He needed to sleep, needed to rest so he could get the pick-up arranged for first thing in the morning and get Kelly and that little boy out of his mind, out of his life, out of his heart once and for all.

Of course, his mind refused to obey.

Next to him, the woman in question succumbed to exhaustion and slept. Moonlight turned her complexion to porcelain, her hair to silk. She hadn't bothered to dress after their lovemaking and her body was warm and soft against his. At his age, Buzz had thought he'd experienced it all when it came to sex.

Tonight had proven him dead wrong.

He wanted to believe the emotions that had pounded through him when he'd been inside her, the power of the physical sensations coursing through his blood had been so intensified because it had been so long since he'd had sex.

Only he knew better.

Every time he closed his eyes he saw the way she'd looked at him when he'd been inside her. She hadn't wanted to surrender. She'd fought him tooth and nail and body and soul. But neither of them could deny the magic or stop the inevitable.

How could something that felt so right be so wrong? How the hell was he going to handle this? How was he going to handle having a son when the mother of his child didn't want him in their lives?

"If brooding were dangerous, we'd both be in dire straits right now."

He hadn't realized Kelly had wakened and for a moment he felt embarrassed that she'd caught him embroiled in such intimate thoughts. Shifting slightly, he turned to her, felt something inside him soften at the sight of her. "You sneaked up on me," he said.

"You were a hundred miles away."

"Actually, I was right here."

"Ah, you like to keep your troubles close."

Reaching out, he tucked a strand of hair behind her ear. "Very close." He smiled. "Safer that way."

A smile touched her mouth. She was so pretty when she smiled. He wondered when she'd stopped doing it. Wondered if maybe it had something to do with him.

"You used to smile all the time," he said.

"You used to make me laugh."

He suddenly had the crazy notion to lean forward and kiss her. The memory of their lovemaking floated through his mind. The feel of her beneath him. The sensation of wet heat wrapped around him. Arousal stirred hotly in his groin, making his sex heavy and uncomfortable.

As if realizing his thoughts, she sat up, holding the sleeping bag to her breast. "I need to check on Eddie."

"I checked on him a few minutes ago." He didn't mention he'd spent twenty minutes inside the tent, watching his little boy sleep, and thinking about a future that could never be. "He's wiped out," he said.

"I guess he should be." She glanced down at her watch. "Most little boys are wiped out at 3:00 a.m."

"I guess it's just us troubled adults who are left sleepless."

"I guess so."

He propped himself up on an elbow and met her gaze. "I'm not sure how we're going to work this out, Kel."

She stared back at him, solemn and sweet and so beautiful he wanted to gather her into his arms and make all the problems standing between them go away forever. If only life were that simple, he thought.

"Maybe we're not," she said.

"I'll do what you want," he said, shocked when his voice faltered. "If you think it's best that I walk away... from you. From Eddie..." Not trusting his voice, he took a deep breath. "I'll do it. I'll walk away."

"I don't want Eddie hurt. I don't want his life in turmoil."

"It doesn't have to be that way."

"We've tried this once before," she said. "I gave it my best shot. You did, too, Buzz. It wasn't enough."

He thought about that for a moment, felt the blade of hurt cut him a little more deeply.

"Why does this have to hurt so much?" she asked, her eyes filling.

"For God's sake, don't cry," he said, but the tears spilled over her lashes to glisten on her cheeks like broken diamonds.

"There aren't any easy answers," she said.

"No. There aren't."

He didn't expect her to reach for him, but when she did he was ready. His arms wrapped around her. He tasted tears and a hint of desperation when she kissed him. Then she moved tentatively against him. He became aware of soft flesh and secret curves and the sweet promise of her desire. The blood rushed from his head to his groin so quickly he was dizzy. He knew they weren't going to settle anything tonight. It was almost as if they'd mutually agreed that they would never reconcile their differences. Not when it came to their relationship. Not when it came to the child he'd already come to think of as his son.

He'd thought the first round of lovemaking would have taken off the edge, but it hadn't. As his blood pumped furiously through his veins and his breaths turned labored, he realized that clench of desperation would never leave him when it came to this woman. Because as surely as he was holding her tightly within his embrace, she was slipping through his arms. It was an unbearable sensation for a man who liked to be in control.

She gasped when he rolled on top of her. Her hair spread out behind her like a blanket of fine satin. The sleeping bag had slipped, exposing the beauty of her breasts. She stared up at him, her nostrils flaring, her mouth glistening with the remnants of their kisses.

"Tell me you want this." Taking her hands in his, he slid her arms above her head.

She watched him, her eyes cautious and dark with passion. "I want this," she said simply. "You make me crazy with wanting you."

He pushed into her, felt her wet heat close around him as tightly as a surgical glove, and ground his teeth together to keep his concentration. He began to move, slowly, concentrating not only on his pleasure, but on hers. He watched her eyes glaze. Perspiration slicked her forehead. She rose to meet him, strength for strength, stroke for stroke, desperation for desperation.

"Tell me," he said, not sure what he was asking, wanting to hear her say the words that were in her heart, wishing he could reach inside her instead, look into that heart and see if she had anything left for him.

She came apart in his arms a moment later. He watched her crest, awed and amazed and humbled that he could do that to her. That she would share the most intimate of moments with him. Never taking his eyes from hers, he continued stroking her, steady and deep and all-encompassing. He felt his own completion approach, and fought it, but he knew it was a losing battle. He didn't want this moment to end, but he couldn't stop the inevitable.

A moment later the pleasure took him over the top. He slipped over the edge like a man falling off a cliff, not sure what awaited him at the bottom.

"I love you, Kelly," he whispered. "I never stopped loving you."

Vaguely, he was aware of her stiffening in his arms, but he was beyond interpreting, beyond comprehension. With a final thrust and a guttural cry wrenched from somewhere deep inside him, he emptied his seed into the deepest reaches of her.

And he tried desperately not to think about what he'd just done.

Chapter 14

Dawn broke cold and gray. Buzz woke at first light to an empty sleeping bag and the disturbing memory of making a confession he'd spent the last few years denying. A confession consisting of three words he'd spent the same amount of time trying to exorcise from his heart as if they were some evil demon.

Raising up on an elbow, he looked around and tried not to think about the stiffness in his arms and legs or the stabbing pain in the small of his back. His shoulder creaked as he worked out a kink. His neck was stiff as a board.

But worse than any physical pain, he felt the aftermath of a very bad mistake he'd sworn he wouldn't make again.

I love you.

His own damning words rang like a death knell in his head. How could he have been so stupid? Saying something like that in the heat of the moment to a woman who wanted nothing more than to sever all ties to him wasn't exactly smooth.

Snippets of the night before came to him like flashes of memory to a drunk after a blackout. The beauty of her body. The body he'd missed so desperately for all these years. The way her eyes had glazed with pleasure when he'd moved within her. The tight sheath of her when he'd been inside her heat. The memory of the magic they'd shared, both physically and emotionally, made him shake inside.

I love you.

God, how could he be such an idiot? Best to face reality now, he thought darkly. The bottom line was she hadn't reciprocated the words. Not that he'd expected her to. That he'd wakened alone said it all, he realized. And for the first time in a long time he felt vulnerable and stupid and incredibly alone.

He must have been asleep when she'd sneaked out of his sleeping bag and climbed back into the tent with Eddie. She hadn't bothered to tell Buzz she was leaving. Or kiss him goodbye. He told himself she hadn't had a choice but to go back to Eddie. Of course, she didn't want her little boy—*their* little boy—to see her sleeping in the arms of a man he barely knew. Something like that could be confusing to a child. Still, it bothered him that she hadn't seen fit to wake him.

Realizing there was nothing he could do about the mistakes he'd made the night before except try like hell not to make the same ones all over again today, he unzipped the bag and stood. He tried to stretch, ended up wincing instead. He needed to check in with RMSAR. The winds had died down. They should be able to get the chopper in to pick them up.

"I'm hungry."

Buzz actually jolted at the sound of the little voice. He spun to see Eddie standing a few feet outside the tent with his hair sticking up and the stuffed bear clutched in his grasp. The sight of his child, so soft and vulnerable and innocent, struck him squarely in the gut. For a moment, he could do nothing but stare, telling himself it didn't hurt to stand there and look at him and know that in a few short hours he would be gone forever.

"What are you hungry for?" he managed after a minute.

Eddie rubbed his eyes. "Fat egg."

Buzz didn't have a clue what a fat egg was. "How about some granola and hot chocolate?"

"Okay, but I gotta pee first."

"Right." Buzz wiped a hand over his jaw to hide the smile. "You ever been camping before?"

"No."

"You ever been a Boy Scout?"

"I'm gonna join Cub Scouts as soon as we move to Tahoe."

On instinct Buzz offered his hand. "In that case, let me show you where the restroom is."

Eddie took his hand. "They got a bathroom way out here?"

"Well, sort of. Just don't do this when you're at home, okay?"

Kelly woke to voices. Groggy and disoriented, she reached for Eddie. Her heart thumped hard when she found the sleeping bag next to her empty. She sat up quickly, her forehead grazing the top of the tent.

"Eddie?" she said in a sleep-clogged voice.

A familiar fear gripped her. Fighting her way out of the sleeping bag, she scrambled to the zippered entrance of the tent and into the soft light of dawn.

Her heart was still pounding furiously when she spotted Buzz and Eddie sitting near the fire twenty feet away. Both males were sitting on logs with their elbows on their knees and steaming cups in their hands. The same heart that had been pounding with fear a moment ago slowed to a soft, familiar ache.

Eddie was mimicking his father. If Buzz was aware of it, he made no indication. The sight of her son watching him with such adoration in his young eyes brought tears to her eyes. And a different kind of fear to her heart.

"Morning."

She hadn't realized Buzz had spotted her. She blinked, suddenly, painfully aware of his eyes skimming over her. Everything that had happened the night before, everything they had done played quickly through her mind. The heat of his hands roaming her body. The urgency of his mouth. The sensation of being filled by him, emotionally, physically. Whispered words that could never be taken back....

She prayed he didn't notice the hot blush that crept into her cheeks. Abruptly, she was aware of how she must look. Her hair looked like a rat's nest. Her shirt was wrinkled. She told herself it didn't matter, but for several interminable seconds she wished she'd at least taken the time to finger-comb her hair.

"Mommy!"

Before she could say anything, Eddie jumped up from his place on the log and ran over to her, throwing his arms around her hips. "Buzz and I had candy bars for breakfast!"

"Oh, well..."

"Do you want one? He fixed me some hot chocolate, too. Do you want some?"

She hugged her son to her and tried desperately to find her voice, all the while feeling self-conscious because she knew Buzz was looking at her. "I think I might just have some coffee this morning, sweetheart."

"Buzz! Fix her some coffee. She likes milk and sugar."

Buzz smiled as he looked away. "Coming right up."

Eddie turned back to her and looked proud for a moment. "Buzz and I had to whiz this morning."

Whiz? It took her a moment to figure out what he was referring to, then it dawned on her. "Oh," she muttered, realizing now that her little boy had learned the word *whiz* he was never going to use *tinkle* again. That was a female term, and evidently Eddie was hungry for the male stuff.

Despite everything that had happened—the mistake she'd made the night before, the danger of their situation, the pain in her heart, she laughed. God, she loved this child. Kneeling, she looked into his guileless gray eyes that were so much like Buzz's, and thanked God he was safe and sound. Dirt smudged his left cheek. He had a scratch on his chin. There was a blade of buffalo grass in his hair, so she plucked it out.

"I love you, puppy face." Pulling him close, she kissed him on the cheek.

"I'm not a puppy face."

"Are, too."

He giggled and wiped the wetness of her kiss from his cheek. "I love you, too, Mommy."

She kissed the tip of his upturned nose, then hugged him to her, trying not to let the moment get too serious. She breathed in his scent, let it fill her and calm her and she knew that no matter what else happened, as long as she had her son everything would be okay.

"It's black."

She pulled away at the sound of Buzz's voice and stood. She'd known she would eventually have to face him, have to face what they'd done the night before.

I love you.

She imagined the warmth of his breath against her ear as she stood and accepted the cup of coffee. Her stomach felt jittery. And when she looked into his slate-gray eyes she knew he was remembering, too, because for an instant he didn't meet her gaze.

"Thank you." She took the coffee and, because she desperately needed something to do, sipped even though it was much too hot.

He gazed back at her, steadier now but cautious. His walls were back up, she realized. High, thick impenetrable walls he used to keep her out of his head, out of his heart. He'd done it when they were married, kept her out as if she were a thief out to steal his emotions, and he was doing it now.

But last night…last night she'd seen those same walls obliterated.

"It looks like the winds have died down," he said. "I don't know how long that will last, so I need to radio RMSAR and set up the pick-up."

She glanced toward the north. Smoke tinged the sky gray and an odd shade of pink, but there was no longer ash floating down. That was a good sign. "Maybe the fire's under control."

"I hope so. Hard to tell. It's so damn dry."

He started to turn away, but before she could stop herself she reached out and touched his arm. Pausing, he turned back to her, hitting her with those cool eyes.

"Thanks for taking care of Eddie this morning," she said.

"You were exhausted."

"So were you."

Shrugging, he looked over where Eddie was carrying on a conversation and sharing his hot chocolate with Bunky Bear. "He's a great kid."

She smiled despite the burn of tears. For a crazy moment she wanted to say *just like his dad,* but she didn't. Buzz might be his biological father, but he wasn't going to be his dad.

"He likes you," she said.

"Kids aren't afraid to open up their minds and give their hearts."

The words went through her like a bullet searing through flesh and going deep. She stared at him, her heart rolling into a frenetic staccato. "Buzz, about last night—"

"Don't, Kel," he said gruffly.

"But I—"

"You made your position clear. I got it. It's okay. I'd rather not discuss it this morning if you don't mind."

She didn't want to discuss it either, but she knew at some point they would have to. For the life of her she couldn't think of how to make things right. She didn't want Eddie hurt by a man who spent his days jumping out of choppers and scaling sheer cliffs. She didn't want her son following in those lofty footsteps.

She watched Buzz walk over to the radio, wanting desperately to do the right thing. If only she knew what that was. Her heart broke because deep down inside, she knew the only man who would ever matter to her was the only man she could never have.

"Homer One this is Tango Two Niner. Do you read?" Buzz walked several yards away from the makeshift camp, speaking into the radio.

"Homer One standing by."

"Is Eagle available for a pick-up?"

"Stand by."

"Standing by," Buzz said, aware that Eddie had wandered over, his eyes as wide as his open mouth as he watched Buzz speak into the radio.

A few seconds later, Dispatch's voice belched from the radio. "That's affirm, Tango. What's your twenty?"

"I'm a quarter mile north of Woody Creek Pass."

"Terrain sucks, Buzz." Static hissed for an instant. "Eagle, do you read?"

"Roger that, Homer One." Chopper pilot Tony Colorosa's voice crackled over the radio. "How's tricks, Malone?"

"About like the terrain," Buzz grumbled.

"Come again?"

"Never mind. What's your ETA, Eagle?"

"Sixteen minutes if there's a place where I can set this tin can down."

"Negative. We've got trees and rock all over the place up here."

"There's no time for a hike, Buzz. Winds are going to start kicking once the sun heats things up."

"Terrific," Buzz muttered.

"You up to a swoop and scoop?" Tony asked, using the search and rescue term for a pickup made by winching a man down from the chopper and picking up a subject using a steel cable and harness. It was the riskiest kind of rescue, but it was also the fastest.

Buzz didn't even want to think of a swoop and scoop when it came to Eddie. The kid had already been through a lot. But he was even more worried about Kelly. She'd been terrified of helicopters since losing her father and brother in that fiery crash.

"What are the stats on the fire?" Buzz asked.

"We lost four more homes last night. It's contained for now, but the weather service says winds are going to start kicking in a couple of hours."

Buzz cursed, knowing he didn't have a choice but to agree to the winch pick-up. "That's affirm on the swoop and scoop."

"Hold your panties on, ladies, we're gonna rock and roll!" Tony belted out a whoop.

Buzz wasn't in the mood for the pilot's antics, but let it

slide since his mood had nothing to do with the poor taste of words and everything to do with a woman with big brown eyes and a child who'd suddenly become one of the most important people in his life.

"I'll put out a flare," he said.

"Roger that," the pilot replied. "ETA fifteen minutes. Eagle over and out."

Switching off the VHF radio, Buzz crammed it into its case, then spun back toward camp only to find himself facing a curious set of huge gray eyes.

"Is that a real radio?" Eddie asked.

Buzz studied the small, freckled face for a moment, felt his mood shift, lighten. "As real as it gets."

"Can I talk on it?"

"We're on the emergency channel at the moment, and we don't want to clog that particular channel up with conversation."

Eddie shoved his hands into his pockets and looked dejected.

"How about if I let you hold it?" Buzz offered.

"Wow! Really?"

"Sure." Buzz opened the sheath and slid the radio from its nest. "You ever used one of these before?"

The little boy's eyes widened. "Who? Me?"

"You don't see anyone else around, do you?" Buzz handed him the radio.

Eddie accepted it as if it were made of glass, then stared down at it with great reverence. "It sure is heavy."

"See that button right there?" Buzz asked, referring to the Squawk button.

"This one?" He carefully touched it with a small fingertip.

"Press it."

Tentatively, Eddie pressed the button—and nearly dropped the radio when it beeped.

Buzz withheld a smile. "You ever ride in a chopper before?"

Eddie looked up at him. "I rode in a limo once."

"A limo, huh?"

"Yeah, my mom took me. She had to wear a dress."

Buzz didn't want to think about Kelly in a dress. He especially didn't want to sink to the level of asking this child *why* she'd had to wear a dress—or who she'd been with—but he couldn't quite suppress the quick surge of jealousy.

"The limo was cool," Eddie said. "But I'll bet a chopter is better."

Buzz laughed outright. "That's chopper, sport."

"Wow! A real chopter! I can't wait to tell my mommy! Can she come, too?"

Buzz didn't think Kelly would consider a ride in a helicopter very cool. Not after losing her father and brother in a chopper crash.

"I'll have to talk to your mother about—"

"Mommy!" Spinning, Eddie took off running toward Kelly. "Buzz said I can take a ride in the chopter with him!"

Buzz groaned at the way that sounded. Like he was trying to buy the kid's love by offering something she couldn't give him. Sheesh, he didn't have this communicating with kids thing down yet. The key, he realized, was not to say anything you didn't want broadcast in the next ten seconds.

"What's this about him riding in a chopper?"

Buzz looked up to see Kelly approach, her eyes flashing cold and hot, her back ramrod straight. She'd always looked good when she was mad and the years hadn't changed that. He still noticed. And he still felt the same old punch of lust every time he looked at her.

"That's not how it sounds," he said.

"Why don't you explain it to me then?" She folded her arms.

Buzz sighed. "I just radioed RMSAR headquarters. They're going to pick us up in the chopper."

Her stance relaxed marginally. "Oh. Well…"

"Swoop and scoop," he added.

A different kind of tension leaked into her expression, and she paled. "Buzz…"

He glanced down at his son, hoping she knew better than to frighten the little boy. As if realizing she would, indeed, frighten Eddie if she made her argument in front of him, Kelly turned away and knelt in front of Eddie, sweeping the hair off his forehead with the backs of her fingers. "Honey, I want you to go into the tent and put your jacket on and pack Bunky Bear into your backpack, okay? And tie your shoes. Double-knot, like I showed you. We're going to leave in a little bit."

"Mo-om…"

"Give Buzz back his radio."

"Jeez. I didn't even get to talk."

"Don't jeez me. And be sure to thank him."

Sighing heavily, he handed the radio to Buzz. "Thanks," he mumbled.

Clearing his throat, Buzz accepted it and shoved it into the sheath. "Any time," he said.

Eddie lingered until Kelly put her hands on his slim shoulders and turned him in the direction of the tent. "Put your jacket on please. Go."

Casting a final I-can't-believe-she-would-do-this-to-me look at Buzz, Eddie folded his arms and tromped toward the tent, clearly not happy that he'd been relegated to packing his stuff and tying his shoes.

Buzz waited while Kelly rose to her full height. He felt the familiar tightening in his chest when she turned back to him and raked him with those pretty brown eyes. "Why a swoop and scoop? Why can't they designate a pick-up point and land, for God's sake?''

"Too many trees. Terrain is too rough. There's no place for miles to land that big 412.''

"In that case, we can hike to a suitable pick-up point.''

"Winds are expected to start kicking again in about an hour. We don't have time to hike to a decent pick-up point.''

"I don't want Eddie dangling from the end of a cable a hundred feet above the ground.''

"I'll be with him," Buzz cut in. "He and I go up first, then I'll come back down and get you.''

She stared at him as if he'd just asked her to jump out of a plane without a parachute. "There has to be some other way.''

"There isn't," he said firmly. "I thought about it all night. We don't have time to hike down to the valley. It would take us half the day. By the time we get there the winds would be up again.''

"Buzz, I don't like it.''

"There's no other way.''

"We'll just take an extra day and hike down the way we came.''

"Not with the fire coming this way.''

"Maybe the firefighters have it under control by now. Maybe the winds have—''

"They haven't, Kel. Damn it, I know you don't want to do this, but you don't have a choice.''

"All I want to do is keep my son safe.''

"That's why we're going to do this my way.''

She didn't have anything to say about that. Instead, she stood there, staring at him as if she were the one dangling a hundred feet above the ground—and he'd just cut her cable.

"We don't have a choice," he repeated.

"If anything happens—"

"Nothing's going to happen," he snapped.

Raising her hand to her mouth, she covered it as if to muffle a sound. "I couldn't bear it if anything happened to him," she whispered.

"Kelly...damn it—"

"I'll never forgive you. I swear, if something happens to him, I'll never forgive you."

The urge to go to her was strong, but Buzz knew that would be a mistake. Instead he steeled himself against the fear he saw in her eyes, against the tremulous voice and shaking shoulders—and his own need to make her understand that it would be infinitely more dangerous for them to stay.

Instead, he simply walked away.

Chapter 15

Kelly watched the bright orange smoke from the flare curl into the morning sky only to be swept away by the wind at treetop level. In the distance, she could hear the rumble of the Pratt and Whitney engines and the *whop-whop-whop* of the chopper's rotors cutting through the air. A few feet away, Buzz fitted Eddie with a safety harness the chopper had dropped on a fly-by a few minutes earlier, adjusting it to fit his smaller frame.

"What happens if the cable breaks?" Eddie asked the question with the same unconcerned nonchalance as if he were asking about the weather.

"The cable won't break." Buzz slipped the harness between the boy's small legs, then tightened the straps at his waist. "It's steel. And you're not exactly tubby."

"I weigh forty-two pounds," Eddie put in.

Kelly watched the exchange, wishing desperately they didn't have to use a cable—steel or otherwise, to get her little boy into the chopper. Her hand shook when she reached out and ruffled her son's hair. "How you doing, kiddo?"

"Fine, Mommy. I'm not even scared."

She was feeling the same sick panic as the first time she'd had to leave him at daycare when he was nine months old—only this time it was multiplied exponentially because seeing him dangle from a cable one hundred feet above jagged rock was nothing compared to leaving him with Mrs. Hemmelgarn. She thought it ironic that her son was so brave when she felt as if she were coming apart inside. She glanced at Buzz. "What about a helmet?"

"We don't have one."

"I've got a really hard head, Mommy." As if to prove the point, Eddie rapped on the top of his head with his knuckles while opening and closing his mouth, making hollow sounds.

"That's what I thought," Buzz said.

Eddie looked at him and grinned. "What?"

Buzz grinned back. "Your head is hollow."

"Is not!"

Kelly wasn't sure how she managed it, but she laughed. At least she thought it was a laugh. Anything was better than the terror that had her tied up in little knots. She was so worried she could have lain down on the ground and cried, but the last thing she wanted to do was scare her son at a time like this.

Kneeling in front of Eddie, she zipped his jacket closed then kissed the tip of his little nose. "Buzz is going to take good care of you."

"I know. He showed me his muscles this morning. They're big."

If she hadn't been on the verge of tears, she would have rolled her eyes. As it was, she barely managed a smile.

"Don't be scared, Mommy."

She did laugh then and wondered when her four-year-old child had become so perceptive. "I'm not scared, honey."

"Are, too. The end of your nose is all red."

Blinking back tears she didn't want either male to see, she hugged him to her and held him tight. "You're the smartest little boy in the whole world," she whispered. "I love you, puppy face."

"Love you, too, Mommy."

She pulled away and rose, her eyes seeking Buzz's. He stood several feet away, his head craned up as if trying to spot the chopper. He was wearing a harness. Kelly tried not to notice the way the straps at his hips accentuated his male attributes, but she did and the realization that she could notice something like that at a time like this made her realize just how bad she had it for her ex-husband.

Putting the last touches on his harness, Buzz jerked his gaze to hers and walked over to her. "He's in good hands, Kel."

"Don't let him get hurt," she said, fighting tears.

"He's not going to get hurt."

She nodded, knowing she was being foolish and emotional, and wiped the tears off her cheek with the back of her hand. "He's my life, Buzz."

The muscles in his jaws flexed. "Hey, Kel, come on. I do this for a living, remember? Once we clip on it'll take less than two minutes for us to be winched up to the hatch, another minute to unhook him and another minute for me to get back down to you. Five minutes max and we'll be on our way to RMSAR headquarters."

"I know. I'm just…. God, Buzz, this scares me."

"Everything's going to be fine." Reaching out, he put his hand on her shoulder and squeezed.

The gesture touched her deeply. Kelly wondered if she would ever be able to tell him how much it meant to her at that moment.

"You've got my word." Cupping her chin in his palm, he forced her gaze to his. "You know I always keep my word, don't you?"

The intensity in those stormy eyes stole the answer hovering on the tip of her tongue. Speechless and expectant, her heart racing with fear and anticipation, she stared at him, felt the ground move beneath her feet.

She didn't expect him to kiss her. Not in full view of Eddie. Certainly not in front of his testosterone-laden teammates on board the chopper. But one minute she was standing there wishing with all her heart they didn't have to do this, the next she was swept into his embrace, and his mouth was making love to hers with an intensity that sucked all the oxygen from her lungs and the last vestiges of rational thought from her brain.

Kelly didn't intend to kiss him back, either, but her body reacted instinctively. Fear for her child mingled with a clash of emotions for the man holding her and made her legs tremble. But the pull of his mouth was too strong to resist. She looped her arms around his neck, her body falling full length against his. She heard his breath quicken. Her own stalled in her lungs when he deepened the kiss. Shoving logic and restraint and a hundred other emotions aside, she opened to him. And for a split second the rest of the world ceased to exist. Their hearts beat in a wild, simultaneous rhythm. Once. Twice.

As abruptly as he'd executed the kiss, he broke it. His eyes were dark, his pupils dilated when he eased her to arm's length. He didn't say a word, but he didn't need to. His eyes conveyed all the things she needed to know.

"We're not finished," he said. "With a lot of things."

Logic ordered her to correct him, to tell him they were, indeed, finished. That they'd been finished for a long time. But her brain was scrambled and her heart was beating so wildly she felt as if she couldn't catch her breath.

"Hey, why're you kissing my mom?" came a small voice.

Buzz looked down and grinned at Eddie. "Hang on to me, sport," he said. "We're going up."

"Be careful," Kelly managed, but the words were lost in the maelstrom of wind and debris kicked up by the rotor blades.

Buzz looked up at the belly of the chopper hovering forty feet overhead. "We've got to go." Then he looked at her one last time. "I'll be back for you."

Stepping away from her, he looked over at Eddie, who was staring at them as if they'd just sprouted horns. "Ready, partner?"

Eddie nodded, but Kelly could tell he was still bewildered by the kiss. She wondered how to explain it without confusing him when she couldn't even explain it to herself.

She wanted to touch her son one more time, but Buzz warned her away with his eyes. Turning the little boy toward him, he lifted Eddie so that they were facing each other, then buckled their harnesses together. Looking up toward the chopper, he stuck out his arm and gave a thumbs-up signal. A moment later a cable with a closed hook on the end was lowered by the winch stationed just above the main hatch.

Buzz caught the shank in his hand, then quickly secured it to the carabiner on his harness. He gave another thumbs-up signal and an instant later, the cable went taut. Man and child were jerked off their feet.

Kelly wasn't sure which was louder, the rotor blades or her own heart as she watched Buzz and her son being hoisted upward. She saw them talking, saw Buzz's arms go around her child. Eddie wrapped his little legs around Buzz's body. Upward they went. Twenty feet. Thirty feet. Forty feet. She could see a dark-haired man in an orange flight suit just inside the hatch, waiting for them.

A heavily gloved hand reached out and snagged the cable. A moment later, Buzz and Eddie disappeared inside the hatch. Relief made her legs go weak. The man in the orange flight suit looked down at her. She couldn't see his face because he was wearing a helmet with communication gear, but the thumbs-up said it all.

"Thank you, God," she whispered. "Thank you."

Wind from the rotors whipped her hair into a frenzy. Dust stung her eyes as the chopper hovered. She didn't care about any of those things as long as her son was safe on board. She squinted upward, saw Buzz at the hatch, checking his harness. All the while her heart pounded out a maniacal rhythm because she knew that in another minute she would be face-to-face with him dangling from a cable forty feet off the ground and all this would be over. She could go back to her life the way it was before any of this happened.

We're not finished.

Buzz's words rang in her ears. She tried not to think of them now, about what they meant in terms of how his knowing about Eddie would affect their lives.

Her thoughts were cut short when Buzz backed up to the hatch and dropped down. She watched him, terrified and fascinated and slightly in awe that he was so damn courageous. He was only ten feet down when the chopper jolted and swung hard in a counter-clockwise rotation. She stared in horror as Buzz was swung around and around, like a wildly spinning yo-yo.

"Buzz!" she screamed. "What's happening?! *Buzz!*"

The chopper spun sickeningly. The engines revved. Buzz swung around, his boots actually hitting the uppermost branches of a tall pine. "*Buzz!* Oh, my God!"

Kelly stood motionless, unable to move, unable to tear her eyes away from the monstrous craft or the man dangling from a cable ten feet beneath it. She could see him gripping the straps of his harness. They'd put a helmet on him when he was inside the chopper. But a helmet wasn't going to help if he hit those trees. Or if, God forbid, the chopper went down.

The engines screamed, deafening her. The craft shuddered. The tail rotors groaned. Wind and debris pelted her, blinding her. All Kelly could think was that her little boy was on board that chopper. And the man who'd risked her life to save them both was in very real danger of being killed.

And there wasn't a damn thing she could do about it but stand there and watch it happen.

Buzz knew the instant the cable shuddered that he was in dire straits. Just as he knew what the chances were of his making it back through the hatch before he got slammed into those trees—or the rock face of the cliff on the other side of the stream. He maintained his equilibrium by keeping his eyes on the horizon, but by the fourth or fifth spin he was starting to get disoriented.

"Mayday! Mayday!" Tony Colorosa's voice barked over the VHF radio. "This is Eagle. I've got to put her down. Lake City do you read?"

"What the hell is going on, Flyboy?" Buzz shouted into his own headgear.

"Just stay cool, Buzz." John Maitland's voice came over his communication gear headset. "We're bringing you up."

"Like hell you are!"

The cable jolted and Buzz felt himself being pulled upward toward the hatch. Cursing, forgetting about professionalism and keeping his cool, he looked down at Kelly and realized the chopper was no longer spinning, but moving away from her. He shouted an oath into his mike.

A moment later, he reached the hatch. Maitland snagged

the cable and dragged him inside. Buzz turned on him like a mad, snarling dog.

"I'm not leaving her!" he shouted.

"Steady, Buzz."

"Damn it! We can't leave her out here all alone. You could have cut me loose. You could have left me with her!"

"That's not procedure."

"To hell with procedure!"

"Calm down, Buzz. Just...stay cool."

Only then did he notice Eddie sitting on the litter a few feet away. His face was chalk-white, the tip of his nose was red from crying. Tears streaked his cheeks. He looked up at Buzz with the ravaged eyes of a child who had been terrified. Buzz felt the contact like a bone-shattering blow.

He'd seen too many terrified children in his time. Children he hadn't been able to help. He stared, remembering, remembering so damn much, and he swore this time would be different

"Eddie." Grappling for control, he walked over to the child and pulled him into his arms. "Everything's going to be all right. You hear me?"

"I'm s-scared."

"We're going to be fine." He didn't know that. He could feel the instability in the way the chopper flew. Some kind of mechanical malfunction. Hydraulics, maybe. Or the swash plate. He prayed to God Flyboy could get them down.

"Are we gonna crash, Buzz?"

"No."

"Where's my mommy?"

"We're going to have to go back to get her, son."

Eddie began to cry. "We left my mommy."

"I know. The chopper...." He grappled for a word an

upset child would understand. "The chopper had some kind of mechanical problem."

"You mean it broke?"

"That's right. We just have to go back to base and fix it."

"How are we going to find mommy?"

"We know her coordinates."

The little boy closed his eyes and began crying in earnest.

"Strap in." Tony Colorosa's voice crackled in Buzz's headset. "We're going to put her down at Lake County."

Buzz looked over at John Maitland. "You heard the man. Strap in."

John took the jump seat at the rear and buckled in. "If anyone can get us down, Flyboy can," he said.

Setting Eddie on the seat next to him, Buzz reached into the overhead cabinet and pulled out a helmet. It would be too big for Eddie, but if things got bumpy it would protect his head.

"Here you go, partner." Kneeling before the boy, he slipped the helmet over his small head, then drew the chin strap tight.

"It's too big."

"It fits you just fine."

Eddie's chin trembled. "I want Mommy."

Buzz wanted her, too—in ways that were far too complex to communicate to this child—so he said the next best thing. "I'm going to get her. I promise."

The little boy nodded, but he was still scared. Buzz didn't blame him. Frankly, he was scared, too.

He could only imagine what Kelly was thinking. He would never forget the look of utter horror on her face as he'd been swung wildly around and around before Maitland had been able to winch him up and get him on board.

"Okay, ladies, ETA two minutes," came Tony Colorosa's voice into their headset communication gear. "Hold on. This is going to be rough."

The engines groaned. The chopper shuddered.

"You scared, Buzz?" Eddie asked a moment later.

The need to hold his child was strong, but Buzz knew both of them would be safer strapped into the seats. "A little," he admitted. "How about you?"

"A little. You sure we're not going to crash?"

"I'm sure."

The chopper began to vibrate as they lost altitude and speed. Buzz glanced through the portal of the hatch across from them, saw the familiar roofs of the hangars. They'd reached Lake County airport.

"I want you to lean forward and put your head between your knees," he said to Eddie.

The boy looked at him with huge, frightened eyes.

"Go on." Leaning forward, Buzz demonstrated. "Like this. It'll be okay."

The child obeyed, but he'd started crying again. Buzz leaned close to him, wrapped himself around the small body as best he could. A moment later, the chopper jolted violently. A rooster tail of sparks spewed high outside the portal. The grate of steel against concrete screeched through the cabin as the skids scraped the tarmac.

An instant later the chopper went still. Buzz raised his head, looked wildly around for smoke or flames, but found nothing. Quickly, he worked off the straps, then turned to Eddie. "You okay, partner?" he asked.

Eddie's chin quivered, but he nodded. "I want Mommy."

"I'm going to go get her. Right now."

"I want to go, too."

Kneeling in front of him, Buzz took the boy's small hands in his, rubbed them gently because they were cold, then looked into his eyes. "You're the bravest young man I've ever met," he said.

Eddie grinned, trying desperately to look the part even though he still had tears on his cheeks.

"I want you to stay here," Buzz said. "You're smaller than I am and you'll slow me down. Understand?"

"I want to go with you, Buzz!"

Buzz looked over at Maitland. "Get on the horn. Get me an ATV. I want Jake Madigan looking for her. I want volunteers. I want another chopper. And I want all this yesterday. Got it?"

John started toward the door. "I'm on it."

"I'll meet you at the hangar office in five minutes."

Maitland gave him a mock salute, then swung open the hatch and jumped to the tarmac.

Tony Colorosa looked satisfied with himself as he strutted out of the cockpit. "Not a bad landing job considering hydraulics were at 10 per cent, huh, Buzz?"

Buzz stood, unimpressed. "I'd like you to keep someone entertained while I go find my ex-wife."

Colorosa looked down at Eddie, his smile faltering. "What?"

"You heard me." Buzz might have grinned if he hadn't been so terrified. Big, bad Tony Colorosa going pale at the prospect of watching a four-year-old for a few hours.

"I want to go with you!" Eddie shouted.

Tony laughed, but he was starting to look a little green. "Hey, wait a minute...."

Ignoring him, Buzz eased the boy closer to Tony. "He's hungry and he needs a shower."

"A shower?" Tony shot the kid a horrified look. "Hey, look, Buzz, I don't do—"

"I think you're familiar with the procedure." Buzz started toward the door. "And be sure to get him some dessert."

"Dessert? Malone!"

Buzz slammed the door in his face and sprinted toward the airport office.

The news from the front lines wasn't good. The winds were fanning the flames and driving the fire south at a devastating speed. The fire was burning out of control, consuming everything in its path like a voracious, bloodthirsty beast. It had consumed over ten thousand acres in two days. With no rain in the forecast—and another front grinding down from the north—there was no relief in sight.

Buzz spread the map out on the makeshift table and cradled the cell phone to his ear. "How far is the front line from Woody Creek?" he asked the firefighter on the other end of the line.

"The leading edge is parallel to Woody Creek and runs east for about twenty miles."

Cold fear compressed his chest. "That's impossible. I was just there yesterday afternoon."

"The winds are pumping this fire along at an incredible speed. We're probably going to have to let this one burn itself out or else wait for rain."

Sick with fear, Buzz hung up the phone. He couldn't believe things had gotten so serious in just a few short hours. Last night the fire had been under control. If what the firefighter had said was true, that meant Kelly was less than a mile from the front line. A fire like that could eat up a mile of dry timber in a very short period of time.

"Any place you can think of where we can go in and set a chopper down?" he asked the park ranger standing across from him.

The park ranger was a young man with a crew cut and shoulders like oversized hams. "Negative. You know as well as I do the only way to make an extraction at this point is a swoop and scoop. Anything else would be insane in these winds.''

Buzz cursed. The fear pressing down on him turned cold and ugly and thrashed inside him like a dangerous, wounded animal.

"There's a woman stranded not far from Woody Creek. I need to get her out."

"Firefighters aren't going to want a bunch of yahoos going in there. They don't have the manpower to pull together a rescue if some hero gets into trouble."

Buzz glared at him. "I don't have any yahoos working for me, and I don't necessarily give a rat's ass what the firefighters want or don't want. I'm going in. You got that?"

The ranger's eyes skittered down to the map. "Ranger station not far from there has an ATV."

Buzz's interest piqued at the mention of an ATV. "Can you drive me over there?"

"Sure. They're about to evacuate, so I'll call ahead. They can fuel her up and have her waiting."

Buzz started toward the door.

Chapter 16

Kelly couldn't believe the rescue chopper had nearly crashed right before her eyes. She couldn't get the image of the monstrous craft hovering, then shuddering and spinning wildly out of control from her mind. In those unbearably long moments, her heart had simply stopped because she felt certain her little boy and the only man she'd ever loved were going to die right in front of her.

Unable to tear her eyes away, she'd dropped to her knees, screaming words she couldn't even recall, and watched the horrific scene unfold, certain God was going to take them away from her the same way He'd taken her father and brother.

She'd been giddy with relief when the chopper stabilized and gained altitude, laughing like a mad woman until tears streamed down her face. Even as the chopper had disappeared from view it didn't cross her mind that she was being left behind. All she could do was thank God they hadn't crashed, that no one had been hurt. That no one had died. She hadn't had time to worry about her own predicament.

Until now.

She'd been waiting at the pick-up point for more than an hour. She knew Buzz would return for her. She had enough common sense to know her chances of being found were much higher if she stayed put. But as the minutes ticked by, and the smoke around her thickened, she knew staying wasn't going to be an option much longer.

Kelly didn't want to believe she'd run out of time. She could tell by the amount of ash falling from the leaden sky that the fire was close. Forest fires could travel at an amazing speed during the dry season. Dry wood and grass and brush went up like tinder, when the humidity was low and the winds were fanning the flames. She remembered her father telling stories about the fires outrunning deer and cougar.

She couldn't believe that just a few short hours ago, the sky had been clear and she'd been within minutes of rescue. Looking at the same sky now, it seemed as if a storm had sprung straight from hell and was barreling down from the north to crush her with its black, oppressive weight.

She was going to have to make a decision. Leave the pick-up point where she knew Buzz could find her. Or head south, away from the leading edge of the fire. If she stayed and the fire was moving as quickly as she suspected, Kelly risked being overcome by flames and smoke. If she headed south, however, she risked Buzz not being able to find her.

Studying the roiling black cloud of smoke to the north, Kelly figured her options were quickly dwindling. Deep down inside she knew what she had to do. The thought of moving on terrified her. But the thought of staying—and risking being burned to death—frightened her even more.

"Okay, so we move," she said, trying not to notice the high, tight pitch of her voice as she started an easy pace down the very same trail she and Buzz and Eddie had hiked the day before. Her throat burned, but she wasn't sure if it was from screaming or the smoke. She moved swiftly down the path, setting a rhythm, her hiking boots striking the earth solidly. Fear spurred her on, and she used it to energize her tired body. She felt the press of panic, but refused to let it take hold. The most important thing was that her son was safe, she thought. She knew Buzz and the rest of the RMSAR team would be out looking for her. That was enough, she realized, knowing the best of the best were out there, knowing they would find her.

The irony of the situation didn't elude her. Buzz's need for adrenaline and danger had always been a point of contention between them. She'd had to rely on those very same skills to save her son, and now her own life.

The realization sent a pang of regret through her gut, like a knife slicing clean through her. She told herself it didn't hurt, that she'd come to terms with spending the rest of her life without him. That she hadn't been wrong. That she didn't love him.

"I don't, damn you," she panted as she put one foot in front of the other and ran for her life.

I love you.

Buzz's words rang inside her head, echoing in her heart like a lonely cry in the night. The image of the way he'd looked at her when he said them flashed through her mind. He wasn't a sensitive man; he was hard and uncompromising and rarely revealed his feelings. She told herself he'd said those words in the heat of the moment, a moment when they'd been at their most vulnerable. A moment when their emotions had been running high, their bodies running hot. It had been a long time for both of them. They'd made a mistake. That was all.

But Kelly also knew Buzz Malone never said anything

he didn't mean. That reality frightened her more than any fire.

She couldn't let this change anything. She had the job of her dreams waiting for her in Tahoe. The kind of life she always wanted. She and Eddie would buy a little house there. In another year he would start school. She would make a home for them in Tahoe. A home where Eddie would be secure and she wouldn't lie awake nights wondering if the phone was going to ring and she would be told the man she loved was gone forever.

Closing her eyes against the slash of pain she couldn't allow herself to feel, Kelly continued down the path at a fast clip. She was breathing hard from the exertion of her pace. Sweat cooled her back. She could see the ash floating down all around her like snow. Certain she'd made some headway, she slowed her pace, then stopped to catch her breath. Her muscles already felt jittery, but she felt sure she probably had a very long way to go. Better not to exhaust herself right off the bat.

She walked over to a gnarled juniper and sat down, then looked up. Her entire body jolted when she saw that the sky had gone as black as night. The smoke had thickened in the last minutes and rolled down the mountain like a black avalanche.

She sat there, frozen, her pulse pounding, a jumble of emotions roiling inside her head. She stared at the sky, awed and terrified and oddly calm. Hope jumped through her when in the distance, she thought she heard the rumble of a chopper. Getting quickly to her feet, she cocked her head and listened. Sure enough, a low rumble sounded.

She glanced up at the treetops and desperately wished for a flare. The trees were so thick that even if a chopper flew directly overhead, the spotter might miss her. Realizing she might not have much time before the chopper made a pass, she quickly worked off her jacket. Looking wildly around, she spotted a long, narrow branch. She snatched it up off the ground and tied her jacket around the end so that it formed a makeshift flag.

Feeling diminutively better now that she had somewhat of a plan in place, she stood still and listened for the chopper. Around her the pulse of the forest had changed. No birds sang. She could see the treetops moving, but the rhythm was frantic, like nervous, harried fingers. Even the ground beneath her seemed to tremble.

The chopper must be getting closer, she thought, but the hairs at the back of her neck prickled. Raising the stick above her head, she crashed down the path toward a small clearing where the chopper spotter would have a better chance of seeing her. She clambered up a rocky ravine so steep she had to use her hands to pull herself up, but she dared not let go of her flag.

Kelly's breath rushed between clenched teeth when she reached the summit of the ravine. Using a sapling aspen, she pulled herself up, then jumped to her feet. She raised her flag—and froze. Less than ten yards away, yellow flames plowed through a thicket of juniper, the sap popping and sizzling like hot oil in a pan. Shock made her gasp. Terror burned a path through her body. Her flight instinct kicked in, but she held her ground. Panic threatened, but she held it off by sheer force of will.

She stared at the flames, and wondered if she could make it back to the stream before it overcame her and burned her alive.

The ATV bounced wildly over tree roots and rocks the size of bowling balls. Buzz knew better than to push the vehicle over the rough terrain at such a dangerous speed, but it was fear driving him now. Fear that he wouldn't be able to find her. Fear that he wouldn't reach her in time.

Fear that she would meet the same terrible end as her father and brother.

He prayed that she'd realized just how perilously close she was to the leading edge of the fire and taken flight. While he knew she couldn't outrun the fire, distance would buy her time. Kelly was smart; she knew this land almost as well as he did. But without a compass or communication gear—or even the sky to guide her—it would be easy for her to get disoriented. Buzz had seen it happen even to veteran firefighters.

The ATV lurched. Cursing, he cut the wheel hard to the right and kicked down on the gas. The small vehicle cornered on two wheels, bucked over a fallen log, then grabbed the trail and tore up a steep path as if it were a living creature and on the run from the fire itself. Branches tore at his helmet and jacket. The larger branches bruised, but he barely felt the pain. He should reach the pick-up point soon. Just over the next rise.

Buzz spotted the fire a hundred yards before reaching the site. Flames had engulfed the pick-up point and now shot twenty feet into the air. He could feel the heat coming at him, the hot, stinking breath of the devil himself.

"Kelly!"

Ramming the ATV into Park, he jumped out and ran toward the flames. There was no sign of their camp. The tent had burned. The pit he'd dug for the fire was obscured by flames and smoke.

"*Kelly!* Answer me, damn it!"

Buzz didn't scare easily, and he never panicked. Fourteen years with the Denver PD had taught him the importance of keeping a cool head. His work as the team leader of RMSAR reinforced that belief. It was a rule he lived by. One he never broke. But as he stumbled back to the vehicle, he felt both emotions stabbing into him, cutting him as surely as any knife.

Back on the ATV, he gripped the steering wheel and stared at the fire, felt another emotion unfurl deep in his chest. He refused to believe the fire had taken her. Refused to believe that her life force could simply cease to exist. He could still feel the pulse of her. Like the warm flow of blood through his veins. She was alive; he knew it. He felt her as strongly as he felt the heat of the fire on his face.

Desperation hammered at him as he turned the vehicle around and started back down the path. Cursing with one breath, praying with the next, he pushed the ATV as hard as he dared. A thousand thoughts rushed through his mind. He talked to God, bargained with Him, made promises and confessions and meant every word of both.

Buzz told himself he could live without Kelly in his life. What he couldn't live with was not having her in this world. Kelly made the world a better place. She would give his son a wholesome, secure home filled with love and all the things he couldn't give.

He was so caught up in his thoughts that he didn't see the jut of rock until the ATV was upon it. The left front wheel hit it hard. The momentum sent the front end of the vehicle straight up, then over onto its side. Buzz hit the ground hard on his left shoulder. He heard bone crack. Pain zinged through his brain like a shock of electricity as he rolled.

An instant later, he lay face down on a bed of pine needles, dazed. A few feet away, the ATV lay on its side, the front wheels spinning. Above him, the treetops swayed restlessly against a black sky. He lifted his head to get his bearings, realized he was about ten feet off the path. Quickly, he took stock of his injuries. The pain in his back took his breath. He lay there for a few moments, gasping, struggling to stay calm. He remembered the months of physical therapy he'd had after the shooting. He remembered the physical therapist telling him the best way to ease the pain was to stay relaxed. For a moment, Buzz did just that, trying to relax, trying to catch his breath.

Cautiously, he sat up, grimacing when the muscles in his back seized. The pain was bad, but he could function. Judging from the pain zinging down his arm, he'd also managed to injure his shoulder, maybe even dislocated the joint. But the physical pain was nothing compared to the fear clenching his heart. Kelly was out there, alone and in imminent danger.

Shoving back a rise of panic, Buzz got to his knees then to his feet. Groaning when pain shot through his spine, he straightened and turned toward the ATV. It was going to be a miracle if the thing started, but he had to try.

Buzz grabbed the steering wheel. Using his hip, he pushed until the vehicle rolled and landed steadily on all four wheels. The strain sent his back into another spasm and he went down on one knee. Closing his eyes, he waited for the spasm to pass. Cursing the bastard who'd put the bullet in him, he struggled to his feet.

"Kelly…"

He'd intended to shout, but her name rushed between clenched teeth. Remembering the whistle, Buzz put it to his lips, gripped it between his teeth and blew three times. He climbed onto the ATV and forced his hands to close around the steering wheel. Growling low in his throat, he reached for the key, turned it. The engine coughed once then purred to life.

"Kelly!" His voice was stronger now. The pain was bad, but he could handle it. He could do this, he realized. They were going to get through this. He was going to find her and get her back to safety.

Hope spiked when he heard the crack of wood behind him. "Kelly!" Turning in the seat, he looked up the path from whence he'd just come and found himself staring into the face of hell.

* * *

Kelly's feet pounded the path like pistons driving an engine. She'd heard Buzz's whistle. She was certain of it. He'd come for her just as she'd known he would.

But it seemed as if she'd been running forever and still no sign of him. No sign of anyone.

The path curved sharply to the left, then dipped and ran along the ridge of a small ravine. Kelly ran as fast as she could, hurdling over rocks and fallen trees. Brush and low-growing juniper blurred past. Ahead, the trail ran straight into a face of rock and cut sharply again. She followed the rock wall around to the left and sprinted through the trees, ducking branches as she ran.

The sight of the fire rising up out of the forest floor stopped her cold. Adrenaline surged through her muscles. A few minutes ago the fire had been behind her. How had it gotten in *front* of her?

Realizing she could no longer stay on the path, she turned and started through the trees. She'd only taken a few steps when she heard the whistle again. Closer. Through the trees and around the jut of granite twenty yards away.

"Buzz! Where are you?"

She didn't know if it was Buzz, but it was his name that burst from her lips. Arms outstretched, she ran toward the sound of the whistle, crashing through branches, stumbling over rocks. She ran as she had never run before, the image of him branded into her mind, the sound of his voice ringing in her ears. All the while, the fire consumed the forest around her.

She skirted the jut of granite, blinked back smoke-induced tears. The beams of the ATV's headlights materialized through the black haze. Standing on the driver's seat, holding his helmet at his side, Buzz looked like an apparition.

"*Buzz!* Oh, God! You came!"

She didn't wait for him to respond. She ran toward him. It barely registered in her brain that he wasn't smiling. That he was barely moving. All she wanted to do was feel his arms around her, hear her name on his lips, look into his eyes and tell him all the things she hadn't been able to say before.

Chapter 17

The sight of Kelly running toward him, her face pale with terror, struck Buzz with the mind-numbing shock of a physical blow. The emotions that followed rendered him as utterly useless as any injury. All he could do was stand there, thank God she was alive and wish with all of his heart that things could have worked out differently between them.

Silly thought to have when the fire of century burned all around them.

Happiness and relief and a dozen other emotions he couldn't begin to name zinged through him with such force that he couldn't do anything but stand there silent and still and anticipate the moment when she would touch him, when he could smell her scent, feel her warm and soft against him, hold her just one more time.

There was no longer any doubt in his mind. He was in love with this woman. Crazy, head-over-heels in love no matter how hard he tried not to be. It was a truth he'd denied for too long. A truth that had been eating him alive since the day she'd walked out of his life. And at that moment, it didn't matter to him that she could never love him back. She was alive. That would have to be enough.

She came against him with all the finesse of a Mack truck traveling at a hundred miles per hour. Buzz heard himself grunt. Her arms went around him. The pain in his back and shoulder made him stiffen. But even as the pain ran like a lit fuse up his spine, pleasure infused every nerve ending with a power that stunned him.

"Kelly," he whispered. "Kelly…"

Her essence surrounded him. The softness of her body teased his senses, taunted his sensibilities, made him ache with a need every bit as acute as the pain in his back.

Putting his arms around her, he buried his face in her hair and held her tightly. He heard her name, realized belatedly he'd spoken it again. She smelled like smoke, but he could still discern the sweet essence of her beneath it. He drank it in as if it were clean, cool water, and he was crazed with thirst.

"You came for me," she said breathlessly.

"You knew I would."

"Eddie—"

"He's okay."

He wanted to devour her, hold her so tight that he simply absorbed her. Even surrounded by danger, his brain fogged with pain, he wanted her with a need that was insane. Not just physically, he realized, but for the first time in his life he needed someone on an emotional level. He needed her so desperately he could feel it running through him like a hot thread.

He lowered his mouth to hers. Pleasure sparked like static. He tasted smoke and softness and subtle heat. The mix of flavors intoxicated him. He knew kissing her in the middle of a raging forest fire wasn't very smart. But for the first time in his life, Buzz didn't care. He followed his heart, gave it free rein, let it guide him.

He didn't expect her to kiss him back—Kelly was no more prone to imbecilic behavior than he was. But when his tongue slipped between her lips, she opened to him, purring in the back of her throat like a cat. He kissed her long and hard until he was drunk on pleasure. Until the raging fire and the pain in his shoulder faded into the distance like a spent storm.

Vaguely, he was aware of her arms around his neck, her mouth clinging to his. Desire flared hotly in his veins, racing through his body with every thunderous beat of his heart.

An instant later, sanity intervened with the snap of dry wood and the splintering sound of a tree falling nearby. Buzz pulled away, keenly aware that he was aroused and wanting, annoyed because she did that to him every time he looked at her and he knew how lousy he was going to feel when she walked away for good.

"This is a damn fine time to do this," he growled. "But you taste incredibly good."

Kelly stared at him, caution dawning in her eyes. "So do you," she whispered. "A little smoky."

He smiled. "I'm glad you're all right."

"I'm glad you came. I mean…I'm glad it was you. I was hoping it would be you."

"I couldn't stay away. I couldn't leave you out here."

"Buzz…" She raised her hand, then let it fall as if realizing it would only fan a flame far more dangerous than the fire raging all around.

He wasn't sure what he would do if she touched him again. Kiss her again, maybe. Or maybe he'd do something really stupid like tell her he loved her…

"We don't have much time." Loath to let her go, he

stepped back and motioned toward the ATV. "We've got to go."

"You're hurt."

"I can drive." Taking her shoulders, he guided her over to the ATV. "Get on."

She turned to him, ran her hand lightly over his shoulder. Even though her touch was light, the pain made him wince. She tossed him a worried frown. "My God, you're shoulder feels like it's dislocated."

"It'll keep for a little while."

"Buzz—"

It took tremendous effort, but he climbed behind the wheel without wincing. "Get on."

"You're stubborn as a mule."

"I guess maybe that's one of the things we've always had in common." He stared at her, unmoving, a standoff he was determined to win. "Come on, Kel. We don't have much time."

"What am I going to do with you?" Exasperation laced her voice as she slid onto the seat behind him.

He cut her a look. "I don't think you want me to answer that."

"Probably not."

Keenly aware of the press of her body against him, Buzz jammed the vehicle in reverse, braked hard, then headed in the same direction from which he'd come. An instant later he slammed his foot down on the brake. Fear drizzled through his midsection when he saw knee-high flames flickering over the path he'd taken earlier.

"How are we going to get through?" Kelly asked.

"The same way I came through the first time."

"It wasn't on fire the first time, was it?"

Using his uninjured arm, he worked off his shirt.

"What are you doing?" she asked.

Without answering, he tore off two long strips of material. He opened the canteen, wetted both strips and turned to Kelly. "I'm going to tie this over your nose and mouth."

Kelly held herself perfectly still as he positioned the strip of wet material over the lower half of her face and tied it tightly at the back of her head. He did the same to himself. Then turning in the seat, he sprinkled the remaining water over her, wetting her shirt and jeans and hair.

"What are you doing?" she asked.

"Keeping you from getting burned." He emptied the canteen over her.

"But what about you?"

He turned away from her, set his hands on the steering wheel. "I want you to hold on to me."

"What are you going to do?"

"I'm going to get us out of here."

"Buzz, you don't know what's on the other side. What if there's fire?"

He punched the accelerator. The ATV shot forward, a racehorse plunging from the gate and running for its life. He felt Kelly rock back, then her arms wrapped around his midsection. He shouldn't have enjoyed the sensation considering the circumstances; he wasn't even sure they were going to get out of this alive. But he reveled in the feel of her against him, her closeness. And he couldn't help but wonder if this was the last time he would ever have her this close.

The ATV burst into the wall of flames. Yellow heat scorched his face. Acrid smoke burned the inside of his nose, sent tears to his eyes, blurring his vision. Buzz held the steering wheel steady, kept the pedal to the floor and drove blindly through the flames. He smelled burning rubber and singed hair. Heat streaked up his arm. He looked down, saw the sleeve of his shirt smoldering. Cursing, he slapped at the flames, felt Kelly's hands reach around him to do the same.

An instant later the flames opened up to forest. The smoke thickened, and Buzz knew they were now downwind, heading south, away from the fire. He sucked in a breath, felt his lungs seize. He coughed. Behind him, he could hear Kelly choking. For the first time he felt the pain of a burn on his arm. He wanted to stop, but knew they couldn't linger. The smoke was only going to get worse. The heat would only get more intense.

They were alive, he thought. And for the moment, Buzz knew that was the best he could hope for.

The fire pursued them like a hungry predator for what seemed like an eternity, but eventually the smoke thinned and the trail opened up. Visibility returned, though the pungent smell of burning timber still hung heavy in the air. Kelly held onto Buzz as if her life depended on it as the ATV took them over the terrain at a death-defying speed.

She didn't think they were ever going to reach the campground. Every bump jarred her all the way to her bones. Her face and arms stung from the scratches she'd received from the branches growing into the trail. Even though the smoke was no longer chokingly thick, her throat felt as if someone had taken a rasp to it.

She could only imagine how Buzz felt. He hadn't said a word, but occasionally, when he had to make a sharp turn or they hit a large bump, she could feel his body go rigid with pain. A couple of times, she even thought she heard him groan. Damn stubborn man. She'd been perfectly capable of driving the ATV. Why did he always have to be so damn heroic?

But she knew the answer to that. And with her emotions riding high, she didn't want to examine it too closely.

Dusk had fallen by the time they drove into the parking lot of the campground. A dozen fire department vehicles from several jurisdictions, law-enforcement vehicles from the Gunnison County Sheriff's Department, an ambulance and a big white RMSAR truck hauling a goose-neck horse trailer crowded the small lot. By the time the ATV reached the sidewalk, several people had exited the main building and were rushing toward them. Kelly spotted several police officers, a female park ranger. She caught sight of an RMSAR-emblazoned cap, a television camera and lights. Someone let out a whoop, then a throng of people surrounded them.

A dozen voices came at her at once. She knew it was silly, but she didn't want to let go of Buzz. She wanted to believe it was because he was hurt, because he needed her and she wanted to help him. But she knew her inability to take her hands from around his waist had more to do with her own needs than his.

A moment later, she spotted Eddie. Her heart pinged once against her ribs and she had to choke back a sob. ''Sweetheart,'' she whispered, but the word was barely audible.

''Mommy!''

Her heart swelled at the sound of the little voice she cherished. Tears threatened hotly behind her eyes. Her gaze followed her son's outstretched arm to the tall man holding his hand. She saw black hair, a devilish goatee and dark, mischievous eyes. Tony Colorosa, the chopper pilot, she realized, and choked out a laugh.

Farther back in the throng of people, she spotted several other members of the Rocky Mountain Search and Rescue team and Taylor Quelhorst. Taylor looked out of place amongst all that flannel and denim in his creased slacks and button-down shirt. Kelly should have been relieved to see him. She should have been relieved that the nightmare was over and she was free to get on with her life. Strangely, she felt nothing more than an odd sense of melancholy.

Buzz cut the ATV's engine. Kelly was still pressed up

against him, with her arms wrapped around his waist. It took a good bit of discipline to disengage herself and slide back.

More than anything, she wanted to see her son. She wanted to hold him and thank God they'd made it through the ordeal alive and unharmed. But before she could walk away, she realized there was something she wanted to say to Buzz first.

Numb with the remnants of fear and sheer exhaustion, she slid from the seat onto shaky legs. She stood there, trying to regain her equilibrium as Buzz slid off. When he turned to her, their eyes met, held—and the rest of the crowd melted away.

His eyes were as gray and hard as the mountain as they studied her. Cool as stone. Uncompromising as granite. And as unpredictable as a mountain storm. There was no sign of the pain that was surely racking his body. No sign of the tenderness he'd shown her the night before. No sign that anything that had happened in the last twenty-four hours had affected him one way or the other.

She stared at him, the festering wound of emotions inside her throbbing, about to burst. Suddenly, all the words that had been pounding to get out dried in her mouth. Her chest was so tight she couldn't speak. It stunned her to realize she was close to tears. She didn't want to cry here. Not in front of all these people. Certainly not in front of this man; she didn't want him to get the wrong idea.

"You okay?" Buzz asked.

Because she couldn't manage anything else, she raised her hand and pressed her fingers lightly to his cheek. He flinched at her touch, but he didn't look away.

"I just wanted to thank you," she whispered. "For everything."

The words weren't adequate, but for the life of her she couldn't think of anything else to say.

For a moment, he looked as if he wanted to say some-thing more. Kelly found herself leaning toward him, want-ing to hear his voice, desperate to know what was going on inside that hardened exterior.

"Mommy!"

The moment vanished. Kelly started, feeling as if she'd just been wakened from a deep sleep. Turning, she saw Eddie rushing toward her, Tony Colorosa in tow.

She knelt just in time for Eddie to fling himself into her arms. Closing her eyes, she enveloped him in her arms and squeezed him as tightly as she dared.

"Hi, sweetheart." Pressing her face against his hair, she breathed in his little-boy scent. Her heart ached with love for him.

"Mommy, you're squeezing me!"

Struggling to control her emotions, Kelly mustered a smile and eased her child to arm's length. "How's my puppy face?"

He grinned. "I'm not a puppy face."

She choked out a laugh.

He was wearing a black RMSAR cap that was too big even though it was cinched to the smallest size. She figured it was Tony Colorosa's. She could only imagine how Tony had kept her son entertained for the day while Buzz and the rest of the team had been out looking for her.

"Mommy, we were scared because you were lost in the woods, but Flyboy told me Buzz was going to save you just like in the movies!"

Kelly didn't know what to say to that. "He did, honey."

"Flyboy showed me his chopter. He let me sit in the pilot's seat and everything!"

Tony smiled down at him and winked. "That's chopper, sport."

"And I got to sit on the horse! Man! When I grow up I want to be a Search and Rescue pilot only I'm gonna have horses, too!'' He squirmed in her arms and looked at Tony. ''Where's Jake? I want to show Mommy the horse!''

Unable to keep herself from it, Kelly pulled Eddie close again and looked at Tony over his shoulder. She mouthed the words *thank you* and gave up on trying to withhold the tears.

''Kelly.''

She should have been comforted and relieved to hear Taylor Quelhorst's voice. He represented her future. A secure life in Lake Tahoe. The job of her dreams. The future she'd always wanted for herself and her son. But for the life of her she couldn't figure out why the sound of his voice filled her with dread. Why she didn't want to see him. Why she didn't want to talk to him. Why she felt vaguely annoyed that he was there at all.

Shoving the irrational feelings to the back of her mind where they belonged, she stood and faced him. His blue eyes swept swiftly down the front of her. He was smiling, but she saw distaste flash across his expression and realized he was reacting either to the stench of smoke or the way she looked.

''I must look like a walking disaster,'' she heard herself say.

''You look terrific.''

Kelly looked over her shoulder, telling herself she wasn't looking for Buzz, spotted several RMSAR team members talking to him.

''I'm really glad you're all right.''

She turned back to Taylor and forced a smile, only giving him half her attention. ''Thank you.''

He must have decided she didn't look *that* bad, because in the next instant, he stepped forward and pulled her into an embrace.

''Taylor...'' she said, surprised.

''I was so worried about you.''

Kelly closed her eyes and let herself be held, trying not to think about how cold his arms felt around her. She tried not to compare this with the heat of Buzz's embrace. Or think about how wrong it felt to be held by another man. Most of all, she tried not to acknowledge the pain knifing through her heart because as much as she didn't want to admit it, she was pretty sure it was broken.

And she knew there wasn't a damn thing she could do about it because it was nobody's fault but her own.

Buzz watched the other man's arms go around her and felt the primal urge to walk over and rearrange that pretty-boy face. Blood streaked through his veins like lighted jet fuel as Quelhorst's hands skimmed over the small of her back. Dangerous thoughts streaked through his mind, possessive thoughts that belied the fact that he was an enlightened and civilized man.

She made her choice, a little voice told him. *Be a man about it and let her go.*

He looked over at the child whose hand she clutched so with a white-knuckled hand, and a different kind of pain broke open in his chest. The kind of pain a man never quite learned to live with.

"Easy does it, partner."

He turned his head at the sound of the voice to see John Maitland standing next to him, a grim, knowing expression on his face.

"Let it go," Maitland said.

Buzz answered with a nasty curse. He might be furious and hurting and maybe even a little desperate, but his pride wouldn't let him do anything as stupid as take a swing at a man over a woman who'd made her position perfectly clear.

"Come on," John said. "I'll drive you over to Lake County to get that shoulder looked at."

Pain ground in his shoulder every time he moved. The burn on his arm throbbed with every beat of his heart. But the pain splitting his chest was infinitely worse than those two physical pains combined.

Buzz took one last look at Kelly and Eddie. At the woman who'd once been his, who'd turned his life upside-down. At the child who'd changed everything—and made him realize for the first time in his life just how wrong a man could be, how at odds a man could be about what he wanted and what he really needed.

Regret lay like a steel ball in his gut. He would find a way to get to know his son, he vowed. He would travel to Lake Tahoe as often as possible. Eddie could visit during summer vacation and spring break. They could play softball down at the school in the evenings. Hike the trails and camp during the warm summer months. Ski when the mountains were lush with snow.

But the thought of seeing that child only two or three times a year hurt. It wasn't enough, he realized. It would never be enough. He wanted more. Not just his son, but the woman. He wanted his wife back. A house with a white picket fence and a hedge and a Labrador retriever.

He wanted a family.

The realization shocked him. Frightened him. That it was five years too late shattered him.

Feeling himself tumbling into a black pit of despair, Buzz turned away. He was breathing hard, nearly doubled over with pain. John Maitland looked away, and Buzz realized the other man knew it wasn't just the physical pain that was about to send him to his knees.

Hanging on to the last of his dignity by a thread, Buzz started toward the RMSAR truck across the lot. "Let's get the hell out of here."

Chapter 18

Rock and roll blared through the hangar. A serenade of screaming guitar, bass drums and a lilting male voice echoed off the corrugated steel walls, vibrating everything in between.

Tony Colorosa spouted off about his date the night before as he walked around his first love—the pretty Bell 412 chopper—and did the pre-flight check. John Maitland rolled his eyes from his place at the hatch while he inventoried the med kits stowed in the overhead compartments. Twenty feet away, at the north side of the hangar where a small, impromptu meeting area had been set up, Jake Madigan unrolled a laminated terrain map and pinned it to a wallboard.

Buzz sat at the makeshift desk in the glassed-in office and stared unseeingly down at the chopper maintenance reports in front of him. It was the fourth or fifth time he'd had to start reading the same report, and already he'd forgotten what he'd read. He wanted to believe his lack of concentration was because of the lingering pain in his shoulder. He wanted to blame it on the pain killers the doctor had prescribed. But he knew neither of those things had a damn thing to do with his concentration. First, he hadn't taken any of the pain medication for almost a week. Second, he was honest enough with himself to admit his inability to concentrate had more to do with a pretty brunette with dark eyes and the kind of smile a man never quite got over. If Buzz figured right, she was on her way to the airport about now.

Yeah, so much for concentration.

He told himself he could handle living without her. As long as she was happy. As long as Eddie was happy. That was all that really mattered. He had his work here and the cabin. Of course, she would have to tolerate him on occasion because there was no way in hell he was going to let Eddie grow up without knowing his father. He didn't give a damn what that pencil-neck Quelhort had to say about it.

Two weeks had passed since that last day on the mountain. Buzz didn't want to admit it, but already he could feel her disappearing, as if a little piece of him had been cut out every day he didn't see her, and an open wound had been left to bleed out.

As much as he hated to admit it, he missed her, damn it. He missed Eddie. Two facts that ticked him off almost as much as they hurt.

Cursing, he threw the pen across the room. He looked up in time to see Colorosa and Maitland standing at the doorway, exchanging knowing glances. The two men pretended not to have noticed the pen caper, but Buzz figured his team had already figured out what was going on with their surly team leader.

Hell, what a mess.

"Can I help you ladies?" Scowling at the two men, he walked around the desk and was in the process of picking up the pen when he heard the outer hangar door open. Straightening, he looked through the glass partition to see an all-too-familiar female figure silhouetted against the bright sunlight beyond—and felt his knees go weak. Next to her the smaller figure of a boy strained to extricate his hand from his mother's.

Kelly stood motionless for a moment, and in less than two seconds all activity in the hangar screeched to a halt as five sets of male eyes darted toward the hangar door. The tension broke when Eddie, wearing blue jeans, a Captain Kudos T-shirt and his RMSAR cap, darted into the hangar and blinked the sunlight from his eyes.

"Mommy, look! There's the chopter! Can I go see it?" Even as he asked for permission, he sprinted toward the behemoth craft. "Flyboy! Can I sit in the pilot's seat again?"

"How's it going, sport?" came Colorosa's voice as he started toward the boy.

Buzz frowned when Colorosa cast him a glance over his shoulder, moving his brows up and down like Groucho Marx. Maitland combed a hand through his hair and ducked quietly out of the office.

Idiots, Buzz thought, and braced for what he figured was going to be a very difficult goodbye.

Why couldn't she have come by his cabin so they could have a little privacy, for God's sake? How was he supposed to say goodbye to his son with his entire team watching? How was he supposed to let the only woman he'd ever loved walk out that door without making a damn fool of himself by dropping to his knees and begging her to stay?

Vaguely, he was aware of Kelly approaching the chopper and talking briefly to Colorosa. He saw Tony point toward the office where Buzz stood. Kelly looked over at him, and his mouth went dust-dry. He told himself it wasn't nerves that had his heart pounding, his palms slicking with sweat.

But damn it, there were certain things a man liked to do without an audience.

Buzz watched her approach, trying not to notice the subtle sway of her hips or the habit she had of opening and closing her hands when she was nervous. He loved the way she walked. Loved the way her hair fell over her shoulders. She smiled when she got close enough for him to see her face, but he could plainly see the nerves behind it. Damn, this was going to be tough.

He worked hard to shore up his defenses in the seconds before she reached him. But for the first time in his life, Buzz couldn't quite manage. He felt unbearably vulnerable. Stripped bare. As if all his protective outer layers had been peeled away and his heart lay in plain view, beating and bleeding and hurting a lot more than he wanted anyone to see.

She stepped into the doorway a moment later. Buzz took a deep breath, felt her scent fill his lungs, and wished for the thousandth time things could have worked out differently. In the back of his mind he wondered if Mr. Pencil-Neck was outside, waiting, smirking because in five minutes she would walk away from the father of her child and the door would open for him to step in and take over.

"Hi," she said.

"Hi." Brilliant response, but for the life of him he couldn't think of anything else. What could a man say when the woman he loved was about to walk out of his life forever?

"I tried to call you." Nervously, she shoved her hands into the pockets of her jeans. "Kept getting your answering machine."

Buzz tried not to notice the way the gesture made the fabric of her shirt stretch across her breasts. Everything they'd shared up on the mountain flashed in his mind. The ensuing emotion moved him, shook him, and the regret tasted bitter at the back of his throat.

"I've been busy," he said after a moment.

She nodded. "How's the shoulder?"

He looked down at the sling. "Should be good as new in about four weeks."

"Hurt?"

"Not much." Not nearly as much as this is going to hurt, he thought.

Moving slightly, he looked over her shoulder. Colorosa and Maitland had Eddie in the pilot's seat and were showing him the safety harness. On the other side of the hangar, Jake was in the process of marking the park ranger stations and RMSAR headquarters on the topographical map.

Confident he had some relative privacy, Buzz looked at Kelly. "I want to be part of Eddie's life," he blurted out.

She blinked. "Buzz..."

"I mean it, Kel," he said, more firmly. "I can handle your having a relationship with Quelhort."

"Quelhorst. And for the tenth time, I'm not—"

"I don't care about that." God, that was a pathetic lie. "I don't. I just...want to see Eddie. I can fly out to Tahoe. I can drive once or twice a year. He can come here to see me in the summer. Maybe on spring break if you can spare him."

"Buzz..."

"I have a right to see my son, Kel. I know I told you I never wanted children." His voice broke and a sharp pang of humiliation washed over him. Jesus! He was losing it. Buzz Malone, hard as steel and cold as stone, losing his cool. He couldn't believe it. Couldn't believe his emotions were going to betray him and humiliate him in front of the woman whose opinion had suddenly become of vast importance to him.

"Damn it." He turned away from her and paced over to

a dented steel file cabinet. He didn't need anything in the freaking cabinet, but he yanked the drawer open anyway. He stared blindly into the drawer because he desperately needed a few moments to pull himself together.

"I'm not going to Tahoe," Kelly said.

It took a moment for the words to register in his brain. When they did, he turned to her, not understanding, and waited, not daring to hope the explanation had anything to do with him, with those precious hours they'd spent together on the mountain. Hours when he'd finally realized what it could mean for a man and a woman and a child to be together as a single strong unit, a family, one powerful force bound together by love.

Her brown eyes were luminous in the glare of the fluorescent lights of the office. He stared at her, felt his emotions burgeon, his throat lock up, his chest compress his heart until he thought it would explode.

He never would have believed he could break like this. For the first time in his life, he felt...fragile. As fragile as glass, and he wondered if this woman would shatter him.

"I've been wanting to tell you something I didn't tell you before," she said. "That's why I'm here."

He looked at her, felt the pull to her, worked hard to hold his ground. He wanted to speak, just to let her know he could, but for the life of him he couldn't think of anything to say.

"I came here to tell you I love you," she said simply.

The words shattered him. Buzz felt himself coming apart, like glass thrown to the floor. He felt the pieces scatter and cut and he knew they would never go back the same way they were before.

He stared at her, not sure what to do next, terrified to let himself feel because he knew once he did there was no turning back.

She stared back at him with eyes that weren't merely

luminous, but filled with tears. Crystal tears that pooled and sparkled. Tears of hope for a future and the hurt of the past and terrible fear that things had already moved beyond the point of no return.

Suddenly, he knew he needed to let her know that it wasn't too late. That it was never too late.

Clamping his jaws together to hold his own emotions at bay, he crossed to her. "Come here," he growled.

He didn't wait for her to acquiesce. His uninjured arm wrapped around her and pulled her against him, and he wished fervently that his other arm wasn't in a sling.

"Put your arms around me," he said.

"You're bossy."

"Damn straight I am."

Her arms went around his neck. "I love you," she repeated. "I came here to tell you that."

"Say it again."

"I love you. I've always loved you. God, Buzz, I've missed you."

He buried his face in her hair. Closing his eyes, he breathed in her scent, let it fill his senses. "I've missed you, too," he said.

"I've spent the last two weeks agonizing over what to do. But this is the only thing that felt right. The only thing that makes me truly happy," she said.

"I never stopped loving you."

"I hurt you." Pulling back slightly, she looked into his eyes. "I'm sorry for that. I mean it."

"I couldn't give you what you wanted. I hurt you, too."

"You had good reasons for not wanting children."

"Fear is never a good reason, Kel."

"I know that now."

He kissed her. The pleasure jolted him. The rightness of it sent a zing of happiness through him. The kind of happiness some men search for their entire lives and sometimes never find.

She pulled away again, put one hand against his cheek. "It was incredibly selfish of me to demand you give up your career because I was afraid."

"You lost your brother and your father. That kind of loss doesn't leave a person unaffected."

"It almost cost us everything," she whispered.

"But it didn't."

She blinked rapidly, fighting tears that continued to stream unacknowledged down her cheeks. "You risked your life for a son you'd never met. You would have risked your life even if he hadn't been your son. I never realized what that meant before."

"I'm just a man, Kel. I'm the same man I've always been. Stubborn. Uncompromising—"

"Courageous and decent and kind."

He kissed her mouth, her temple, her nose. "Keep going."

"Buzz, you're not the same man you were before."

Pulling back slightly, he met her gaze, felt the power of it shake him so profoundly he raised his hand to touch her cheek, just to make sure she was really there.

"I've seen the way you look at Eddie," she whispered. "I know you love him."

Buzz stared at her, awed and shaken and so moved he couldn't draw a breath. "I do," he said. "I love him with all my heart. I want to be his father, Kel." His voice broke, but he trudged on before he lost his nerve. "I want you to be my wife."

She trembled in his arms. Even before she spoke Buzz saw the answer in her eyes. He felt the answer coming through her body and into his.

"Marry me," he said.

She smiled through her tears. "That would make me incredibly happy. I know it would make Eddie happy, too."

"I've only got two bedrooms in the cabin, but I've been meaning to add an extra bedroom. Maybe I could just make it two."

"Eddie's always wanted a little brother or sister."

"Maybe both."

She laughed. "Okay, two bedrooms."

"And a dog."

"You'll love Brandy."

"You got yourself a deal, Mrs. Malone."

The rise of applause spun them around. Buzz looked up to see his entire team standing just outside the glassed-in office. Eddie was perched on Tony Colorosa's shoulders, clapping his hands.

"Buzz just kissed my mommy!" he squealed. "Flyboy, did you see that?"

Tony Colorosa raised his hand and Eddie slapped his palm in a high five. Madigan and Maitland broke into raucous laughter.

Grinning, Buzz crossed the room, closed the door and lowered the mini blinds. "Idiots," he muttered, then turned to his new fiancée and took her into his arms. "Where were we?"

*   *   *   *   *